A loud yowling broke out from the clearing. It was the sound of many cats raising their voices in a terrible screech of fear. Fireheart spun around and raced out of Bluestar's den.

The center of the clearing was almost deserted, bathed in bright light where the normally leafy cover had been burned away. Cats crouched around the edges in the scant shelter of the charred fern walls. Fireheart caught a glimpse of Goldenflower and Willowpelt pushing their kits into the nursery. Brackenfur was nudging a couple of the elders toward their den, urging them to hurry.

The cats at the edge of the clearing were staring up at the sky, their eyes huge with fear. As he looked upward, Fireheart heard the beating of wings and saw a hawk circling above the trees, its harsh cry drifting on the air. At the same time he realized that one cat had not taken shelter; Snowkit was still tumbling and playing in the middle of the open space.

"Snowkit!" Speckletail yowled desperately.

WARRIORS

A DANGEROUS PATH

ERIN
HUNTER

AVON BOOKS

An Imprint of HarperCollinsPublishers

Library of Congress Catalog Card Number 2003013962
ISBN 0-06-052565-7

First Avon edition, 2005

AVON TRADEMARK REG. U.S. PAT. OFF. AND IN OTHER COUNTRIES,
MARCA REGISTRADA, HECHO EN U.S.A.

❖

Visit us on the World Wide Web!
www.harperchildrens.com
11 12 13 LP/BR 30 29 28 27 26

To the real Bramblepaw

Special thanks to Cherith Baldry

WARRIORS

A DANGEROUS PATH

ALLEGIANCES

THUNDERCLAN

LEADER

BLUESTAR—blue-gray she-cat, tinged with silver around her muzzle

DEPUTY

FIREHEART—handsome ginger tom
APPRENTICE, CLOUDPAW

MEDICINE CAT

CINDERPELT—dark gray she-cat

WARRIORS

(toms, and she-cats without kits)

WHITESTORM—big white tom
APPRENTICE, BRIGHTPAW

DARKSTRIPE—sleek black-and-gray tabby tom
APPRENTICE, FERNPAW

FROSTFUR—beautiful white coat and blue eyes

BRINDLEFACE—pretty tabby

LONGTAIL—pale tabby tom with dark black stripes
APPRENTICE, SWIFTPAW

MOUSEFUR—small dusky brown she-cat
APPRENTICE, THORNPAW

BRACKENFUR—golden brown tabby tom

DUSTPELT—dark brown tabby tom
APPRENTICE, ASHPAW

SANDSTORM—pale ginger she-cat

APPRENTICES

(more than six moons old, in training to become warriors)

SWIFTPAW—black-and-white tom

CLOUDPAW—long-haired white tom

BRIGHTPAW—she-cat, white with ginger splotches

THORNPAW—golden brown tabby tom

FERNPAW—pale gray (with darker flecks) she-cat, pale green eyes

ASHPAW—pale gray (with darker flecks) tom, dark blue eyes

QUEENS

(she-cats expecting or nursing kits)

GOLDENFLOWER—pale ginger coat

SPECKLETAIL—pale tabby, and the oldest nursery queen

WILLOWPELT—very pale gray she-cat with unusual blue eyes

ELDERS

(former warriors and queens, now retired)

ONE-EYE—pale gray she-cat, the oldest she-cat in ThunderClan; virtually blind and deaf

SMALLEAR—gray tom with very small ears; the oldest tom in ThunderClan

DAPPLETAIL—once-pretty tortoiseshell she-cat with a lovely dappled coat

SHADOWCLAN

LEADER   **TIGERSTAR**—big dark brown tabby tom with unusually long front claws, formerly of ThunderClan

DEPUTY   **BLACKFOOT**—large white tom with huge jet-black paws, formerly a rogue cat

MEDICINE CAT   **RUNNINGNOSE**—small gray-and-white tom

WARRIORS   **OAKFUR**—small brown tom

    LITTLECLOUD—very small tabby tom

    DARKFLOWER—black she-cat

    BOULDER—silver tabby tom, formerly a rogue cat

    RUSSETFUR—dark ginger she-cat, formerly a rogue cat
    APPRENTICE, CEDARPAW

    JAGGEDTOOTH—huge tabby tom, formerly a rogue cat
    APPRENTICE, ROWANPAW

QUEENS   **TALLPOPPY**—long-legged light brown tabby she-cat

WINDCLAN

LEADER   **TALLSTAR**—black-and-white tom with a very long tail

DEPUTY   **DEADFOOT**—black tom with a twisted paw

MEDICINE CAT   **BARKFACE**—short-tailed brown tom

WARRIORS

MUDCLAW—mottled dark brown tom

WEBFOOT—dark gray tabby tom

TORNEAR—tabby tom

TAWNYFUR—golden brown she-cat

ONEWHISKER—brown tabby tom
APPRENTICE, GORSEPAW

RUNNINGBROOK—light gray she-cat

QUEENS

ASHFOOT—gray queen

MORNINGFLOWER—tortoiseshell queen

WHITETAIL—small white she-cat

RIVERCLAN

LEADER

CROOKEDSTAR—huge light-colored tabby with a twisted jaw

DEPUTY

LEOPARDFUR—unusually spotted golden tabby she-cat

MEDICINE CAT

MUDFUR—long-haired light brown tom

WARRIORS

BLACKCLAW—smoky black tom

HEAVYSTEP—thickset tabby tom
APPRENTICE, DAWNPAW

STONEFUR—gray tom with battle-scarred ears

MISTYFOOT—gray she-cat with blue eyes

SHADEPELT—very dark gray she-cat

LOUDBELLY—dark brown tom

GRAYSTRIPE—long-haired gray tom, formerly of ThunderClan

CATS OUTSIDE CLANS

BARLEY—black-and-white tom that lives on a farm close to the forest

RAVENPAW—sleek black cat who lives on the farm with Barley

PRINCESS—light brown tabby with a distinctive white chest and paws; a kittypet

SMUDGE—plump black-and-white kittypet who lives in a house at the edge of the forest

CARRIONPLACE

SHADOWCLAN
CAMP

THUNDERPATH

THUNDERCLAN
CAMP

GREAT
SYCAMORE

SANDY
HOLLOW

SNAKEROCKS

TALLPINES

TREECUT PLACE

TWOLEGPLACE

THUNDERCLAN

RIVERCLAN

SHADOWCLAN

WINDCLAN

STARCLAN

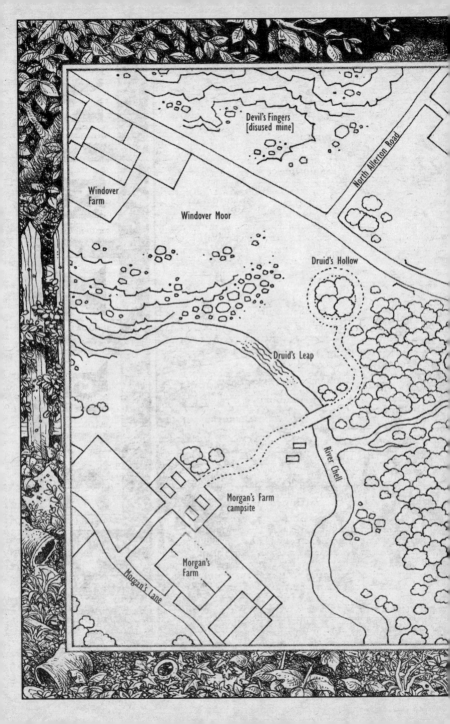

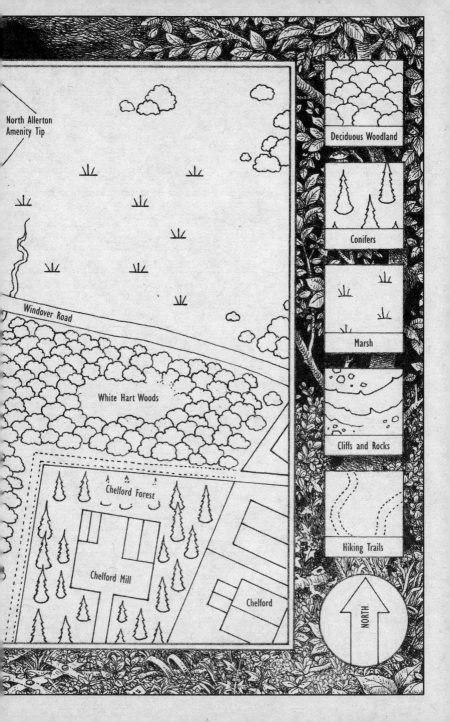

North Allerton
Amenity Tip

Windover Road

White Hart Woods

Chelford Forest

Chelford Mill

Chelford

Deciduous Woodland

Conifers

Marsh

Cliffs and Rocks

Hiking Trails

NORTH

PROLOGUE

❧

Inside the kennel-that-moves, everything was dark. The pack leader could hear the scrabbling of claws and feel the sleek pelt of the dog next to him, but he could see nothing. Dog scent filled his nostrils, and beyond that the smell of the burned forest.

The pack leader sat uncomfortably on the vibrating floor until the kennel-that-moves bounced to a halt. Outside, he could hear Man voices. He understood some of the words. "Fire . . . keep watch . . . guard dogs."

The pack leader picked up the Men's fear-scent, along with the bittersweet smell of cut wood. He remembered coming here the night before, and the night before that, more than four paws' worth of nights. He had prowled the compound with the rest of the pack, sifting through the scents for intruders, ready to drive them away.

The dog snarled softly, his lips drawn back from sharp teeth. The pack was strong. They could run, and kill. They craved warm blood, and the terror-scent of prey before it died. But instead they were penned up, they ate the food the Man threw to them, and they obeyed the Man's orders.

The dog rose to his powerful paws, rattling the doors as he

butted them with his massive black-and-tan head. He lifted his voice in a bark that sounded all the louder in the confined space. "Out! Pack out! Out now!"

The rest of the pack added their voices. "Pack out! Pack run!"

As if in answer, the doors of the kennel-that-moves were flung open. In the twilight the pack leader could see the Man standing there, barking an order.

The leader jumped down first, close to a pile of logs stacked in the middle of the compound. His paws threw up little puffs of ash and soot. The rest of the pack followed in a stream of black-and-brown bodies. "Pack follow! Pack follow!" they barked. The leader padded restlessly along the fence that separated them from the forest. Beyond the fence, burned-out tree trunks leaned against each other or lay on the ground. Farther away a barrier of undamaged trees rustled in the breeze.

Scents flowed enticingly from the leaf-thick shadows. The dog's muscles tensed. Out there, in the prey-filled forest, the pack could run free. There would be no Man to chain or command them. They would feed as often as they wanted, because they would be the strongest and most savage of all.

"Free!" the lead dog barked. "Pack free! Free soon!"

He walked up to the fence and pressed his nose against the mesh links, drawing the smells of the forest deep into his lungs. Many of the scents he had never smelled before, but there was one he knew well, stronger than the rest, the scent of his enemy and his prey.

Cats!

❈ ❈ ❈

Night had fallen; the leafless branches of the blackened trees were silhouetted against a full moon. In the darkness the dogs ranged to and fro, deep shadows in the night. Paws padded softly among soot and sawdust. Muscles rippled under shining coats. Their eyes gleamed. Their jaws were parted, revealing sharp teeth, and their tongues lolled.

The pack leader sniffed along the bottom of the fence, searching for a special place on the opposite side of the compound from where the Man stayed at night. Three nights ago the dog had discovered a narrow hole leading under the fence. He knew at once that this would be the route to freedom for the pack.

"Hole. Where hole?" he growled.

Then he spotted the place where the earth floor of the compound fell away into a hollow. One massive paw scraped at the ground. The dog raised his head to bark to his followers. "Here. Hole, hole. Here."

He could feel their eagerness in his own mind, sharp as thorns, hot as carrion. They came bounding up to the lead dog, answering his bark. "Hole. Hole."

"Bigger, hole bigger," the pack leader promised. "Run soon."

He began scraping at the ground again with all the strength in his lean, powerful body. Earth scattered as the hole under the chain-link fence grew wider and deeper. The remaining dogs milled around, snuffling at the night air that carried scents from the forest. They drooled at the thought of sinking their teeth into the warm bodies of living prey.

The pack leader stopped, ears pricked for the sound of the Man coming to check on them. But there was no sign of him, and his scent drifted from far away.

The lead dog flattened himself on the ground and squirmed down into the hole. The bottom of the fence scraped along his pelt. The dog thrust hard with his hind paws, propelling himself forward until he could scramble up and stand in the forest outside.

"Free now," he barked. "Come! Come!"

The hole grew deeper still as each dog forced his way through, to stand beside his leader among the burned-out trees. They padded back and forth, pushing their muzzles into the holes at the roots of trees, gazing into the darkness with eyes that glowed with a cold fire.

As the last dog dragged itself under the fence, the pack leader raised his head and let out a triumphant bark. "Run. Pack free. Run now!"

Turning toward the trees, he bounded away, powerful muscles working in a smooth rhythm. The pack streamed behind, their dark shapes flashing through the forest night. *Pack, pack,* they thought. *Pack run.*

The whole of the forest was theirs, and in their minds, there was a single instinct. *"Kill! Kill!"*

CHAPTER 1

✿

Fireheart's fur bristled with disbelief and fury as he gazed up at the new leader of ShadowClan standing on the Great Rock. He watched as the cat swung his massive head from side to side. Muscles rippled under his gleaming pelt and his amber eyes seemed to glow with triumph.

"Tigerclaw!" Fireheart spat. His old enemy—the cat who had tried to kill him more than once—was now one of the most powerful cats in the forest.

The full moon rode high above Fourtrees, shedding its cold light over the cats of the four Clans, assembled there for the Gathering. They had all been shocked to learn of the death of Nightstar, the ShadowClan leader. But no cat in the forest had expected that ShadowClan's new leader would be Tigerclaw, the former ThunderClan deputy.

Beside Fireheart, Darkstripe was rigid with excitement, his eyes glittering. Fireheart wondered what thoughts were going through the mind of his black-pelted Clan mate. When Tigerclaw had been banished from ThunderClan, he had invited his old friend to go with him, but Darkstripe had refused. Was he regretting that decision now?

Fireheart caught sight of Sandstorm weaving her way toward him. "What's going on?" the pale ginger she-cat hissed as she came into earshot. "Tigerclaw can't lead ShadowClan. He's a traitor!"

For several heartbeats, Fireheart hesitated. Shortly after he had joined ThunderClan, Fireheart had discovered that Tigerclaw had murdered Redtail, the deputy. Once Tigerclaw became deputy himself, he had led rogue cats to attack the ThunderClan camp, trying to murder their leader, Bluestar, so that he could take her place. As punishment, he had been banished from their Clan and the forest. It was hardly a noble history for a leader of any Clan.

"But ShadowClan don't know about all that," Fireheart reminded Sandstorm now, keeping his voice low. "None of the other Clans know."

"Then you should tell them!"

Fireheart glanced up at Tallstar and Crookedstar, the leaders of WindClan and RiverClan, respectively, who stood beside Tigerstar on the Great Rock. Would they listen if he told them what he knew? ShadowClan had suffered so much from Brokentail's bloodthirsty leadership, followed by a devastating sickness, that they probably wouldn't care *what* their new leader had done, as long as he could forge them into a strong Clan again.

Besides, Fireheart couldn't help feeling a guilty relief that Tigerclaw had satisfied his hunger for power in a different Clan. Maybe now ThunderClan could stop waiting for him to attack, and Fireheart could walk the forest without constantly glancing over his shoulder.

Yet, as he struggled with his conflicting emotions, he knew that he would never forgive himself if he let Tigerclaw come to power without even making a protest.

"Fireheart!" He turned to see Cloudpaw, his long-furred white apprentice, padding quickly toward him with the wiry brown warrior Mousefur just behind. "Fireheart, are you just going to stand there and let that piece of fox dung take over?"

"Quiet, Cloudpaw," Fireheart ordered. "I know. I'll—"

He broke off as Tigerclaw paced to the front of the Great Rock.

"I am pleased to be here with you at the Gathering this night." The huge tabby spoke with quiet authority. "I stand here before you as the new leader of ShadowClan. Nightstar died of the sickness that took so many of my Clan, and StarClan have named me as his successor."

Tallstar, the black-and-white leader of WindClan, turned to him. "Welcome, Tigerstar," he meowed, nodding respectfully. "May StarClan walk with you."

Crookedstar meowed agreement as the new ShadowClan leader dipped his head in acknowledgment.

"I thank you for your greetings," Tigerstar replied. "It's an honor to stand here with you, although I wish the circumstances could have been different."

"Wait a moment," Tallstar interrupted him. "There should be four of us here." He peered down at the crowd of cats below. "Where's the leader of ThunderClan?"

"Go on." Fireheart felt a cat nudge him, and glanced around

to see that Whitestorm had joined the other ThunderClan warriors. "You're taking Bluestar's place, remember?"

Fireheart nodded to him, suddenly unable to speak. He bunched his muscles and got ready to spring. A heartbeat later he was scrambling to the top of the Great Rock to stand beside the three leaders. For a moment the unfamiliar viewpoint took his breath away. He seemed to be far above the hollow, watching the changing patterns of light and dark on the cats below as the moon shone through the branches of the four massive oak trees. Fireheart shivered as he caught the pale gleam reflected from countless pairs of eyes.

"Fireheart?" He looked up as Tallstar spoke. "Why are you here? Has something happened to Bluestar?"

Fireheart dipped his head respectfully. "Our leader breathed smoke in the fire, and she's not yet well enough to travel. But she'll recover," he added hastily. "It's nothing serious."

Tallstar nodded, and Crookedstar broke in testily, "Are we ever going to start? We're wasting moonlight."

Without waiting for a reply, the pale tabby RiverClan leader gave the yowl that signaled the beginning of the meeting. When the murmuring of the cats below had died away, he meowed, "Cats of all Clans, welcome to the Gathering. Tonight we are joined by a new leader, Tigerstar." He beckoned to the massive warrior with a flick of his tail. "Tigerstar, are you ready to speak now?"

Thanking him with a courteous nod, Tigerstar stepped forward to address the assembled cats. "I stand here before you by the will of StarClan. Nightstar was a noble warrior, but he was old, and he did not have the strength to fight the sickness when it came. His deputy, Cinderfur, died too."

Fireheart felt his fur prickling with unease as he listened. Clan leaders received nine lives when they went to share tongues with StarClan at Mothermouth, and Nightstar had become leader only a few seasons ago. What had happened to his nine lives? Had ShadowClan's sickness been so violent that it had taken all of them?

Looking down, Fireheart caught sight of Runningnose, the ShadowClan medicine cat, sitting with his head bowed. Fireheart could not see his face, but his hunched posture suggested that he was lost in misery. It must be hard for him, Fireheart thought, to know that all his skill had not been enough to save his leader.

"StarClan brought me to ShadowClan when its need was greatest," Tigerstar continued from on top of the Great Rock. "Not enough cats survived the sickness to hunt for the nursing queens and the elders, or to defend their clan, and no warrior was ready to take on the leadership. Then StarClan sent an omen to Runningnose that another great leader would arise. I swear by all our warrior ancestors that I will become that leader."

Out of the corner of his eye, Fireheart noticed that Runningnose was shifting uncomfortably. For some reason he looked unhappy at the mention of the omen.

Fireheart suddenly realized that his own task had become much harder. If there had been an omen, then StarClan themselves must have chosen Tigerstar as the new leader of

ShadowClan. Surely it was not the place of Fireheart or any other cat to question their decisions. What could he say now that would not seem to challenge the will of their warrior ancestors?

"Thanks to StarClan," Tigerstar went on, "I had other cats to bring with me who have proven themselves willing to hunt and fight for their new Clan."

Fireheart knew exactly which cats Tigerstar meant—the band of rogues who had attacked the ThunderClan camp! He could see one of them just below the Great Rock, a huge ginger tom, sitting with his tail curled around his paws. The last time Fireheart had seen him, he had been grappling with Brindleface, trying to break into the ThunderClan nursery. Ironically, some of these rogues had grown up in ShadowClan and had supported the tyrannical leader, Brokentail. They had been driven out with their leader when ThunderClan had come to the aid of the oppressed Clan.

Tallstar stepped forward, a doubtful look in his eyes. "Brokentail's allies were cruel and bloodthirsty, just as he was. Is it really wise to let them back into the Clan?"

Fireheart could understand Tallstar's misgivings, since these very cats had driven WindClan from their territory and had almost destroyed them. He wondered how many ShadowClan warriors shared his concern. After all, Brokentail's own Clan had suffered almost as much as WindClan had from their murderous leader's rule; he was surprised they would take the outlaws back.

"Brokentail's warriors obeyed him," Tigerstar replied

calmly. "Which of you wouldn't do the same for your own leader? The warrior code says that a leader's word is law." He swiped his tongue around his muzzle before continuing. "These cats were loyal to Brokentail. They will be loyal to me now. Blackfoot, who was Brokentail's deputy, is my deputy now."

Tallstar still looked suspicious, but Tigerstar met his gaze steadily. "Tallstar, you are right to hate Brokentail. He did great harm to your Clan. But let me remind you that it was not my decision to take him into ThunderClan and care for him. I spoke against that from the first, but when Bluestar insisted on giving him sanctuary, loyalty to my leader meant that I had to support her."

The WindClan leader hesitated and then bowed his head. "That's true," he meowed.

"Then all I ask is that you trust me, and give my warriors a chance to show that they can honor the warrior code, and prove their loyalty to ShadowClan once more. With the help of StarClan, my first task is to make ShadowClan well and strong again," Tigerstar vowed.

Perhaps, Fireheart thought hopefully, now that Tigerstar had achieved his ambition, he really would become a great leader. He had said that the outlaws deserved another chance; perhaps the same was true of Tigerstar himself. Yet every hair in Fireheart's pelt was prickling. He still wanted to make it clear to Tigerstar that ThunderClan was not his for the taking.

He was so deep in thought that he hardly realized that Tigerstar had finished addressing the assembled Clans.

"Fireheart?" Tallstar meowed. "Do you want to speak now?"

Fireheart swallowed nervously and padded forward, the rock cool and smooth beneath his paws. Below, he could see Sandstorm and the other ThunderClan cats looking up at him expectantly; the pale ginger she-cat was watching him with a glow of admiration in her eyes.

Feeling encouraged, Fireheart began to speak. He wasn't going to pretend that the ThunderClan camp had not been devastated by the recent fire, but he did not want to give the impression that the Clan was weak. Leopardfur, the River-Clan deputy, was listening intently. As Fireheart glanced at her she narrowed her eyes as if she were measuring his words carefully. RiverClan had helped ThunderClan escape from the fire, and no cat knew better than Leopardfur how vulner-able they were.

"A few dawns ago," Fireheart reported, "fire started in the Treecut place and swept through our camp. Halftail and Patchpelt died, and the Clan honors them. And we especially honor Yellowfang. She went back into the burning camp to rescue Halftail." He bowed his head, memories of the old medicine cat threatening to overwhelm him. "I found her in her den, and I was with her when she died."

Wails of dismay broke out among the listening cats. Not only ThunderClan had reason to grieve for Yellowfang's death. Fireheart noticed Runningnose sitting erect and gazing upward, his eyes clouded with sorrow. He had been Yellowfang's apprentice when she was ShadowClan's med-icine cat, before Brokentail drove her out.

"Our new medicine cat will be Cinderpelt," Fireheart went on. "Bluestar suffered from breathing in smoke, but she is recovering. None of our kits were harmed. We are rebuilding our camp." He did not mention the shortage of prey in the burned stretch of forest, or the way that the camp was still open to attack in spite of their efforts to rebuild the walls. "We must thank RiverClan," he added, with a respectful glance at Crookedstar. "They gave us shelter in their camp during the fire. Without their help, more of our cats might have died."

As Crookedstar acknowledged his words with a nod, Fireheart couldn't resist glancing down at Leopardfur again. The RiverClan deputy hadn't shifted her amber gaze from him.

Pausing to take a deep breath, Fireheart turned to Tigerstar. "ThunderClan accepts that StarClan has approved your leadership," he meowed. "As rogues, your followers stole from all four Clans while they roamed the forest, so it is good that they have their own Clan again. We trust that they will be bound by the warrior code and will keep to their own territory." He thought he could see a gleam of surprise in Tigerstar's eyes, and continued firmly, "But we will not tolerate any invasions into ThunderClan territory. In spite of the fire, we are strong enough to drive out any cat who sets a paw over our borders. We have no fear of ShadowClan."

One or two yowls of agreement rose from his own warriors below. Tigerstar gave a slight dip of his head, and spoke in a low rumble that carried no farther than the other cats on

WARRIORS: A DANGEROUS PATH 14

top of the Great Rock. "Brave words, Fireheart. You have nothing to fear from ShadowClan."

Fireheart wished that he could believe him. Bowing his head in acknowledgment, he stepped back again, his fur flattening in relief that his turn to speak was over, and listened while Tallstar and Crookedstar gave the news from their own Clans—word of new apprentices and warriors, and a warning of extra Twolegs by the river.

When the formal part of the meeting was over, Fireheart sprang down to the group of ThunderClan warriors at the base of the rock.

"You spoke well," meowed Whitestorm. Sandstorm's eyes shone as she looked at Fireheart, and she pressed her muzzle against his neck.

Fireheart gave her cheek a quick lick. "It's time to go," he meowed. "Say your good-byes, and if any cat asks, tell them that ThunderClan is doing fine."

Throughout the clearing, the groups of cats were breaking up as all four Clans prepared to leave. Fireheart began looking around for the rest of his warriors. He caught sight of a familiar blue-gray shape and bounded across the hollow to join her.

"Hi, Mistyfoot," he meowed. "How are you? How's Graystripe? I didn't see him here tonight."

Graystripe had been Fireheart's first friend in ThunderClan; they had trained together as apprentices. But then Graystripe had fallen in love with Silverstream, a young RiverClan warrior, and she had died bearing his kits. Graystripe had left his own

Clan to go with them to RiverClan, and though seasons had passed, Fireheart still missed him.

"Graystripe didn't come." The RiverClan queen sat down and curled her tail neatly around her paws. "Leopardfur wouldn't let him. She was furious about the way he behaved during the fire. She says that in his heart, he's still loyal to ThunderClan."

Fireheart had to admit that Leopardfur was probably right. Graystripe had already asked Bluestar if he could come back to ThunderClan, but she had refused. "So how is he?" Fireheart repeated.

"He's fine," Mistyfoot meowed. "So are the kits. He asked me to find out how you were doing after the fire. Bluestar's not seriously ill, you say?"

"No, she'll be better soon." Fireheart tried to sound confident. It was true that Bluestar was recovering from the effects of breathing smoke, but for some moons now the ThunderClan leader's mind had been clouded. She had begun to doubt her own judgment, and even to question the loyalty of her warriors. The discovery of Tigerstar's treachery had shaken her to her core, and Fireheart couldn't help worrying about how she would react to the news that the deputy she had exiled was now leader of ShadowClan.

"I'm glad to hear that she is recovering." Mistyfoot's mew broke into his thoughts.

Fireheart twitched his ears. "How's Crookedstar?" he asked, changing the subject. The RiverClan leader had seemed frail when he had allowed ThunderClan to shelter in his camp, and tonight, next to Tigerstar, he looked even older than Fireheart remembered. But maybe that wasn't surprising. The River-Clan leader had had to cope with floods that had driven his cats out of their camp and with a shortage of prey because Twoleg rubbish had poisoned the river. More than all that, Graystripe's beloved Silverstream had been Crookedstar's daughter, and her death had caused him much grief.

"He's okay," meowed Mistyfoot. "He's been through a lot recently. Mind you, I'm more concerned about Graypool," she added, naming the cat who had raised her from kithood. "She seems so old now. I'm afraid she'll go to StarClan soon."

Fireheart would have liked to give the young queen a comforting lick, but he was not sure how the RiverClan cat would take that from a cat of another Clan. Apart from Graypool, Fireheart was the only cat who knew that the frail RiverClan elder was not the real mother of Mistyfoot and her brother, Stonefur. Their father, Oakheart, had brought them to RiverClan when they were tiny kits, and Graypool had agreed to take care of them. Their real mother was Bluestar.

As Fireheart murmured sympathetically and said his good-byes to Mistyfoot, he couldn't help feeling that trouble was still in store for both Clans because of Bluestar's secret.

CHAPTER 2

❧

The sky was growing pale with the first light of dawn when Fireheart and his warriors returned to the ThunderClan camp. Although Fireheart knew what he would find, it was still a shock to reach the top of the ravine and gaze down at the devastation. All the covering of gorse and fern had been stripped away by the fire. The earth floor of the camp was left exposed, surrounded by the blackened remains of the wall of thornbushes that was shored up with branches where the Clan cats had begun to repair it.

"Will it ever be the same?" Sandstorm meowed softly as she came to stand beside him.

A wave of exhaustion flooded over Fireheart as he thought of how much time and work it would take before the camp was fully rebuilt. "One day," he promised. "We've been through bad times before. We'll survive." He pressed his muzzle against Sandstorm's flank, taking comfort from her reassuring purr, before he led the way down the ravine.

The bush where the warriors slept was still there, but the thick canopy of twigs had been burned away. Only a few charred branches remained, the gaps between them interwoven with sticks. Brackenfur was crouched outside, while Longtail sat on watch near the entrance to the nursery, and Dustpelt paced back and forth in front of the elders' den.

Brackenfur sprang to his paws as Fireheart and the others appeared, only to relax a moment later. "It's you," he meowed, relief in his voice. "We've been expecting Tigerclaw all night."

"Well, you can stop worrying," Fireheart meowed. "He's too busy to worry about us. Tiger*star* is the new leader of ShadowClan."

Brackenfur stared in astonishment. "Great StarClan!" he said with a gasp. "I don't believe it!"

"*What* did you say?" Fireheart turned to see Longtail loping across the clearing. "Did I hear you right?"

"You did." Fireheart could see the shock in the tabby warrior's face. "Tigerstar has taken over ShadowClan."

"And they let him?" meowed Longtail. "Are they mad?"

"Not mad at all," Whitestorm replied, coming up to stand beside Fireheart. The elderly warrior scraped the bare earth with his paws and settled down on his haunches with a tired sigh. His thick white fur was stained with soot after the journey back through the forest. "The sickness almost destroyed the ShadowClan cats. They were desperate for a strong leader. Tigerstar must have seemed like a gift from StarClan."

"It sounds like that's just what he was," Fireheart agreed heavily. "Apparently StarClan sent an omen to Runningnose to tell ShadowClan that a great leader would arise."

"But Tigerstar is a traitor!" Brackenfur protested.

"ShadowClan don't know that," Fireheart pointed out.

By this time other cats were appearing. Brightpaw and Swiftpaw ran over from the apprentices' den; Dustpelt padded up with Darkstripe's apprentice, Fernpaw; Speckletail peered curiously out from the nursery. As they pressed around Fireheart with their questions, he had to raise his voice to make himself heard.

"Listen, all of you," he meowed. "There's something you need to hear." *And I have to tell Bluestar*, he added silently, bracing himself for the encounter. "Whitestorm will tell you what happened at the Gathering," he went on, "and then I want a dawn patrol." He hesitated, looking around at the assembled cats. All the warriors were tired; those who hadn't been to the Gathering had stayed awake to guard the camp.

Before Fireheart could decide who to send, Dustpelt spoke. "Ashpaw and I will go."

Fireheart dipped his head gratefully. The brown warrior had never been friendly toward him, but he was a loyal cat to ThunderClan, and he seemed to accept Fireheart's authority as deputy.

"I'll go too," Mousefur offered.

"And me," meowed Cloudpaw.

Fireheart let out a purr of appreciation at his apprentice's words. He was pleased that his sister's son was working harder for the Clan and showing more commitment to Clan life, after the disastrous episode when he was taken away by Twolegs and had to be rescued. "Dustpelt, Mousefur, Cloudpaw, and Ashpaw, then," he meowed. "The rest of you get some sleep. We'll need hunting patrols later on."

"What about you?" asked Darkstripe.

Fireheart took a deep breath. "I'm going to speak to Bluestar."

The curtain of lichen had been burned away from the entrance to Bluestar's den at the base of the Highrock. As Fireheart approached, Cinderpelt, Thunderclan's medicine cat, emerged into the clearing and paused to stretch. Her dark gray fur was ruffled, and she looked worn out from the strain of caring for the Clan in the aftermath of the fire, but the strength of her spirit still shone in her blue eyes. Fireheart was reminded of the time when she had been his eager apprentice, until she had been lured too close to the Thunderpath, in a trap which Tigerclaw had set for Bluestar. The young cat's leg had been permanently injured so she could never be a warrior, but she had always kept her commitment to serving her Clan.

Fireheart padded up to her. "How is Bluestar today?" he asked quietly.

Cinderpelt cast a worried glance back into the den. "She didn't sleep last night," she replied. "I've given her juniper berries to calm her, but I don't know if they'll do any good."

"I need to tell her what happened at the Gathering," Fireheart meowed. "And she's not going to like it."

Cinderpelt's eyes narrowed. "Why not?"

As quickly as he could, Fireheart told her.

Cinderpelt listened in shocked silence, her blue eyes wide with amazement. "What will you do?" she asked when Fireheart had finished.

"There isn't much I *can* do. Besides, it could be a good

thing for ThunderClan. Tigerstar's got what he wants now, and with any luck he's going to be far too busy working his new Clan into shape to bother about us." Seeing that Cinderpelt looked disbelieving, he added hastily, "Who they choose for leader is ShadowClan's business. We'll have to keep a watch on our borders, but I don't believe Tigerstar will be much of a threat, for a while, at least. I'm more worried about how Bluestar is going to take it."

"This is going to make her worse," Cinderpelt meowed anxiously. "I only hope I can find the right herbs to help her. I wish Yellowfang were here."

"I know." Fireheart pressed himself comfortingly against Cinderpelt's side. "But you'll be fine. You're a great medicine cat."

"It's not just that." Cinderpelt's voice dropped to a painful whisper. "I *miss* her, Fireheart! I keep waiting for her to tell me I haven't the sense of a newborn kit—at least when she praised me, I knew she really meant it. I want *her*, Fireheart— her scent and the feel of her fur and the sound of her voice."

"I know," Fireheart murmured. He felt an emptiness inside as memories of the old cat flooded over him. He had been very close to Yellowfang, ever since he had discovered her living as a rogue in ThunderClan territory. "But she hunts with StarClan now."

And perhaps she had found peace at last, he reflected, as he remembered the torment in Yellowfang's voice as she died thinking of her son, Brokentail—the murderous cat she had never stopped loving, even though he had grown up without knowing she was his mother. In the end she had killed him to save her adopted Clan from his bloodthirsty scheming. Yellowfang's pain was at an end, but Fireheart could not imagine that he would ever stop missing her.

"You go to Highstones soon, don't you?" he reminded Cinderpelt. "To meet the other medicine cats? I think you'll feel very close to Yellowfang then."

"Maybe you're right." Cinderpelt pushed away from him. "I can just hear Yellowfang now," she meowed. "'Why are you standing around moaning when there's work to be done?' You go and talk to Bluestar. I'll look in on her again a bit later on."

"If you're sure you're okay," mewed Fireheart.

"I'm fine." Cinderpelt gave his ear a quick lick. "Be strong for her, Fireheart," she urged. "She needs you more than ever."

Fireheart watched the medicine cat as she limped rapidly away, and then turned toward Bluestar's den. Taking a deep breath, he called a greeting and entered through the gap where the lichen used to grow.

Bluestar was crouched on a pile of bedding at the back of the cave, her forepaws tucked under her chest. Her head was raised, but she was not looking at Fireheart. Instead her blue eyes were blank, fixed on something far away that only she could see. Her pelt was rough and unwashed, and she was so thin that Fireheart could see every rib. His heart twisted with pity for her and fear for the rest of his Clan. Their leader had diminished into an old, sick cat, broken by trouble and unable to defend herself, let alone her Clan.

"Bluestar?" Fireheart meowed hesitantly.

At first he thought that Bluestar had not heard him. Then, as he padded farther into the den, she turned her head. Her cloudy blue gaze focused on him, and for a heartbeat she looked puzzled, as if she couldn't remember who he was.

Then her ears pricked and intelligence flooded back into her eyes. "Fireheart? What do you want?"

Fireheart dipped his head respectfully. "I'm just back from the Gathering, Bluestar. I'm afraid there's bad news." He paused.

"Well?" Bluestar sounded irritable. "What is it?"

"ShadowClan has a new leader," Fireheart meowed. He plunged straight on. "It's Tigerclaw—Tiger*star* now."

In an instant, Bluestar leaped to her paws. Her eyes blazed cold fire, and Fireheart flinched at the reminder of the formidable cat she had once been. "That's impossible!" she hissed.

"No, it's true. I saw him myself. He spoke from the Great Rock, with the other leaders."

For a few moments Bluestar did not reply. She paced from one side of the den to the other and back again, her tail lashing. Fireheart backed toward the entrance, not at all sure that Bluestar wouldn't attack him for bringing this terrible news.

"How dare ShadowClan do this?" she spat at last. "How dare they shelter the cat who tried to murder me—and make him their leader!"

"Bluestar, they don't know—" Fireheart began, but the ThunderClan leader was not listening to him.

"And the other leaders?" she demanded. "What did they think? How could they let this happen?"

"No cat knows what Tigerstar did to ThunderClan." Fireheart struggled to make Bluestar think logically. "Crookedstar didn't say much, although Tallstar was unhappy at first that Tigerstar had taken Brokentail's old followers back into the Clan."

"Tallstar!" Bluestar spat. "We should know by now that we can't trust him. After all, it didn't take him long to forget what we did for his Clan, after you and Graystripe risked your lives to find them and bring them home."

Fireheart started to protest, but Bluestar ignored him. "StarClan have abandoned me!" she went on, still pacing furiously. "They told me that fire would save the Clan, but fire has almost destroyed us. How can I ever trust StarClan again—especially now? They have granted a leader's nine lives to that traitor. They care nothing for me or for ThunderClan!"

Fireheart flinched. "Bluestar, listen—"

"No, Fireheart, you listen." Bluestar padded over to him. Her fur was fluffed up and her teeth bared in anger. "ThunderClan is doomed. Tigerstar will lead ShadowClan to destroy us all—and we can expect no help from StarClan."

"Tigerstar didn't seem hostile." Fireheart was desperately trying to get through to his leader. "When he spoke, all he seemed to care about was leading his new Clan."

Bluestar let out a crack of harsh laughter. "If you believe that, Fireheart, you're a fool. Tigerstar will be here before leaf-fall; you mark my words. But he'll find us waiting for him. If we're all going to die, we'll take a few of ShadowClan with us."

She began pacing rapidly back and forth again, while

Fireheart watched, appalled.

"Double the patrols," she ordered. "Set a watch on the camp. Send cats to guard the border with ShadowClan."

"We haven't enough warriors for all that," Fireheart objected. "Every cat is exhausted with the extra work rebuilding the camp. It's all we can do to keep up the regular patrols."

"Are you questioning my orders?" Bluestar whipped around to face him again, drawing her lips back in a snarl. Her eyes narrowed suspiciously. "Or are you going to betray me too?"

"No, Bluestar, no! You can trust me." Fireheart tensed his muscles, half expecting that he would need to dodge Bluestar's slashing claws.

Suddenly the old leader relaxed. "I know, Fireheart. You've always been loyal, not like those others." As if the strength of her fury had exhausted her, she limped back to her bedding.

"Set the patrols," she ordered, sinking down in the soft moss and heather. "Do it now, before ShadowClan makes crowfood of us all."

"Yes, Bluestar." Fireheart saw no point in arguing any more. He bowed his head and backed out of the den. Bluestar's gaze was once more fixed on something unseen. Fireheart wondered if she was looking into the future, and watching the destruction of her Clan.

CHAPTER 3

Fireheart opened his eyes and blinked in the uncomfortably bright sunlight. He still couldn't get used to the way the sun shone straight into the warriors' den now that the thick covering of leaves had gone. Yawning, he uncurled himself and shook the clinging scraps of moss from his coat.

Close beside him, Sandstorm was still asleep; Dustpelt and Darkstripe were curled up a little farther away. Fireheart padded out into the clearing. It was three days since the Gathering and the discovery of Tigerstar's new leadership, and there was still no sign of the attack Bluestar had feared. ThunderClan had used the time to rebuild the camp, and although there was still a long way to go, Fireheart couldn't help feeling pleased when he saw shady walls of fern beginning to grow back around the edge of the camp, and the bramble thicket firmly interlaced with twigs to shelter the nursing queens and their kits.

As Fireheart made his way toward the pile of fresh-kill, he saw the dawn patrol returning with Whitestorm in the lead. Fireheart paused and waited for the white warrior to join him.

"Any sign of ShadowClan?"

Whitestorm shook his head. "Nothing," he meowed. "Just the usual scent markings along their border. There was one thing, though. . . ."

Fireheart's ears pricked. "What?"

"Not far from Snakerocks we found a whole stretch of undergrowth trampled down, and pigeon feathers scattered all over it."

"Pigeon feathers?" Fireheart echoed. "I haven't seen a pigeon for days. Is some other Clan hunting in our territory?"

"I don't think so. The whole place reeked of dog." Whitestorm wrinkled his nose with distaste. "There was dog dirt there too."

"Oh, a dog." Fireheart flicked his tail dismissively. "Well, we all know that Twolegs are always bringing their dogs into the forest. They run around, chase a few squirrels, and then the Twolegs take them home again." He let out a purr of amusement. "The only unusual thing is that it looks as if this one caught something."

To his surprise, Whitestorm continued to look serious. "All the same, I think you should tell the patrols to keep their eyes open," he meowed.

"Okay." Fireheart respected the older warrior too much to ignore his advice, but privately he thought the dog would be a long way away by now, shut up somewhere in Twolegplace. Dogs were noisy nuisances, but he had more important things to worry about.

He was reminded of his anxiety about food supplies as he

followed Whitestorm to the pile of fresh-kill. Brightpaw, Whitestorm's apprentice, and Cloudpaw, who had made up the rest of the patrol, were already there.

"Look at this!" Cloudpaw complained as Fireheart came up. He turned a vole over with one paw. "There's hardly a decent mouthful on it!"

"Prey is scarce," Fireheart reminded him, noticing there were only a few pieces of fresh-kill on the pile. "Any creatures that survived the fire can't find much to eat."

"We need to hunt again," Cloudpaw meowed. He bit into the vole and swallowed. "I'll go as soon as I've finished this."

"You can come with me," mewed Fireheart, selecting a magpie for himself. "I'm going to lead out a patrol later on."

"No, I can't wait," Cloudpaw mumbled through another mouthful. "I'm so hungry I could eat you. Brightpaw, do you want to come with me?"

Brightpaw, who was neatly tucking into a mouse, glanced at her mentor for permission. When Whitestorm nodded she sprang up. "Ready when you are," she meowed.

"All right then," mewed Fireheart. He was slightly annoyed that Cloudpaw hadn't asked for his mentor's permission like Brightpaw, but the Clan did need fresh-kill, and both the apprentices were good hunters. "Don't go too far from camp," he warned.

"But all the best prey is farther away, where the fire didn't reach," Cloudpaw objected. "We'll be fine, Fireheart," he promised. "We'll hunt for the elders first."

Swallowing the last of his vole in one enormous gulp, he

dashed off toward the camp entrance with Brightpaw racing after him.

"Stay away from Twolegplace!" Fireheart called after them, remembering how Cloudpaw had once been all too fond of visiting the Twolegs. The apprentice had paid a harsh price when they had taken him away to their nest on the far side of WindClan's territory. As greenleaf drew to an end, with the prospect of a hungry leaf-bare to come, Fireheart hoped that his apprentice wouldn't be tempted back into his old ways.

"Apprentices!" Whitestorm purred as he watched the two young cats bounding away. "Dawn patrol, and now they're off hunting. I wish I had their energy." He dragged a blackbird a little way from the pile of fresh-kill and crouched down to eat.

As Fireheart finished his magpie, he saw Sandstorm padding across from the warriors' den. The sun shone on her pale ginger coat, and Fireheart admired the ripple of her fur as she moved. "Do you want to come and hunt with me?" he asked as she approached.

"Looks as if we need it," Sandstorm replied, surveying the pitifully few pieces of fresh-kill that remained. "Let's go now—I can wait to eat until we catch something."

Fireheart looked around for another cat to join them and noticed Longtail heading for the apprentices' den, calling for Swiftpaw. "Hey, Longtail!" he meowed as the two cats padded across the clearing. "Come and join our hunting patrol."

Longtail hesitated, as if he wasn't sure whether that was an order from his deputy or not. "We were going to the training hollow," he explained. "Swiftpaw needs to practice his defense moves."

"You can do that later." This time Fireheart made it clear that he was giving an order. "The Clan needs fresh-kill first."

Longtail flicked his tail irritably but said nothing. Swiftpaw was looking more enthusiastic, his eyes bright. The young black-and-white tom had grown almost as big as his mentor, Fireheart noticed; he was the oldest of the apprentices, and he could expect to be made a warrior soon.

I must talk to Bluestar about his naming ceremony, Fireheart thought. *Cloudpaw too, and Brightpaw and Thornpaw. The Clan needs more warriors.*

Leaving Whitestorm to take a well-earned rest, Fireheart led his hunting party out of the camp and up the ravine. At the top, he turned toward Sunningrocks. Doing his best to carry out Bluestar's order about doubling the patrols, he had instructed all the hunting parties to do border duty as well, staying alert for other Clans' scents or any other signs of an enemy presence. In particular, he had warned them to keep a careful watch on the ShadowClan border, but privately he resolved not to neglect RiverClan.

He had an uneasy feeling about their relationship with ThunderClan. With Crookedstar growing old, his deputy, Leopardfur, would have more authority, and Fireheart still expected her to ask for something in return for RiverClan's help on the night of the fire.

As Fireheart led the way toward the river, he noticed plants pushing their way up through the blackened soil. New ferns were beginning to uncoil and green tendrils spread out to cover the earth. The forest was beginning to recover, but as leaf-fall approached, growth would slow down. Fireheart was still worried that his Clan was heading for a cold and comfortless leaf-bare.

When they reached Sunningrocks, Longtail led Swiftpaw into one of the gullies between the rocks. "You can practice listening for mice and voles," he told his apprentice. "See if you can catch something before the rest of us."

Fireheart watched them go approvingly. The pale tabby warrior was a conscientious mentor, and a strong bond had grown between him and Swiftpaw.

Fireheart skirted the rocks on the side that faced the river, where more of the grass and foliage had survived. It was not long before he spotted a mouse scuffling among some brittle grass stems. As it sat up, nibbling a seed clasped in its forepaws, Fireheart sprang and finished it off swiftly.

"Good work," Sandstorm murmured, padding up to him.

"Do you want it?" Fireheart asked, pushing the fresh-kill toward her with one paw. "You haven't eaten yet."

"No, thanks," meowed Sandstorm tartly. "I can catch my own."

She slipped off into the shadow of a hazel tree. Fireheart looked after her, wondering if he'd offended her, and then started to scrape earth over his prey so it could be collected later.

"You want to watch out with that one," a voice meowed behind him. "She'll claw your ears off if you're not careful."

Fireheart spun around. His old friend Graystripe was standing on the border with RiverClan, farther down the slope toward the river. Water gleamed on his thick gray pelt.

"Graystripe!" Fireheart exclaimed. "You startled me!"

Graystripe gave himself a shake and sent droplets sparkling into the air. "I saw you from the other side of the river," he mewed. "I never thought I'd find you catching prey for Sandstorm. Special to you, is she?"

"I don't know what you're talking about," Fireheart protested. His fur suddenly felt hot, and prickled as if ants were crawling through it. "Sandstorm is just a friend."

Graystripe let out a purr of amusement. "Oh, sure, if you say so." He strolled up the slope and lowered his head to butt Fireheart affectionately on the shoulder. "You're lucky, Fireheart. She's a very impressive cat."

Fireheart opened his mouth and then closed it again. Graystripe wouldn't be convinced not matter what he said—and besides, maybe he was right. Maybe Sandstorm was becoming more than a friend. "Never mind that," he meowed, changing the subject. "Tell me how you're getting on. What's the news in RiverClan?"

The laughter died from Graystripe's yellow eyes. "Not much. Every cat is talking about Tigerstar." When Graystripe had been a ThunderClan warrior, he and Fireheart had been the only cats to know the truth about Tigerstar's murderous ambition, and that he had killed the former ThunderClan deputy, Redtail.

"I don't know what to make of it," Fireheart admitted.

"Tigerstar might be different, now he's got what he wants. No cat can deny that he could make a good leader—he's strong, he can fight and hunt, and he knows the warrior code by heart."

"But no cat can trust him," Graystripe growled. "What's the point of knowing the warrior code if all you do is ignore what it says?"

"It's not up to us to trust him now," Fireheart pointed out. "He's got a new Clan, and Runningnose reported an omen that seemed to say StarClan would be sending them a great new leader. StarClan must know that ShadowClan needs a strong warrior to build them up again after the sickness."

Graystripe didn't look convinced. "StarClan sent him?" He snorted. "I'll believe that when hedgehogs fly."

Fireheart couldn't help agreeing with Graystripe that it would be hard to trust Tigerstar. Making his new Clan healthy again might occupy him for a season or two, but after that . . . The thought of the fierce warrior at the head of a strong Clan sent a shudder through Fireheart from ears to tail-tip. He couldn't believe that Tigerstar would settle down to a peaceful life in the forest, respecting the rights of the other three Clans. Sooner or later he would want to extend his territory, and his first target would be ThunderClan.

"If I were you," meowed Graystripe, echoing his thoughts, "I'd keep a very careful watch on my borders."

"Yes, I—" Fireheart began. He broke off as he saw Sandstorm coming toward them, a young rabbit dangling from her jaws. She padded across the pebbles, and dropped her prey at Fireheart's feet. Looking more relaxed, as if she had gotten over her brief annoyance, she nodded to the RiverClan warrior.

"Hi, Graystripe," she mewed. "How are the kits?"

"They're fine, thanks," Graystripe replied. His eyes glowed with pride. "They'll be apprenticed soon."

"Will you mentor one of them?" Fireheart asked.

To his surprise, Graystripe looked uncertain. "I don't know," he meowed. "If it were Crookedstar's decision, maybe . . . but he doesn't do much these days, except sleep. Leopardfur organizes most things now, and she'll never forgive me for the way Whiteclaw died. I think she'll probably give the kits to some other warriors to mentor."

He bowed his head. Fireheart realized he still felt guilty about the death of the RiverClan warrior who had fallen into the gorge when his patrol attacked a small group of ThunderClan warriors.

"That's tough," meowed Fireheart, pressing himself comfortingly against Graystripe's side.

"But you can see her point," Sandstorm pointed out mildly. "Leopardfur will want to make sure that the kits are brought up to be completely loyal to RiverClan."

Graystripe swung his head around to face her, his fur bristling. "That's just what I would do! I don't want my kits to grow up feeling torn between two Clans." His eyes clouded. "I know what that's like."

Pain for his friend flooded over Fireheart. After the fire, Graystripe had shown how unhappy he was in his new Clan, and clearly things were no better now. Fireheart wanted to say, "Come home," but he knew he had no right to offer Graystripe a place in the Clan when Bluestar had already refused.

"Speak to Crookedstar," he suggested. "Ask him yourself about the kits."

"And try to stay on the good side of Leopardfur," added Sandstorm. "Don't let her catch you crossing the ThunderClan border."

Graystripe flinched. "Maybe you're right. I'd better be getting back. Good-bye, Sandstorm, Fireheart."

"Try to come to the next Gathering," Fireheart urged.

Graystripe flicked his tail in acknowledgment and padded off down the slope. Halfway to the river he turned, meowed, "Wait there a moment!" and raced down to the edge of the water. For several heartbeats he sat motionless on a flat stone, gazing down into the shallows.

"Now what's he up to?" Sandstorm muttered.

Before Fireheart could reply, Graystripe's paw darted out. A silver fish shot out of the stream and fell to the bank, where it lay flopping and wriggling. Graystripe finished it off with a single blow of his paw and dragged it back up the slope to where Fireheart and Sandstorm stood watching.

"Here," he meowed as he dropped it. "I know prey must be scarce since the fire. That should help a bit."

"Thanks," meowed Fireheart, and added admiringly, "That was a neat trick back there."

Graystripe let out a purr of satisfaction. "Mistyfoot showed me how."

"It's very welcome," Sandstorm told him. "But if Leopard-fur finds out you've been feeding another Clan, she won't be pleased."

"Leopardfur can go chase her own tail," Graystripe growled. "If she says anything, I'll remind her how Fireheart and I helped feed RiverClan during the floods last newleaf."

He turned away and bounded back to the river. Fireheart's heart ached as he watched his friend launch himself into the water and begin swimming strongly for the opposite bank. He would have given anything to have Graystripe back in ThunderClan, but he had to admit it seemed unlikely that the gray warrior could ever be accepted there again.

Fireheart struggled to carry the slippery fish as the hunting patrol returned to camp, his mouth watering as the unfamiliar scent filled his nostrils. When he entered the camp he saw that the pile of fresh-kill already looked bigger. Cloudpaw and Brightpaw had returned, and were about to go out again with Mousefur and Thornpaw.

"We've fed the elders, Fireheart!" Cloudpaw called over his shoulder as he scampered up the ravine.

"And Cinderpelt?" Fireheart called back.

"Not yet!"

Fireheart watched his young kin dash out of sight and then turned back to the pile of fresh-kill. Perhaps Graystripe's fish would tempt Cinderpelt, he thought. He suspected that the young medicine cat wasn't eating enough, out of grief for Yellowfang, and because she was so busy caring for the smoke-sick cats and Bluestar.

"Are you hungry, Fireheart?" asked Sandstorm, dropping the last of her catch onto the pile. In the end she had waited to eat until they brought the prey back to camp, and she was eyeing the fresh-kill avidly. "We could eat together, if you like."

"Okay." The magpie Fireheart had eaten that morning seemed a long time ago now. "I'll just take this to Cinderpelt."

"Don't be long," meowed Sandstorm.

Fireheart gripped the fish in his jaws and walked toward Cinderpelt's den. Before the fire, a lush tunnel of ferns had separated it from the rest of the camp. Now just a few blackened stalks showed above the ground, and Fireheart could clearly see the cleft in the rock that was the entrance to the den.

He stopped outside, dropped the fresh-kill, and called, "Cinderpelt!"

After a moment the young medicine cat poked her head out of the opening. "What? Oh, it's you, Fireheart."

She padded out of the den to join him. Her fur was ruffled, and her eyes didn't have their usual lively sparkle. Instead she seemed distracted and troubled. Fireheart guessed that her mind was on Yellowfang.

"I'm glad you're here," she mewed. "There's something I want to tell you."

"Have something to eat first," Fireheart urged her. "Look, Graystripe caught a fish for us."

"Thanks, Fireheart," Cinderpelt meowed, "but this is urgent. StarClan sent a dream to me last night."

Something about the way she spoke made Fireheart uneasy. He was still not used to the way that his former apprentice was growing into a true medicine cat, living without a mate or kits of her own, meeting secretly with other medicine cats and united with them through their bond with the warrior spirits of StarClan.

"What was the dream about?" he asked. He had experienced dreams like this more than once, warning him of things that were going to happen. That helped him to imagine, better than most Clan cats, the mixture of awe and bewilderment that Cinderpelt must be feeling now.

"I'm not sure." Cinderpelt blinked in confusion. "I thought I was standing in the forest, and I could hear something large crashing through the trees, but I couldn't see what it was. And I heard voices calling—harsh voices, in a language that wasn't cat. But I could understand what they said. . . ."

Her voice trailed off. She stood gazing into the distance, her eyes clouded, while her front paws kneaded the ground in front of her.

"What did they say?" Fireheart prompted.

Cinderpelt shivered. "It was really strange. They were calling, 'Pack, pack,' and 'Kill, kill.'"

Fireheart couldn't help feeling disappointed. He had hoped that a message from StarClan might have given them some hint about how to deal with all his problems—Tigerstar's reappearance, Bluestar's illness, and the aftermath of the fire. "Do you know what it means?" he asked.

Cinderpelt shook her head, a lingering look of horror in

her eyes, as though she faced a huge threat Fireheart could not see. "Not yet. Maybe StarClan will show me more when I've been to Highstones. But it's something bad, Fireheart, I'm sure of it."

"As if we haven't enough to worry about," Fireheart muttered. To Cinderpelt, he mewed, "I don't know what I can do, unless we find out more. I need facts. Are you sure that's all the dream told you?"

Her blue eyes still wide with distress, Cinderpelt nodded. Fireheart gave her ear a comforting lick. "Don't worry, Cinderpelt. If it's a warning about ShadowClan, we're already watching out for them. Just tell me the moment you get any more details."

He jumped as an irritated yowling sounded from behind him. "Fireheart, are you going to be all day?"

Glancing around, he saw that Sandstorm was waiting for him at the entrance to the burned fern tunnel. "I've got to go," he said to Cinderpelt.

"But—"

"I'll think about it, okay?" Fireheart interrupted her, his rumbling belly urging him to go and join Sandstorm. "Let me know if you have any other dreams."

Cinderpelt's ears twitched in annoyance. "This is a message from StarClan, Fireheart, not just a root digging into my fur or a tough bit of fresh-kill caught in my throat. It could affect the whole Clan. We need to work out what it means."

"Well, you'll be better at that than I am," Fireheart told her, backing away from Cinderpelt's den and tossing the last words over his shoulder.

Bounding across the clearing toward Sandstorm, he wondered briefly what the dream could have meant. It didn't sound like an attack from another Clan, and he couldn't think of anything else that might be a threat. As he tucked into the vole that Sandstorm had saved for him, he managed to put Cinderpelt's dream out of his mind.

CHAPTER 4

Fireheart's flanks heaved as he fought for breath, and his cheek stung where claws had raked across it. As he staggered to his feet, Brightpaw took a couple of steps back.

"I haven't hurt you, have I?" the ginger-and-white apprentice asked anxiously.

"No, I'm fine." Fireheart gasped. "Did Whitestorm show you that move? I never saw it coming. Well done."

Trying not to limp, he padded across the training hollow to where Swiftpaw, Thornpaw, and Cloudpaw were watching. He had been assessing the apprentices' fighting skills, and they had all held their own against him. They had the makings of formidable warriors.

"I'm glad you're all on my side. I wouldn't want to meet you in battle," Fireheart meowed. "I've had a word with your mentors, and they think you're ready, so I'm going to ask Bluestar if you can be made warriors."

Brightpaw, Thornpaw, and Swiftpaw exchanged excited glances. Cloudpaw tried to look nonchalant, but there was a gleam of anticipation in his eyes too.

"Okay," Fireheart went on. "Hunt on your way back to

camp, and see that the elders and the queens are fed. Then you can eat."

"If there's anything left," mewed Swiftpaw.

Fireheart flicked a glance at him. Swiftpaw sometimes picked up discontented rumblings from his mentor, Longtail, who had once been a close ally of Tigerclaw, but on this occasion he seemed to be trying to make a joke. All four young cats sprang up and dashed out of the training hollow. Fireheart heard Brightpaw yowling to Cloudpaw, "Bet I catch more prey than you!"

It seemed a long time since he had been that carefree, Fireheart reflected as he followed more slowly. Under the weight of his responsibilities as deputy, he sometimes felt older than the elders. The Clan was surviving, managing to find food and to rebuild the devastated camp, but all the warriors were overstretched. Fireheart was on his paws from dawn to sunset, and every night he went to his den with tasks still undone. *How long can we go on?* he asked himself. *It'll get harder, not easier, when leaf-bare comes.* Already the few leaves that the fire had left on the trees were turning red and gold. As Fireheart paused at the top of the hollow, he felt a chill breeze ruffle his fur, though the sun shone brightly.

He slipped quietly back into camp and stood for a moment near the entrance, looking around. Darkstripe, who was in charge of the rebuilding, had started to patch the remaining gaps in the branches of the warriors' den. Dustpelt was working with him and the two younger apprentices, Fernpaw and Ashpaw.

On the other side of the camp Fireheart saw Cinderpelt making her way to the elders' den, carrying some herbs in her jaws.

In the center of the clearing, Goldenflower's two kits were playing with Speckletail's kit, while the queens sat watching them near the entrance to the nursery. Willowpelt was there too, carefully guarding her litter, who were much younger, from the rough play of the older kits.

Fireheart's gaze rested on Bramblekit, the bigger of Goldenflower's kits. That strong, muscular body and dark brown pelt were disturbingly familiar; no cat who looked at the kit could doubt that Tigerstar was his father. The thought always made Fireheart uneasy, and he struggled to push it aside. Logically, he knew that he should feel just as suspicious of the kit's sister, Tawnykit, but though she shared the same father, she didn't share the misfortune of looking exactly like him. Fireheart knew it was unfair to blame Bramblekit for his father's crimes.

Yet Fireheart could not banish the memory of the young kit clinging to a branch of a blazing tree, wailing in terror as Fireheart tried to reach him. And he could not forget that while he was rescuing Bramblekit, the fire had trapped Yellowfang in her den. Had he sacrificed Yellowfang to save Tigerstar's son?

Suddenly a shrill squeal came from the group of kits. Bramblekit had bowled over Snowkit and was holding him down on the ground with his claws. The squealing came from the sturdy white kit, who didn't seem to be trying to defend himself.

Fireheart shot forward, barreling into Bramblekit and knocking him away from his victim. "Enough!" he snarled. "What do you think you're doing?"

The dark tabby kit picked himself up, amber eyes glaring with shock and indignation.

"Well?" Fireheart demanded.

Bramblekit shook dust off his fur. "It's nothing, Fireheart. We're only playing."

"Only playing? Then why was Speckletail's kit crying out like that?"

The glow died from Bramblekit's amber eyes and he shrugged. "How should I know? He can't play properly anyway."

"Bramblekit!" It was Goldenflower who spoke, coming to stand beside her kit. "How many times do I have to tell you? If somebody squeals, you let go. And don't be so rude to Fireheart. Remember, he's the deputy."

Bramblekit's eyes flicked to Fireheart and away again. "I'm sorry," he mumbled.

"Yes, well, make sure it doesn't happen again," Fireheart snapped.

Bramblekit padded past him to where Snowkit still crouched on the ground. Speckletail was giving his white fur a brisk lick. "Come on, get up," she meowed. "You're not hurt."

"Yeah, come on, Snowkit," Bramblekit mewed, swiping his tongue over the kit's ear. "I didn't mean it. Come and play, and you can be Clan leader this time."

Bramblekit's sister, Tawnykit, was sitting a couple of tail-lengths away, her tail curled around her paws. "He's no fun," she mewed. "He never has any good games."

"Tawnykit!" Goldenflower cuffed her lightly across one ear. "Don't be so nasty. I don't know what's gotten into the pair of you today."

Snowkit was still crouched on the ground, and got up only when his mother nudged him to his feet.

"Maybe you should let Cinderpelt check him," Fireheart advised the pale tabby queen. "Make sure he's not hurt."

Speckletail swung her head around and glared at her Clan deputy. "There's nothing wrong with my kit!" she growled. "Are you saying that I can't look after him properly?" Turning her back on Fireheart, she herded Snowkit back into the nursery.

"She's very protective of her kit," Goldenflower explained. "I think it comes of having only the one." She blinked fondly at her two kits, now scuffling together on the ground.

Fireheart went to sit beside her, feeling uncomfortable about the harsh way he had spoken to Bramblekit. "Have you told them that their father is leader of ShadowClan now?" he asked quietly.

Goldenflower gave him a quick glance. "No, not yet," she admitted. "They would only boast about it, and then some cat would tell them the rest of the story."

"Sooner or later they'll find out," meowed Fireheart.

The ginger queen vigorously washed her chest fur for a few moments. "I've seen the way you look at them," she mewed at last. "Especially Bramblekit. It's not his fault that he looks exactly like Tigerstar. But other cats look at him like that too." Thoughtfully she licked her paw and drew it over her ear. "I want my kits to grow up happy, not feeling guilty because of something that happened before they were born. Maybe there's more hope of that now, if Tigerstar becomes a great leader. Maybe they'll even be proud of him in the end."

Fireheart twitched his ears uncomfortably, unable to share her optimism.

"They both respect you, you know," Goldenflower went on. "Especially since you saved Bramblekit from the fire."

For a moment Fireheart didn't know what to say. He felt guiltier than ever about his hostile feelings toward Bramblekit, yet however hard he tried he could not help seeing the murderous father in the young kit.

"I think *you* should tell them about Tigerstar," Goldenflower meowed, turning an intense gaze on him. "You're the deputy, after all. They would take it well from you—and I know you would tell them the truth."

"You . . . you think I should tell them now?" Fireheart stammered. The way Goldenflower spoke made it sound like a challenge.

"No, not now," replied Goldenflower calmly. "Not until you're ready. And when you think *they're* ready," she added. "But don't leave it for too long."

Fireheart dipped his head. "I will, Goldenflower," he promised. "And I'll make it as easy for them as I can."

Before Goldenflower could reply, Bramblekit came skidding

up to his mother with Tawnykit just behind him. "Can we go and see the elders?" he asked, eyes shining. "One-eye promised to tell us some great stories!"

Goldenflower let out an indulgent purr. "Yes, of course," she meowed. "Take her something from the pile of fresh-kill—that's good manners. And mind that you're back here by sunset."

"We will!" meowed Tawnykit. She dashed off across the camp, calling over her shoulder, "I'm going to fetch a mouse for One-eye!"

"No, you're not, I am!" Bramblekit yowled, scampering after her.

"Well," Goldenflower meowed, turning back to Fireheart, "if you can see anything wrong with those kits, tell me what it is, because I can't."

She got up, obviously not needing an answer, and shook each paw in turn before retreating into the nursery. Fireheart watched her go. Somehow he had managed to make himself unpopular with both Speckletail and Goldenflower; even though Goldenflower trusted him, she clearly found it hard to forgive him for his conflicting feelings about Bramblekit—and he was no nearer to sorting them out.

Sighing, he got to his paws, realizing it was time he sent out the evening patrol. As he turned away from the nursery he caught sight of Brackenfur, who was hovering nearby as if he wanted to speak to him.

"Is there a problem?" he asked the young warrior.

"I don't know," Brackenfur replied. "It's just that I saw

what happened there, with Speckletail's kit, and—"

"You're not going to tell me I was too hard on Bramblekit, are you?"

"No, Fireheart, of course not. But . . . well, I think there might be something wrong with Snowkit."

Fireheart knew that the golden brown tom wouldn't make a fuss about nothing. "Go on," he urged.

"I've been keeping an eye on him," Brackenfur explained. He scuffed the ground with his forepaws, an embarrassed look on his face. "I . . . I sort of hoped Bluestar might choose me to mentor him, and I wanted to get to know him. And I think there's something the matter with him. He doesn't play like the others. He doesn't seem to respond when any cat talks to him. You know kits, Fireheart—noses into everything—but Snowkit's not like that. I think Cinderpelt ought to have a look at him."

"I suggested that to Speckletail and practically got my ears clawed."

Brackenfur shrugged. "Maybe Speckletail won't admit there could be anything wrong with her kit."

Fireheart thought for a moment. Snowkit *did* seem slow and unresponsive compared with the other kits. He was much older than Goldenflower's litter, but nothing like as well developed. "Leave it with me," he meowed. "I'll have a word with Cinderpelt. She'll find a way of taking a look at the kit without upsetting Speckletail."

"Thanks, Fireheart." Brackenfur sounded relieved.

"Meanwhile," Fireheart mewed, "can you lead the evening

patrol? Ask Mousefur and Brindleface to go with you."

Brackenfur straightened up. "Sure, Fireheart," he replied. "I'll go and look for them now."

He set off across the camp with his tail held high. When he had gone a few fox-lengths, Fireheart called him back. "Oh, and Brackenfur," he mewed, pleased for once to impart good news, "when Snowkit is ready, I'll speak to Bluestar about letting you mentor him."

Before Fireheart went to find Cinderpelt, he visited Bluestar to tell her about the apprentices' assessment. The Clan leader was seated outside her den in a patch of sunshine, and Fireheart thought hopefully that she might be feeling more like her old self. But her blue eyes looked tired as she blinked at him, and a piece of fresh-kill lay beside her, only half-eaten.

"Well, Fireheart?" she asked as he approached. "What can I do for you?"

"I've got good news, Bluestar." Fireheart tried to sound cheerful. "I assessed all four of the older apprentices today. They did well. I think it's time they were made into warriors."

"The older apprentices?" Bluestar's eyes clouded with confusion. "That would be Brackenpaw, and . . . and Cinderpaw?"

Fireheart's heart sank. Bluestar couldn't even remember which cats were apprentices! "No, Bluestar," he mewed patiently. "Cloudpaw, Brightpaw, Swiftpaw, and Thornpaw."

Bluestar shifted a little. "That's who I meant," she snapped. "And you want them to be warriors? Just . . . just remind me who their mentors are, will you?"

"I'm Cloudpaw's mentor," Fireheart began, trying to keep his increasing dismay out of his voice. "The others are Longtail—"

"Longtail," Bluestar interrupted. "Ah, yes . . . one of Tigerclaw's friends. Why did we give him an apprentice, when we can't trust him?"

"Longtail chose to stay in ThunderClan when Tigerclaw left," Fireheart reminded her.

Bluestar snorted. "That doesn't mean we can trust him," she repeated. "We can't trust any of them. They're traitors and they'll train more traitors. I won't make warriors of any of their apprentices!" She paused as Fireheart stared at her, appalled, then added, "Only yours, Fireheart. You alone are faithful to me. Cloudpaw can be a warrior, but not those others."

Fireheart didn't know what to say. Even though the Clan seemed happy to have Cloudpaw back after his escapade with the Twolegs, Fireheart could foresee trouble if his apprentice was made a warrior and the other apprentices were not. Besides, it wouldn't do Cloudpaw any good to be singled out for an honor that the others deserved just as much as he did.

Fireheart fought with rising panic as he realized that meant *none* of the apprentices could be made into warriors yet. Even though the Clan needed them so desperately, he knew there was no reasoning with Bluestar in this mood.

"Er . . . thanks, Bluestar," he meowed at last, starting to back away. "But maybe we'll wait awhile longer. A bit more training won't hurt."

He made his escape, leaving Bluestar looking after him with the same vague expression in her eyes.

CHAPTER 5

The sun was going down, casting long shadows across the clearing, by the time Fireheart went to look for Cinderpelt. He found the medicine cat in her den, checking her supplies of healing herbs, and sat just outside the entrance to talk to her.

"Speckletail's kit?" she meowed when Fireheart had told her about Brackenfur's suspicions. She narrowed her eyes thoughtfully. "Yes, I can see what he means. I'll take a look."

"You'll have to be careful of Speckletail," Fireheart warned her. "When I suggested she might let you check Snowkit, she practically bit my nose off."

"I'm not surprised," remarked Cinderpelt. "No queen wants to believe her kits aren't perfect. I'll deal with it, Fireheart; don't worry. But not right away," she added, patting her store of juniper berries into a neater pile. "It's too late to disturb them tonight, and tomorrow I have to go to Highstones."

"So soon?" Fireheart was surprised; he hadn't realized how quickly the days were slipping by.

"Tomorrow night is the new moon. All the other medicine cats will be there too. StarClan will give me my full powers."

Cinderpelt hesitated and then added, "Yellowfang should have come with me, to present me to StarClan as a fully trained medicine cat. Now I'll have to go through the ceremony without her." Her eyes grew wide and remote as she spoke. Fireheart felt that she was moving far away from him, into a land of shadows and dreams where he could not follow her.

"You'll need to take a warrior with you," he meowed. "Last time Bluestar tried to go to Highstones, WindClan wouldn't let her pass through their territory."

Cinderpelt looked at him calmly. "I'd like to see the patrol that would dare to stop a medicine cat. StarClan would never forgive that." Her expression changed and her eyes glinted mischievously. "You can come as far as Fourtrees if you like. Assuming you can spare the time from Sandstorm."

Fireheart felt uncomfortable. "I don't know what you mean," he muttered. But he remembered leaving to go and eat with Sandstorm while Cinderpelt was telling him about her dream, and he guessed that the medicine cat had felt unfairly dismissed. "Sandstorm can lead the dawn patrol without me," he mewed out loud. "I'll come with you to Fourtrees."

The next day dawned damp and misty. Tendrils of fog curled between the trees as Fireheart and Cinderpelt made their way to Fourtrees. The clinging white clouds dampened the sound of their pawsteps and beaded their fur with tiny droplets. In the silence Fireheart jumped at the sudden alarm call of a bird above his head. He felt half-afraid that they might lose their way in this eerily unfamiliar-looking forest.

But by the time they crossed the stream and began to climb the slope to Fourtrees, the mist had begun to clear, and at the top of the hollow they emerged into bright sunlight. The four massive oaks stood straight ahead of them, their leaves turning red-gold with the approach of leaf-fall.

Cinderpelt let out a noisy breath and shook the moisture from her fur. "That feels good! I was starting to think I'd have to scent my way to Highstones, and I've only been there once before, with Yellowfang."

Fireheart too enjoyed the feeling of warm sun on his fur. He stretched luxuriously and opened his jaws to taste the air, hoping to pick up the scent of prey.

Instead, the scent of other cats flooded over him. *ShadowClan!* he thought, his muscles tensing as his gaze flicked from side to side. A moment later he relaxed as he spotted Runningnose, the ShadowClan medicine cat, padding up to the hollow from ShadowClan territory with another cat beside him. This was no hostile warrior. StarClan raised medicine cats above the level of Clan rivalry.

"It looks as if you won't have to travel alone after all," he meowed to Cinderpelt.

They waited until the ShadowClan cats came up to them. As they drew nearer, Fireheart recognized the other cat. It was Littlecloud, a small tabby tom who had almost died in his Clan's recent sickness. He and another warrior, Whitethroat, had tried to seek refuge with ThunderClan. Bluestar had refused to take them in, but Cinderpelt had secretly sheltered them and cared for them until they were fit enough to travel back to their own territory.

Whitethroat had died soon after, when Tigerstar and his rogues had attacked a ThunderClan patrol. A monster had cut the young cat down on the Thunderpath as he was fleeing from the fight. Reliving the shock of that moment, Fireheart was glad to see that Littlecloud at least looked strong and healthy again.

"Hello, there!" Runningnose greeted the ThunderClan cats cheerfully. "Well met, Cinderpelt. It's a good day to travel."

Littlecloud nodded respectfully to Fireheart and went to touch noses with Cinderpelt.

"It's good to see you on your paws again," she meowed.

"All thanks to you," Littlecloud replied. With a touch of pride he added, "I'm Runningnose's apprentice now."

"Congratulations!" Cinderpelt purred.

"And that's because of you too," Littlecloud went on enthusiastically. "When we were ill, you knew just what to do. And then you gave us healing herbs to take back to the Clan—and they worked! I want to do more stuff like that."

"He has real talent," Runningnose mewed. "And it took courage to come back to us with the herbs. I'm only sorry Whitethroat didn't come back with him."

"He didn't?" Fireheart asked, seizing the chance to find out how much the ShadowClan cats knew about the young warrior's fate.

Sadly, Littlecloud shook his head. "He wouldn't come back with me to camp. He was scared of catching the sickness again, even though we had the healing herbs with us." He blinked as if the memory caused him pain. "We found his body beside the Thunderpath a few days later."

"I'm sorry," Fireheart meowed. He wondered whether to tell him the truth about how Whitethroat had died, but decided it would be too harmful to reveal that Littlecloud's new leader had been partly responsible for his friend's death. It was clear that Whitethroat must have joined the rogues for a short time, and paid with his life.

Cinderpelt pressed her muzzle comfortingly against Littlecloud's flank. Settling down on the warm grass, she beckoned with her tail for the apprentice to sit beside her and began to ask him about his training.

"Are things better now?" Fireheart carefully asked Runningnose. He would have liked to warn the medicine cat about Tigerstar, but there was so little he could say without revealing what had happened in ThunderClan.

"It seems so," meowed Runningnose, sounding equally guarded. "The apprentices are getting a proper training for the first time in moons, and our bellies are always full."

"That's good news," Fireheart mewed, forcing himself to add, "What about the rogues?"

Runningnose frowned. "Not every cat was happy about their coming into our Clan," he admitted. "I wasn't happy about them myself. But they haven't caused any trouble—and they're strong warriors; no cat can deny that."

"Then maybe Tigerstar will be a great leader, just like the omen said," Fireheart mewed.

The medicine cat met his gaze evenly. "It seems strange that ThunderClan got rid of a strong cat like that."

Fireheart took a deep breath. Perhaps he should take this chance to tell Runningnose the truth about Tigerstar. "It's a long story," he began.

"No, Fireheart," Runningnose interrupted. "I'm not asking you to betray your Clan's secrets." He edged closer to Fireheart, then scraped the ground with his paws and crouched down beside him. "Whatever happened in ThunderClan, I'm certain of one thing," he mewed softly. "StarClan did send Tigerstar to us."

"You mean the omen?"

"Actually, there's something else." Runningnose glanced sideways at Fireheart. "Our last leader was never accepted by StarClan," he admitted. "When Nightstar became leader, StarClan did not grant him nine lives."

"What?" Fireheart stared at the medicine cat in disbelief. If Nightstar had had only one life, it explained why the sickness had claimed him so quickly. Fireheart found his voice again. "Why didn't he get nine lives?"

"StarClan have not explained that to me," meowed Runningnose. "I wondered if it was because Brokentail was still alive, and StarClan still recognized him as Clan leader. By the time we learned that Brokentail had died, Nightstar was too weak to make the journey to the Moonstone to receive his nine lives. And since Tigerstar came, I think maybe he was StarClan's choice of leader for us all along. Nightstar was not the right cat."

"Yet the Clan still accepted him as leader?" Fireheart asked.

"The Clan never knew that he had not been given his nine lives," Runningnose confessed. "Nightstar was a noble cat, and loyal to his Clan. We decided to keep StarClan's rejection a secret. What else could we do? There was no other cat fit to be leader. If we had told the truth, the Clan would have panicked."

There was a kind of relief in Runningnose's voice as he told the story. Fireheart guessed how relieved the medicine cat must have felt to be able to share the secret at last.

"The Clan cats thought the sickness was so bad it took all of Nightstar's lives at once," Runningnose continued. "They were scared—very scared. They had never been in greater need of a strong leader."

So they accepted Tigerstar without question. Fireheart added what the medicine cat had not said. But there was no need for Runningnose to voice his doubts about his new leader. "Has Tigerstar said anything about attacking ThunderClan?" Fireheart asked hesitantly.

Runningnose let out a purr of amusement. "Do you really expect me to answer that? If he *was* planning anything, I'd be betraying my Clan if I told you. As far as I know, you haven't anything to worry about, but whether you believe me or not is up to you."

Fireheart discovered that he believed him—at least, he believed that Runningnose knew nothing about any plans that Tigerstar might be making. Whether the medicine cat was right was another question altogether.

"Fireheart!" The voice was Cinderpelt's. She had risen to her paws and was gazing across the hollow to the swell of moorland beyond. This was the WindClan territory that the medicine cats would have to cross to reach Highstones for the ceremony. "Are you and Runningnose going to sit there gossiping all day like a couple of elders?"

Her paws worked impatiently in the grass. Littlecloud was standing beside her, his head raised and his eyes shining eagerly.

"All right," Runningnose meowed, getting up and going to join them. "We've got all day, you know. Highstones isn't going anywhere."

The four cats padded around the top of the hollow until they reached the edge of the windswept moor. Cinderpelt paused and touched noses with Fireheart. "I'll be fine from here," she meowed. "Thanks for coming this far. I'll be back tomorrow night."

"Take care," Fireheart replied.

He had stood here once before and said good-bye to Cinderpelt when she first went to face the mysteries of the Moonstone. A shiver ran through his fur as he thought of her plunging down through the underground tunnels to the glittering crystal for her silent communion with StarClan. He said nothing more, only gave the gray she-cat's ear a swift lick in farewell, and stood watching as she limped across the moorland turf with the two ShadowClan cats.

CHAPTER 6

❧

The forest was dark. No moon shone down that night, and when Fireheart looked up he could see nothing but a faint pattern of branches against the sky. The trees looked taller than he remembered, hemming him in. Brambles and ivy tangled around his paws.

"Spottedleaf!" he mewed. "Spottedleaf, where are you?"

There was no answer to his cries, only the rush of water from somewhere ahead of him. He was afraid of stepping forward and finding nothing but black emptiness under his paws as the raging torrent swept him down with it.

In some part of his mind Fireheart knew he was dreaming. He had lain down in the warriors' den in the hope that he would be able to meet with Spottedleaf in sleep. When Fireheart had first come to ThunderClan, Spottedleaf had been the medicine cat, but she had been killed by one of Brokentail's vicious followers. Now she visited Fireheart in his dreams, so that once again he could find in her gentle wisdom the answers to much that troubled him.

But now, though he searched more and more desperately in the black forest, he could not find her. "Spottedleaf!" he cried again. This was not the first time in his recent dreams that she had been invisible to him. The last time, he had only heard her voice, and he fought with the terrible fear that she was drawing away from him. "Spottedleaf, don't leave me!" he begged.

A heavy weight landed on him from behind. Fireheart writhed on the forest floor, trying to free himself. Then the scent of another cat was in his nostrils, and he opened his eyes to find himself scuffling in his mossy bedding with Dustpelt cuffing him around the shoulders.

"What's the matter with you?" Dustpelt growled. "No cat can get a wink of sleep with you yowling like that."

"Leave him alone." Sandstorm put her head up from her nest, blinking sleep from her eyes. "It was only a dream. It's not his fault."

"You would say that," Dustpelt sneered. He turned his back on them and made his way out through the overhanging branches.

Fireheart sat up and began grooming scraps of moss out of his coat. Through the charred branches overhead, he could see that the sun was already up. Whitestorm must have left already with the dawn patrol; there were no other warriors sleeping in the den.

The darkness of his dream was fading, but he could not forget it. Why had the forest seemed so black and terrifying? Why had Spottedleaf not come to him, not even as a scent or the sound of her voice?

"Are you all right?" asked Sandstorm, anxiety showing in her green eyes.

Fireheart shook himself. "I'm fine," he meowed. "Let's go and hunt."

The day was bright, though the chill of leaf-fall was in the air. Fireheart was relieved to see that grass and ferns were growing back thickly as the forest recovered. If only the fine weather would last! Then the growth could continue and prey would return.

He led the way up the ravine and through the forest toward Tallpines. Since the fire, most cats had avoided the stretch of territory closest to Treecutplace, where the devastation was worst. The fire had started there, and whole stretches of the forest had been reduced to nothing but gray ash, dotted with tree stumps. Fireheart wondered if there was a chance of prey there yet, but as he and Sandstorm approached the edge of Tallpines he guessed that he was going to be disappointed.

The pines, charred to tapering trunks, were still a jumble, with fallen trees caught up against others that still stood. The few remaining branches stirred uneasily in the breeze. The ground was black, and no birds sang.

"It's useless here," Sandstorm meowed. "Let's go and—"

She broke off as another cat appeared through the trees, a small tabby-and-white shape stepping nervously over the debris of the fire. With a gasp of surprise Fireheart recognized his sister, Princess.

She spotted him at the same moment and bounded toward him, calling, "Fireheart! Fireheart!"

"Who's *that*?" Sandstorm spat. "She'll scare off all the prey between here and Fourtrees."

Before Fireheart could reply, his sister came up to him. She was purring as if she would never stop, pressing her face against his and covering him with licks. "Fireheart, you're alive!" she mewed. "I was so frightened when I saw the fire! I thought you and Cloudpaw were dead."

"Yes, well, I'm okay," Fireheart meowed awkwardly, giving Princess a quick lick in return and taking a step back, acutely conscious of Sandstorm's eyes on him. "And Cloudpaw's fine too."

Glancing at Sandstorm, he saw that a look of disgust had appeared on the ginger warrior's face and her fur was fluffed out. "That's a *kittypet*," she snarled. "She's got kittypet scent all over her."

Princess gave her a scared look and edged closer to Fireheart. "Is . . . is this one of your friends, Fireheart?" she stammered.

"Yes, this is Sandstorm. Sandstorm, this is my sister, Princess, Cloudpaw's mother."

Sandstorm took a step or two away from them, though she let the fur lie flat on her neck again. "Cloudpaw's mother?" she repeated. "She still sees you both, then?" She shot a glance at Fireheart, clearly wondering how much he had told Princess about Cloudpaw's escapade with the Twolegs.

"Cloudpaw is doing really well," Fireheart meowed. "Isn't he?" He met Sandstorm's gaze, silently willing her not to say anything tactless about the wayward apprentice.

"He hunts well," Sandstorm admitted. "And he's got the makings of a fine fighter."

Princess didn't realize how much Sandstorm was leaving unsaid. Her eyes glowed with pride and she meowed, "I know he'll be a good warrior with Fireheart to mentor him."

"But you haven't told me what you're doing out here," Fireheart mewed, eager to change the subject. "You're a long way from your Twoleg nest."

"I was looking for you. I had to know what had happened to you and Cloudpaw," explained Princess. "I saw the fire from my garden, and then you didn't come to see me, and I thought—"

"I'm sorry," Fireheart meowed. "I would have come, but we've been so busy since the fire. We have to rebuild the camp, and there's not much prey left in the forest. And I have more duties since I was made deputy."

"You're deputy now? Of the whole Clan? Fireheart, that's marvelous!"

Fireheart felt hot with embarrassment as Princess gazed at him.

Sandstorm gave a dry little cough. "There's prey to be caught, Fireheart. . . . "

"Yes, you're right," Fireheart mewed. "Princess, you're very brave to have come so far, but you'd better get home now. The forest can be dangerous if you're not used to it."

"Yes, I know, but I—"

The roar of a Twoleg monster interrupted her, and at the same moment Fireheart's nostrils were blasted with its harsh reek. The roaring grew louder, and a moment later the monster burst out of the trees, bouncing along the rutted track.

Instinctively, Fireheart and Sandstorm crouched beneath a blackened tree trunk, waiting for the monster to pass. Princess merely sat watching it curiously.

"Get *down!*" Sandstorm hissed at her.

Princess looked puzzled, but she pressed herself obediently to the ground next to Fireheart.

Instead of passing, the monster stopped. The roaring was abruptly cut off. Part of the monster unfolded, and three Twolegs jumped out of its belly.

Fireheart exchanged a glance with Sandstorm and flattened himself even further. Princess might feel at home with the Twolegs and their monster, but they were too close for his liking, and the undergrowth was still not thick enough to provide decent cover. All Fireheart's instincts were to run, but curiosity kept him pinned to the ground.

The Twolegs wore matching dark blue pelts. They had no Twoleg kits with them, or dogs, unlike most of the Twolegs who came to the forest. They spread out among the burned trees, yowling and stamping so that their paws threw up puffs of dust and ash. Sandstorm lowered her head and stifled a sneeze as one of them passed within a fox-length of where the three cats were crouching.

"What are they doing?" Fireheart murmured.

"Frightening off all the prey," hissed Sandstorm, spitting out dust. "Honestly, Fireheart, who cares what Twolegs do? They're all mad."

"I don't know. . . ." Fireheart couldn't help feeling that these Twolegs had a purpose, even if he didn't understand what it was. The way they pointed with their paws and yowled at each other seemed to suggest they were moving deliberately through the forest.

Another Twolegs stamped past. He had picked up a branch and was using it to poke into hollows and under clumps of charred undergrowth. It almost looked as if he were hunting for prey, except for the noise he was making, which would have scared away the deafest rabbit.

"Do you know what it's all about?" Fireheart asked Princess.

"I'm not sure," his sister replied. "I understand a bit of their Twoleg talk, but it's not words that my housefolk use. I think they're calling for somebody, but I don't know who."

As Fireheart watched, the Twolegs threw the branch down. There was frustration in the movement. He yowled again, and the other Twolegs appeared from the trees. All three of them went back to the monster and climbed into its belly. The roar started up again, and the monster jerked into motion and vanished into the trees.

"Well!" Sandstorm sat up and began licking fastidiously at her ash-stained fur. "Thank StarClan they've gone!"

Fireheart got to his paws, keeping his gaze fixed on the place in the trees where the monster had disappeared. The sound had died away and the acrid smell was fading. "I don't like it," he meowed.

"Oh, come on, Fireheart!" Sandstorm padded to his side and gave him a nudge. "Why are you bothering about Twolegs? They're weird, and that's all there is to it."

"No, I think *they* know what they're doing, even if it looks weird to us," Fireheart replied. "They usually bring their kits or their dogs to the forest—but these Twolegs didn't. If Princess is right and they were looking for something, they didn't find it. I'd like to know what it was." He paused and then added, "Besides, we don't normally see Twolegs in this part of the forest. They're too close to the camp for my liking."

Sandstorm's impatient look softened, and she pressed her muzzle reassuringly against his shoulder. "You can tell the patrols to keep a lookout," she reminded him.

"Yes." Fireheart nodded thoughtfully. "I'll do that."

As he said good-bye to Princess, he struggled to push his growing anxiety out of his mind. Something was going on in the forest that he didn't understand, and he could not help fearing that it meant danger for his Clan.

Cutting across the corner of Tallpines, Fireheart and Sandstorm made for the river and Sunningrocks. There was no sign of prey anywhere among the scorched trees; the noise made by the Twolegs had seen to that.

"We'll follow the RiverClan border up toward Fourtrees," Fireheart decided. "There might be something there worth catching."

But as they came within sight of Sunningrocks, Fireheart stopped at the sound of a familiar voice calling his name. He looked up to see Graystripe poised on top of the nearest rock; the gray warrior scrambled down and bounded over to him.

"Fireheart! I was hoping to catch you."

"A good thing a patrol didn't catch *you*," Sandstorm growled. "You're very comfortable in our territory, for a RiverClan warrior."

"Come off it, Sandstorm," Graystripe meowed, giving her a good-natured push. "This is me, Graystripe, remember?"

"Only too well," retorted Sandstorm. She sat down, licked a paw, and started washing her face.

"What's the problem, Graystripe?" Fireheart asked, worried that his old friend wouldn't have ventured into ThunderClan territory without good reason.

"It's not exactly a problem," replied the gray warrior. "At least, I hope it isn't. Just something I thought you ought to know."

"Spit it out, then," meowed Sandstorm.

Graystripe flicked his tail at her. "Crookedstar had a visitor yesterday," he told Fireheart. He narrowed his amber eyes. "It was Tigerstar."

"What? What did he want?" Fireheart stammered.

Graystripe shook his head. "I don't know. But Crookedstar is very weak now. The whole Clan knows he's on his last life. Tigerstar spent only a short time with him, but he had a long talk with Leopardfur."

The mention of the RiverClan deputy increased Fireheart's fears. What did she and Tigerstar have to say to each other? Visions of an alliance between ShadowClan and RiverClan raced through his mind, with ThunderClan trapped between the two of them. Then he tried to tell himself he was worrying unnecessarily. He had no reason to think that the two cats were planning anything.

"It's not unknown for leaders to visit each other," he pointed out. "If Crookedstar is dying, Tigerstar might want to pay his last respects."

"Maybe." Graystripe snorted. "But then why spend so much time with Leopardfur? I tried to get close enough to listen, and I heard Tigerstar say something about coming again to our camp."

"Was that all he said?" Fireheart asked.

"That's all I heard." Graystripe ducked his head in embarrassment. "Leopardfur saw me and told me to stay out of her fur."

"Perhaps Tigerstar's just getting to know her," Fireheart guessed. "She'll be Clan leader, after all, when Crookedstar dies."

He turned as he heard another cat calling his name, and saw Mistyfoot pulling herself up out of the river.

"Oh, great StarClan!" exclaimed Sandstorm. "Are we going to have all of RiverClan over here?"

"Fireheart!" Mistyfoot panted, shaking off her fur; Sandstorm jumped back crossly as some of the spinning drops spattered against her paws. "Fireheart, have you seen Graypool anywhere?"

"Graypool?" Fireheart echoed, picturing the short-tempered elder whom Mistyfoot believed to be her mother. Fireheart still felt gratitude to the RiverClan queen for telling him the truth about the two ThunderClan kits she had brought up as her own, but he hadn't seen her for a long time. "What would Graypool be doing here?"

"I don't know." Mistyfoot padded up the slope from the river, her face creased with anxiety. "I can't find her in the camp. She's so weak and confused these days, I'm afraid she's wandered off and doesn't know what she's doing."

"She won't be here," Graystripe objected. "She's not strong enough to swim the river."

"Then where has she gone?" Mistyfoot's voice rose into a wail. "I've looked in all the places I can think of near the camp, and she isn't there. Besides, the river's low just now, and it's not too hard to swim across."

Fireheart thought rapidly. If Graypool had somehow crossed the river into ThunderClan territory, she would need to be tracked down as soon as possible. His Clan mates were scared enough already of an invasion. He didn't like to imagine what would happen if an aggressive cat like Darkstripe found her first.

"Okay," he meowed. "I'll follow the border up to Fourtrees to see if she's gone that way. Sandstorm, you go back to camp. Tell the others what's happened, and warn them not to attack Graypool if they see her."

Sandstorm rolled her eyes. "All right," she mewed as she got to her paws. "I'll hunt on the way back, though. It's time someone caught some fresh-kill for the Clan." With her tail high she stalked off into the trees.

Mistyfoot dipped her head gratefully toward Fireheart. "Thank you," she meowed. "I won't forget this. And Fireheart—if you need to cross onto RiverClan territory to bring

Graypool home, you can tell any cat who sees you that I gave you permission."

Fireheart nodded his thanks. He could just imagine what would happen if he were caught on the wrong side of the border by a RiverClan patrol with Leopardfur at its head.

"Come on, Mistyfoot," Graystripe meowed encouragingly. "I'll swim back with you. We'll check the camp again."

"Thanks, Graystripe." Mistyfoot pressed her nose briefly to the gray warrior's fur, and both RiverClan cats bounded down the bank toward the river.

Graystripe glanced back swiftly to yowl good-bye, then launched himself into the water behind Mistyfoot. Fireheart watched them swimming strongly for the far bank before heading upstream toward Fourtrees.

He followed the border, renewing the scent markings as he went, until he was not far from Fourtrees. He found it hard to believe that the fragile elder could have made it this far. But then, looking down a rocky slope toward the river, he caught sight of a skinny gray shape limping slowly over the Twoleg bridge that crossed the river on the route that RiverClan cats took to Fourtrees.

Graypool!

Fireheart opened his jaws to call out to her, and closed them again without making a sound. The old cat had crossed the bridge and was tottering along the very edge of the river. He was afraid that if she heard a strange cat calling to her, she would slip and fall to her death. Instead he began to make his way down the slope, creeping carefully under cover of the rocks in a hunting crouch so she would not see him and be startled.

After a few moments, he saw to his relief that Graypool had turned away from the river and was trying to climb the steep slope toward Fourtrees. Her claws scrabbled feebly on the boulders, and Fireheart wondered where she thought she was going. Did she imagine it was full moon and she was on her way to a Gathering?

Fireheart straightened up and opened his mouth once more to call to her, but again he bit back her name and slipped rapidly into the shelter of the nearest rock. Another cat had appeared, bounding confidently from the direction of Fourtrees. There was no mistaking that huge, muscular body and dark tabby coat.

It was Tigerstar!

CHAPTER 7
❧

Fireheart peered out from behind his rock. Tigerstar had spotted Graypool and had changed direction toward her. As the dark tabby approached, Graypool reared back in surprise and fell, only to struggle back onto her paws and face Tigerstar. The ShadowClan leader padded up to her and meowed something, but Fireheart was too far away to make out the words.

Flattening his belly to the ground, he crept toward them, using all his hunting skills to stay undetected. Fortunately the wind was blowing toward him, so Tigerstar was unlikely to scent him. Fireheart was unwilling to meet the ShadowClan leader unless he had to. With any luck, Tigerstar was on his way to visit Leopardfur again and would help Graypool back to the RiverClan camp.

Fireheart prowled closer, flattening himself against the turf until he reached the shelter of another rock almost on a level with the other two cats. Graystripe had said that Tigerstar had visited RiverClan the day before. Why should he need to return so soon?

"Don't pretend you don't know me." Fireheart hardly recognized the quavering voice as Graypool's. "I know who

73

you are, right enough. You're Oakheart."

Fireheart stiffened. Oakheart was the name of the cat who fathered Mistyfoot and Stonefur, and took them to RiverClan when Bluestar gave them up. He had been killed in battle just before Fireheart joined ThunderClan, but he had looked a little like Tigerstar—a big tom with a dark pelt.

With infinite caution, Fireheart raised his head to peer over the rock where he was sheltering. Graypool was crouched on a sparse patch of grass just above an outcrop of stones. She was looking up at Tigerstar, who loomed over her a couple of tail-lengths farther up the slope.

"I haven't seen you for moons," Graypool went on. "Where have you been hiding yourself?"

Tigerstar stared down at her with narrowed eyes. Fireheart waited for him to tell the elderly she-cat that she had made a mistake. His blood ran cold when Tigerstar just meowed, "Oh . . . here and there."

What in StarClan's name is he playing at? Fireheart wondered.

"You might at least have come to see me," Graypool complained. "Don't you want to know how those kits are doing?"

The massive tom's ears pricked up, and his amber eyes glowed with interest. "What kits?"

"What kits, he says!" Graypool broke into rusty laughter. "As if you didn't know! The two ThunderClan kits that you asked me to take care of."

Fireheart froze. Graypool had just given away Bluestar's most deeply buried secret!

Tigerstar's muscles tensed, and he gazed at Graypool more

intently still, his interest clear in every line of his body. He thrust his head forward and meowed something so softly that Fireheart could not catch it.

"Seasons ago," replied Graypool, sounding puzzled. "Don't tell me you've forgotten. You . . . No, Oakheart wouldn't need to ask that." She staggered forward a couple of steps to peer more closely at Tigerstar.

"You're not Oakheart!" she exclaimed.

"Never mind that," Tigerstar mewed soothingly. "You can still tell me all about it. What ThunderClan kits? Who was their real mother?"

Fireheart was close enough to see the dazed look in Graypool's eyes. She put her head on one side, gazing confusedly at the ShadowClan leader. "They were beautiful kits," she meowed vaguely. "And now they're fine warriors."

She broke off as Tigerstar thrust his muzzle into her face. "Tell me whose kits they were, old crowfood," he demanded, losing his patience.

Fireheart stared in horror as, flustered, Graypool took a step back. Her paws slid from under her. She rolled down the steep slope in a scramble of legs and tail, and landed hard against one of the rocks that poked out of the turf. There she lay, and did not move again.

Dismay and fury pulsed through Fireheart. As Tigerstar padded down to Graypool's motionless body and sniffed it, he sprang to his paws and raced across the slope. But before Fireheart reached him the ShadowClan leader spun around, without seeing his former enemy, and bounded away in the direction of Fourtrees and his own territory.

Fireheart reached Graypool and gazed down at her. A trickle of blood came from her small gray head where it had struck the rock. Her eyes stared sightlessly at the sky. The she-cat was dead.

Fireheart lowered his head. "Good-bye, Graypool," he mewed softly. "StarClan will honor you."

He stood in silent grief, wishing he had known Graypool better. Her sharp tongue and noble heart reminded him of Yellowfang, and he would never stop feeling grateful to the RiverClan queen for sharing her deepest secret with him, even though he came from another Clan.

His sad reverie was interrupted by the voices of two cats, and he looked up to see Mistyfoot and Graystripe racing toward him from the river. Mistyfoot let out a desperate wail when she saw the dead elder and flung herself down on the turf to press her nose against Graypool's side.

"What happened?" asked Graystripe.

In an instant, Fireheart decided to keep quiet about Tiger-star. Any mention of the ShadowClan leader would risk exposing the truth about Bluestar's kits, and Fireheart knew Graypool would never want that, not even within her own Clan. He glanced at the still gray body and asked forgiveness from StarClan for the half-truth he was about to tell.

"I saw Graypool climbing the slope," he replied. "She slipped, and I couldn't reach her in time. I'm sorry."

"It's not your fault, Fireheart." Mistyfoot looked up at him, her blue eyes filled with sorrow. "I have been afraid for a while that something like this would happen."

She bent her head to touch Graypool's body again. Fireheart felt sympathy well up inside his chest. Graypool had taken Mistyfoot and Stonefur when Bluestar, their real mother, had given them up. Without Graypool they would have died. She had suckled them and reared them until they were ready to become apprentices. She was the only mother they had ever known, and no cat could have done more for them.

"Come on, Mistyfoot." Graystripe gently nudged his friend. "Let's take her back to camp."

"I'll help you," Fireheart offered.

Mistyfoot sat up. "No," she meowed. "You've done enough, Fireheart. Thank you, but this is for her own Clan to do."

With great care she grasped Graypool's scruff in her jaws. Graystripe took hold of the elder's body, and together the two cats carried her down the slope toward the Twoleg bridge. Graypool's limp form sagged between them, and her tail trailed in the dust.

When they reached the other side of the river, Fireheart turned away, back to his own territory and the ThunderClan camp. His thoughts were churning. Tigerstar had found out that two RiverClan warriors had come from ThunderClan! Fireheart had no idea what Tigerstar would do with this knowledge. But he knew, as sure as the sun would rise the next morning, that the ShadowClan leader would make some use of it, and he had a sinking feeling the outcome could be disastrous for Bluestar and the whole of ThunderClan.

❊   ❊   ❊

Fireheart stopped to hunt on the way home and arrived at the top of the ravine with a rabbit clamped firmly in his jaws. Looking down at the entrance to the camp, he saw that Goldenflower had brought her kits out into the bottom of the ravine; the two of them were chasing each other among the rocks, pretending to attack Brightpaw, who flicked her tail at them and frisked about just out of their reach. As Fireheart padded down the ravine and dropped the rabbit to watch for a moment, Bramblekit bounded up to him and laid a mouse at his paws.

"Look, Fireheart!" he meowed triumphantly. "I caught it all by myself!"

"His first prey," Goldenflower added with a fond look at her son.

Bramblekit's amber eyes blazed with excitement. "Mother says I'll be just as good a hunter as my father," he told Fireheart.

Fireheart felt an unpleasant jolt in his belly. His eyes narrowed, and he gave Goldenflower a sharp glance. Goldenflower kept her eyes fixed on her son, but Fireheart could tell from her twitching tail tip that she knew he was watching her.

"Fireheart?" Bramblekit was looking puzzled. "May I give my mouse to the elders?"

Fireheart shook himself angrily. The kit had done very well to catch a mouse when he was still so young, and he deserved a bit of praise. Yet Fireheart couldn't help remembering Tigerstar bending over Graypool's limp body, and he had a hard struggle not to vent his fury on the innocent Bramblekit.

"Yes, of course," he mewed. "And well done for catching it. See if One-eye would like it. She might think it's worth a story."

Bramblekit's eyes lit up. "Good idea!" he yowled. He snatched up the mouse and tore down the ravine to the camp entrance. His sister, Tawnykit, scampered after him.

Goldenflower was looking fiercely at Fireheart, and he knew that she saw very clearly how forced his praise had been. Frostily she mewed, "I told you before, Fireheart, I won't tell the kits anything bad about their father. We're loyal to the Clan—*all* of us."

She spun around, switching her tail across Fireheart's face as she did so, and stalked back to the camp.

Fireheart retrieved his rabbit and followed, deciding that he would take his prey to Cinderpelt and talk to her about Bramblekit at the same time. She might have some ideas about how best to handle the kit. The gray she-cat had limped back into the camp very late the night after the medicine-cat gathering at Highstones; Fireheart knew that she had been exhausted, but it had seemed that the light of the Moonstone still glimmered in her eyes.

As Fireheart pushed his way into the clearing through the newly growing gorse tunnel, he saw that Cinderpelt was sitting with Speckletail outside the nursery. The medicine cat was watching Snowkit, who patted at something on the ground a few tail-lengths from his mother.

Good, Fireheart thought. *Now we should be able to find out if there's something wrong with Snowkit.* He padded over to the two she-cats and dropped the rabbit beside Cinderpelt. "That's for you," he meowed. "How do you feel after your journey?"

Cinderpelt turned to look at him. Her blue eyes were tranquil. "I'm fine," she purred. "Thanks for the rabbit. Speckletail and I were just having a chat about Snowkit."

"There's nothing to chat about," Speckletail muttered, hunching her shoulders. She sounded cranky, but there was a new sense of authority about Cinderpelt, and Fireheart guessed that the older she-cat hadn't dared to refuse outright to talk to her.

Cinderpelt dipped her head. "Just call him to you, would you?" she asked.

Speckletail snorted and called out, "Snowkit! Snowkit, come here!"

She beckoned with her tail as she spoke. Snowkit got up, abandoning the ball of moss he had been playing with, and padded over to his mother. Speckletail bent down and gave his ear a lick.

"Good," meowed Cinderpelt. "Now, Fireheart, go over there and call him to you, will you?" She nodded toward a spot a few fox-lengths away. In a lower voice she added, "Don't move. Just use your voice."

Puzzled, Fireheart did as she asked. This time, although Snowkit was looking straight at him, he didn't move. There was no response from him at all, even when Fireheart called three or four times.

A few other cats paused on their way to the pile of fresh-kill and came to see what was going on. Bluestar—roused by the sound of voices, Fireheart guessed—emerged from her den and sat watching near the base of the Highrock. Dappletail, who was strolling back to the elders' den, stopped beside Speckletail and said something to her. Speckletail spat an irritated reply, but Fireheart was too far away to hear what the two cats had said to each other. Dappletail ignored Speckletail's snappishness and sat down next to Cinderpelt to watch closely.

Fireheart kept on calling Snowkit until Speckletail gave the kit a nudge, nodding in his direction, and the kit came bounding across.

"Well done," Fireheart meowed, and repeated his praise when Snowkit looked at him blankly.

After a pause the kit mewed, "S'all right," but the words sounded so distorted that Fireheart could hardly understand him.

He led Snowkit back to his mother and Cinderpelt. By now he was beginning to suspect what the trouble was, and he felt no surprise when Cinderpelt turned to Speckletail and meowed, "I'm sorry, Speckletail—Snowkit is deaf."

Speckletail worked her paws on the ground in front of her. Her expression was a mixture of grief and anger. "I know he's deaf!" she snapped at last. "I'm his mother. Do you think I wouldn't know?"

"White cats with blue eyes are often deaf," Dappletail mewed to Fireheart. "I remember one of my first litter . . ." She sighed.

"What happened to him?" Fireheart asked, relieved that Cloudpaw, who was also white with blue eyes, had good hearing.

"No cat knows," Dappletail told him sadly. "He disappeared when he was three moons old. We thought a fox must have gotten him."

Speckletail gathered Snowkit closer to her, fiercely protective. "Well, a fox won't get this one!" she vowed. "I can look after him."

"I'm sure you can," Bluestar mewed, padding over to them. "But I'm afraid he can never be a warrior."

This was one of Bluestar's good days, Fireheart realized. Her voice was sympathetic but determined, and her eyes were clear.

"Why can't he be a warrior?" Speckletail demanded. "There's nothing else wrong with him. He's a good, strong kit. He gets on just fine if you signal what he's got to do."

"That's not enough," Bluestar told her. "A mentor couldn't teach him to fight or hunt by signals. He couldn't hear commands in a battle, and how could he catch prey if he can't listen, or hear the sound of his own pawsteps?"

Speckletail leaped to her paws with her fur bristling, and for a few moments Fireheart thought she might spring at Bluestar. Then she whipped around, nudged Snowkit to his paws, and vanished with him inside the nursery.

"She's taking it badly," Dappletail remarked.

"How do you expect her to take it?" asked Cinderpelt. "She's getting old. This could well be her last kit, and now she learns he can't ever be a warrior."

"Cinderpelt, you must talk to her," Bluestar ordered. "Make her see that the needs of the Clan must come first."

"Yes, of course, Bluestar," Cinderpelt mewed, with a respectful nod to her leader. "But I think it's best for her to have a little time alone with Snowkit first, to let her get used to the idea that the rest of the Clan knows about his deafness."

Bluestar grunted agreement and padded back toward her den. Fireheart couldn't help feeling disappointed. Not long ago Bluestar would have talked to Speckletail herself, and perhaps considered some options about Snowkit's future in the Clan. *Where had that compassion and understanding gone?* Fireheart wondered. His fur prickled as he realized that his leader hardly seemed to care about the deaf kit or his mother.

CHAPTER 8

The sun was rising over the trees as Fireheart and his patrol approached Snakerocks, on the opposite side of the territory to the river. The fire had not reached this far; the undergrowth was still lush and green, though leaves had begun to fall.

"Hold on," Fireheart meowed to Thornpaw as the apprentice dashed toward the rocks. "Don't forget there are adders around here."

Thornpaw skidded to a halt. "Sorry, Fireheart."

Since Bluestar had refused to make them warriors, Fireheart had made a point of spending time with all the apprentices in turn, including at least one of them in every patrol, in an attempt to show them that the Clan still valued them. Swiftpaw's scowl suggested that he was resentful of the delay, but Thornpaw did not seem to mind waiting for full warrior status.

Mousefur, Thornpaw's mentor, padded up to him. "Tell me what you can smell."

Thornpaw stood with his head raised and jaws parted, drinking in the air. "Mouse!" he mewed almost at once, swiping his tongue around his mouth.

"Yes, but we're not hunting now," Mousefur reminded him. "What else?"

"The Thunderpath—over there." Thornpaw gestured with his tail. "And dog."

Fireheart, who had been lapping water from a hollow in the ground, pricked up his ears. Tasting the air, he realized that Thornpaw was right. There was a strong scent of dog, and it was fresh.

"That's odd," he commented. "Unless the Twolegs were up very early, that scent should be stale. Last night at the latest."

He remembered Whitestorm's report of finding trampled undergrowth and scattered pigeon feathers near Snakerocks. The place had smelled of dog then, but that scent would not have survived for this long.

"We'd better take a good look around," he meowed.

Ordering Thornpaw not to leave his mentor, Fireheart sent the other cats into the trees while he crept closer to the rocks. Before he reached them, he was called back by Mousefur.

"Come and look at this!"

Skirting a bramble thicket, Fireheart joined the brown warrior and looked down into a small, steep-sided clearing. There was a stagnant pool of greenish water at the bottom, choked with fallen leaves. The sharp scent of crushed ferns reached Fireheart's scent glands, but it was barely noticeable under the overpowering stench of dog. Pigeon feathers were scattered all around, and scraps of fur that might have been squirrel or rabbit. A little way down the slope, Thornpaw sniffed at a pile of dog dung, and recoiled with a snort of disgust.

Fireheart forced himself to take in every detail of the scene. Twoleg dogs didn't usually stay in the forest long enough to leave this many traces, trampling the undergrowth and scattering the remains of prey until the forest reeked like a fox's hole. Seeing it with his own eyes made him realize that something was definitely wrong.

"What do you think?" asked Mousefur.

"I don't know." Fireheart was reluctant to voice his worries. "It looks as if there might be a dog loose in the forest, free from the Twolegs."

Was that *what those Twolegs had been looking for?* he wondered, suddenly remembering the three who had come in the monster when he was hunting in Tallpines with Sandstorm. But that had been a long way from here, on the other side of ThunderClan territory.

"What are we going to do?" Thornpaw piped up, looking unusually serious.

"I'll report it to Bluestar," Fireheart decided. "If there is a dog wandering around in our territory, we'll need to do something about it. Maybe we can lead it away somehow."

The dog was clearly taking prey that ThunderClan couldn't spare, and Fireheart didn't like to think of what might happen if it met one of the Clan warriors face-to-face.

As he turned away from the clearing and led the way back toward the camp, Fireheart could not help feeling that the forest around him had become strangely hostile. He knew every tree and stone, yet there was something in its depths—not quite a scent, nor a sound, more like an echo on the edge of hearing—that he did not understand. Was it just a dog? Or were Bluestar's fears about to come true after all? Did StarClan have some other disaster in mind for ThunderClan?

The patrol had almost reached the camp when Fireheart scented ThunderClan cats behind him. Turning, he saw Whitestorm, Brightpaw, and Cloudpaw picking their way through the blackened debris on the forest floor. All of them were carrying fresh-kill.

"Good hunting?" Fireheart asked as they caught up with him.

Whitestorm dropped the rabbit he was carrying. "Not bad," he replied. "But we had to go all the way to Fourtrees to find it."

"Still, it looks good and fat," Fireheart meowed approvingly. "Well done," he added to Brightpaw and Cloudpaw, who were both dragging squirrels.

"We saw something I think you ought to know about," mewed Whitestorm. "Let's get back to camp."

The white warrior picked up his rabbit again and fell in behind Fireheart as he led the way down the ravine. Once they had deposited the fresh-kill on the pile and Fireheart had sent the apprentices off to feed the elders, he took a piece for himself and crouched beside Whitestorm to eat it. Mousefur picked out a blackbird from the heap and came to join them.

"So what did you see?" Fireheart asked, when a few mouthfuls of vole had taken the edge off the hunger in his belly.

He saw Whitestorm's expression darken and guessed the answer before the white warrior spoke. "More scattered prey," Whitestorm meowed. "Scraps of rabbit fur. And more dog scent. Not far from Fourtrees this time, near the border with RiverClan."

"Fresh scent?"

"Yesterday's, I'd guess."

Fireheart nodded, anxiety prickling in his paws. Clearly the dog had ranged much farther than he had first thought. Gulping down the last of his vole, he told Whitestorm what his dawn patrol had found that morning.

"The whole place stank," Mousefur contributed, looking up from her meal. "There's a dog in our territory, isn't there, killing our prey?"

"Yes, I think so." Fireheart turned to Whitestorm. "When you told me about the first lot of scent you found, I hoped that the dog would have gone home by now with its Twolegs. But it obviously hasn't."

"We'll have to get rid of it somehow," Whitestorm meowed grimly.

"I know. I'm going to report it to Bluestar. She'll probably want to hold a Clan meeting."

Leaving Whitestorm and Mousefur, Fireheart padded across the camp toward the Highrock. As sunhigh approached, the life of the camp went on peacefully around him. Ashpaw and Swiftpaw were scuffling outside the apprentices' den.

Near the warriors' den, Frostfur and Brindleface were sharing tongues, both of them looking half-asleep after taking the watch the previous night. In the center of the clearing Speckletail was signaling with paws and tail to her kit, while Brackenfur looked on. A pang of fear struck deep into Fireheart as he imagined the havoc that the stray dog could create if it found the camp.

He had almost reached Bluestar's den when Brackenfur got up and bounded across to him. "Fireheart, may I have a word?"

Fireheart paused. "If it's quick. I have to speak to Bluestar."

"It's Speckletail," Brackenfur explained. "I'm worried about her. She thinks Snowkit should be an apprentice, and she's trying to mentor him herself. She thinks that if Bluestar sees that he can learn, she'll have to make him into a warrior."

Now that Fireheart looked more closely at the mother and her kit, he could see that they weren't just playing—at least, Speckletail wasn't. She was showing Snowkit the hunting crouch. Snowkit seemed to be having fun, rolling over and batting at his mother with his paws, but he wasn't copying her movements with any accuracy.

Fireheart watched them with growing sadness. "It might be for the best." He sighed after a moment. "If Speckletail realizes for herself that Snowkit can't learn, it might help her accept that he'll never be a warrior."

"Maybe." Brackenfur didn't sound convinced. "I'd like to watch them for a bit, anyway, and see if there's anything I can do to help."

Fireheart studied him approvingly. Though Brackenfur had not been a warrior for many moons, he had the serious air of a much older cat. He was ready for an apprentice, and Fireheart was sure he would make a fine mentor—patient and responsible. But not for Snowkit. Fireheart knew that the deaf kit could never have a mentor, would never travel to Gatherings, or know the fierce joy of being a warrior in the service of his Clan.

However, as long as there were no other kits in need of mentors, it wouldn't hurt to let Brackenfur take an interest in Snowkit. "That's fine, provided it doesn't interfere with your warrior duties," Fireheart mewed. "If you think of anything, let me know. I'll talk to Cinderpelt again."

"Thanks, Fireheart," meowed Brackenfur. He settled himself on the ground, paws tucked neatly under his chest, and went on watching Speckletail and Snowkit.

Fireheart hesitated, feeling sad for the deaf kit and his mother, and for Brackenfur, whose hopes of becoming a mentor would be disappointed this time. Then he turned away to go and find Bluestar.

The Clan leader was lying on her bedding in the far corner of her den. The sunlight did not reach her there, and she looked like a gray shadow. But the remains of a squirrel showed that she had eaten, and as Fireheart paused on the threshold, she was twisting her head around to wash her back. Fireheart felt encouraged by these signs of a normal routine.

He scraped his claws on the ground to draw her attention, and when she turned to look at him he meowed, "Bluestar, may I come in? I've something to report."

"Nothing good, I suppose," Bluestar mewed sourly. Fireheart flinched at her tone, and the leader seemed to relent. "All right, Fireheart, come in and tell me what's on your mind."

"We think there's a dog loose in the forest." Fireheart described the first time Whitestorm had discovered the scattered prey near Snakerocks, what his patrol had seen that morning, and the rabbit remains that Whitestorm had found near Fourtrees.

Bluestar sat in silence, staring at the wall, until Fireheart finished. Then her head snapped around to face him. "Near Fourtrees? Where?"

"By the RiverClan border, Whitestorm said."

Bluestar let out a snarl and dug her claws into the floor of her den. "Yes—I see it all!" she spat. "WindClan have been hunting on our territory."

Fireheart stared at her. "I'm sorry, Bluestar. I don't understand."

"Then you're a fool!" Bluestar growled. Suddenly she seemed to relax. "No, Fireheart, you are a good and noble warrior. It's not your fault that you can't imagine the treachery of others."

What does she mean? Fireheart thought. *Has she forgotten that I was the one who told her about Tigerstar?*

His mind spinning, he realized that this wasn't one of Bluestar's good days. Her eyes were staring and her fur bristling as if rows of enemies stood in front of her. Perhaps, in her confusion, she thought they were.

"But Bluestar," Fireheart protested, "everywhere we found the scraps of prey, we scented dog. There's no reason to think that other Clans are responsible."

"Mouse-brain!" Bluestar hissed, her tail lashing from side to side. "Dogs don't behave like that. They come here with their Twolegs, and their Twolegs take them away again. Whoever heard of a dog roaming free in the forest?"

"Just because it hasn't happened before, doesn't mean it can't happen now," Fireheart meowed desperately. "Why do you believe it was WindClan?"

"Can't you see?" Bluestar's voice was taut with fury. "WindClan warriors were hunting rabbits, and the rabbits must have crossed the RiverClan border by Fourtrees. RiverClan's territory is narrow there. The WindClan cats chased their prey across both borders, onto ThunderClan territory, before they caught it and killed it." She spoke with absolute certainty, as if she had witnessed it herself. "It's so obvious, a kit could see it." Her paws started working again. "Well, WindClan had better watch out!"

Fireheart's heart lurched. It sounded as if Bluestar were planning to attack WindClan. *We can't bear any more trouble!* he thought despairingly. An image popped into his head, of Tigerstar on his way to visit Crookedstar and Leopardfur. With a possible alliance in the air between RiverClan and ShadowClan, the last thing they needed right now was a war with WindClan.

"You may be right, Bluestar," he admitted diplomatically, "but we shouldn't blame WindClan without any real proof.

It could have been RiverClan, couldn't it?"

"Nonsense!" Bluestar's voice was scornful. "The cats of RiverClan would never cross a border in pursuit of prey. They know the warrior code better than that. Have you forgotten how they helped us in the fire? We would all have been burned or drowned if not for RiverClan."

Yes, and Leopardfur won't let us forget it in a hurry, Fireheart added silently. He couldn't help thinking that RiverClan might believe a few rabbits were only the beginning of payment for their help.

Fireheart shook his head to clear it. There was no point in trying to blame RiverClan. He knew what scents he had picked up. A dog was responsible for the scattered prey, and he had to make Bluestar see that. "Bluestar, I really think—" he began.

Bluestar dismissed his words with a sweep of her tail. "No!" she insisted. "It was you, Fireheart, who came to me after the last Gathering and told me how Tallstar welcomed Tigerstar as leader of ShadowClan."

"Hardly welcomed!" Fireheart tried to protest, but Bluestar ignored him.

"Have you forgotten how WindClan warriors stopped me from traveling to Highstones? And how they attacked you when you brought Cloudpaw home? They show no gratitude, none, for what ThunderClan did for them, when you and Graystripe brought them home from exile! Tallstar is working with StarClan against me! He has allied himself with my greatest enemy, and now he and his warriors invade my territory. He's a disgrace to the name of warrior; he . . . " Her eyes were wild and her voice sank to a rough choking, as if she could hardly get the words out.

Thoroughly alarmed, Fireheart started to back out of the den. "Bluestar, don't," he begged. "You've been ill; this is bad for you. I'm going to fetch Cinderpelt."

But before he could leave, a loud yowling broke out from the clearing. It was the sound of many cats raising their voices in a terrible screech of fear. Fireheart spun around and raced out of Bluestar's den.

The center of the clearing was almost deserted, bathed in bright light where the normally leafy cover had been burned away. Cats crouched around the edges in the scant shelter of the charred fern walls. Fireheart caught a glimpse of Goldenflower and Willowpelt pushing their kits into the nursery. Brackenfur was nudging a couple of the elders toward their den, urging them to hurry.

The cats at the edge of the clearing were staring up at the sky, their eyes huge with fear. As he looked upward, Fireheart heard the beating of wings and saw a hawk circling above the trees, its harsh cry drifting on the air. At the same time he realized that one cat had not taken shelter; Snowkit was still tumbling and playing in the middle of the open space.

"Snowkit!" Speckletail yowled desperately.

She was just emerging from behind the nursery, the place where the queens went to make dirt, and she darted toward her kit as soon as she realized what was happening. In the same heartbeat the hawk plunged down toward the clearing.

Snowkit screamed as the cruel talons fastened onto his back. The great wings flapped. Fireheart raced forward, but Speckletail was faster still. As the hawk lifted off, she sprang upward and snagged her claws in the white kit's fur.

For a couple of agonizing moments both cats dangled from the hawk's claws. Fireheart launched himself into the air, but they were too high. Then the hawk released the kit with one foot and scored its talons across Speckletail's face. The she-cat lost her grip and fell back, landing heavily on the ground. Without her weight, the hawk mounted rapidly to treetop height and flew off toward Fourtrees. Snowkit's terrified crying died away.

"No!" Speckletail threw her head back and let out a yowl of pure desperation. "My kit! Oh, my kit!"

Brackenfur dashed past Fireheart, leaping the camp wall at a place where the rebuilding had barely started, and vanished into the forest. Even though Fireheart knew the pursuit was hopeless, he swung around and caught the eye of the nearest cat. "Swiftpaw, go with him."

Swiftpaw opened his mouth to protest, clearly aware that the pursuit would be hopeless, then closed it again and took off after Brackenfur. The rest of the cats, stunned by shock, gradually crept out into the clearing again and formed a ragged circle around Speckletail.

"He couldn't hear," Sandstorm murmured, touching her nose to Fireheart's cheek. "He couldn't hear the hawk, and he couldn't hear us when we tried to warn him."

"It's my fault!" Speckletail wailed. "I left him . . . and now he's gone. The hawk should have taken me instead!"

Sandstorm moved closer to the tabby queen, pressing herself comfortingly against her side, and Cinderpelt came up and gave her ears a gentle lick. "Come to my den," she mewed softly. "We'll look after you. We won't leave you."

But Speckletail refused to be comforted. "He's gone and it's my fault," she whimpered.

"It's not your fault," meowed Bluestar.

Fireheart turned to see his leader pacing toward them. The broad-shouldered gray she-cat looked strong and determined, more like a warrior than any of the other cats, crushed as they were by the tragedy of Snowkit's loss.

"It's not your fault," she repeated. "Whoever heard of a hawk that dared to swoop down and take a kit from the middle of a camp, with so many other cats around? This is a sign from StarClan. I cannot deny the truth any longer." Bluestar gazed at her shocked, assembled Clan, and her voice vibrated with anger. "StarClan is at war with ThunderClan!"

CHAPTER 9

❧

As her Clan stared at her in horror, Bluestar spun around and stalked away to her den. Fireheart took a pace after her, but without turning her head she snapped, "Leave me alone!" There was so much venom in her voice that Fireheart stopped in his tracks.

What am I supposed to do now? he asked himself. He could see that the Clan was on the edge of panic. The shock of the hawk's attack, and Bluestar's interpretation of it, was turning them into frightened kits. His own legs were shaking, but he pushed his fears away and sprang onto the Highrock.

"Listen!" he called. "Gather 'round, all of you."

Gradually the cats obeyed him, creeping into a huddle at the base of the rock. Several of them glanced fearfully up at the sky, as if they expected the hawk to return. Fireheart noticed Fernpaw pressing close to Dustpelt, and Longtail crouched on the ground as if he thought StarClan were going to start raining fire on them there and then.

And then Fireheart spotted Cloudpaw. The apprentice was gazing around in bewilderment. "What's all the fuss about?" he meowed to Brightpaw. "Every cat knows StarClan is just a tale for kits. They can't really do anything to us."

Brightpaw faced him with shock in her eyes. "Cloudpaw, that's not true!" she exclaimed.

"Come on!" Cloudpaw gave her an affectionate flick with his tail. "You don't really believe that load of thistledown, do you?" He showed his indifference by sitting down and giving his paws a thorough wash.

Fireheart stared down at his apprentice with cold dread chilling the blood in his veins. He had known for a long time that Cloudpaw had no respect for the warrior code, but he had not realized that his apprentice did not believe in StarClan at all.

On the other side of the clearing, Cinderpelt and Brindleface were gently guiding Speckletail in the direction of Cinderpelt's den. Cinderpelt stopped, mewed something rapidly to Brindleface, and came limping back toward the rock.

"I think you might need me, Fireheart," she mewed. "But make it quick. I have to take care of Speckletail."

Fireheart nodded. "Cats of ThunderClan," he began, raising his voice, "we've just seen something terrible. No cat can deny that. But we have to be careful about what meaning we give to this tragedy. Cinderpelt, is Bluestar right? Does this mean that StarClan have abandoned us?"

Cinderpelt spoke up clearly from where she sat at the base of the rock. "No," she meowed. "StarClan haven't shown me anything to suggest this. The camp is more exposed since the fire, so it's not surprising that the hawk could see its prey."

"So it was just an accident that we lost Snowkit?" Fireheart prompted.

"Just an accident," Cinderpelt repeated. "Nothing to do with StarClan."

Fireheart saw the Clan begin to relax and realized that Cinderpelt's certainty had reassured them. The cats still looked shocked and grief-stricken that Snowkit had been snatched away, but the wild stares of panic were fading.

But along with his relief came the worry that once the Clan had recovered from their shock, they would start asking themselves why Bluestar had gone so far as to declare war on their warrior ancestors in StarClan. "Thank you, Cinderpelt," Fireheart meowed.

Cinderpelt flicked her tail and limped quickly toward her den.

Fireheart took a step forward on top of the rock and gazed down at the upturned faces. "There's something else I need to tell you," he began. He wasn't at all sure he should be saying this, since Bluestar insisted that WindClan was responsible for the dead rabbits, but with the safety of the Clan at stake he couldn't keep silent. "We think there's a loose dog on ThunderClan territory. We haven't seen it, but we've scented it at Snakerocks and near Fourtrees."

An anxious murmur rose from the cats, and Sandstorm called out, "What about the dogs at the farm beyond WindClan territory? Maybe it's one of those."

"Maybe," Fireheart agreed, remembering how the savage creatures had chased him and Sandstorm while they were searching for Cloudpaw. "Until it goes away again," he went on, "we all have to be especially careful. Apprentices mustn't go out without a warrior. And all cats who leave camp have an extra duty. Look for traces of this dog—scent, pawmarks, scattered scraps of prey. . . . "

"And dung," Mousefur put in. "The filthy creatures never think of burying it."

"Right," meowed Fireheart. "If you come across anything like that, report it to me right away. We need to find out where the dog has made its den."

As he gave his orders he did his best to hide his growing sense of dread. He could not stifle the feeling that the forest was watching him, concealing a deadly enemy somewhere among the trees. At least the threat from Tigerstar was a straightforward fear of attack from a known enemy. This hidden dog was another matter, unseen and unpredictable.

Dismissing the Clan, Fireheart leaped down from the Highrock and made his way toward Cinderpelt's den. On the way, he spotted Brackenfur limping back into the camp with Swiftpaw just behind him. The ginger warrior's fur was torn where he had forced his way through briers and undergrowth in his pursuit of the hawk. One look at his lowered head and dejected expression told Fireheart all he needed to know, but he waited for Brackenfur to come up and make his report.

"I'm sorry, Fireheart. We tried to keep up, but we lost it."

"You did your best," Fireheart replied, pressing his head against the younger warrior's shoulder. "There was never much hope."

"A waste of time and effort right from the start," Swiftpaw growled, though his eyes betrayed his frustration at their failure to save the kit.

"Where's Speckletail?" asked Brackenfur.

"With Cinderpelt. I'm just going to check on her. You two help yourself to fresh-kill and then get some rest."

He waited to see that the two cats obeyed his order before continuing to Cinderpelt's den. Sandstorm fell into step beside him. When they reached the clearing outside the medicine cat's den, they found Speckletail lying there with Brindleface crouched beside her, licking her gently.

Cinderpelt emerged from the cleft in the rock carrying a folded leaf in her mouth, which she set down on the ground in front of Speckletail. "Poppy seeds," she mewed. "Eat them, Speckletail, and they'll make you sleep."

At first Fireheart thought Speckletail had not heard her; then she half sat up, turned her head, and slowly licked up the poppy seeds from the leaf.

"I'll never have any more kits," she mewed, her voice hoarse. "I'll be going to join the elders now."

"And they'll welcome you," Sandstorm murmured, crouching beside the older cat as the poppy seeds took effect and her head gradually lowered into sleep. Fireheart glanced admiringly at Sandstorm; she was a skilled warrior, and he had reason to know the sharpness of her tongue, but she had a gentle side too.

He was roused from his thoughts when he heard Cinderpelt clearing her throat, and he saw that the medicine cat had padded over to sit beside him. From the look she was giving him he realized that she must have spoken to him and was waiting for a response.

"Sorry—what?" he mewed.

"*If* you're not too busy to listen," Cinderpelt meowed dryly, "I said that I'll keep Speckletail with me overnight."

"Good idea, thanks." Fireheart remembered that Cinderpelt had been with Speckletail when he had been telling the Clan about the loose dog. "There's something else you need to know, and I'd like you to have another look at Bluestar."

"Oh? What's the matter with her?"

Speaking softly so that Sandstorm did not hear him, Fireheart told Cinderpelt about the evidence that a dog was loose in the forest, and how Bluestar was convinced that it must be WindClan invading ThunderClan territory to steal prey. "She's so confused," he finished. "She must be, to declare war on StarClan like that. And there's a Gathering in a few nights. What's going to happen if she starts accusing WindClan in front of the other cats?"

"Now wait a minute," Cinderpelt meowed. "This is your Clan leader you're talking about. You should respect her opinions even if you don't agree with them."

"This isn't just a disagreement!" Fireheart protested. "There isn't a scrap of proof for what she suggests." His raised voice made Sandstorm prick up her ears as she lay beside Speckletail, and he lowered it again as he added, "Bluestar was a great leader. Every cat knows that. But now . . . I can't trust her judgment, Cinderpelt. Not when she isn't making any sense."

"You should still try to understand her. Show her a bit of sympathy, at least. She deserves that from every cat."

For a few heartbeats Fireheart felt outrage that Cinderpelt, who had once been his apprentice, should be talking to him like this. It wasn't Cinderpelt who had to defend Bluestar's decisions and try to hide her confusion so that her own Clan still trusted her. Not to mention making excuses for her to all the other Clans so that no cat would guess the weakness at ThunderClan's heart.

"Do you think I haven't tried?" he snapped. "If I'm any more sympathetic, my fur will fall out!"

"Your fur looks fine to me," Cinderpelt remarked.

"Look . . ." Fireheart made one last effort to suppress his annoyance. "Bluestar missed the last Gathering. If she doesn't go to the next one, every cat in the forest will know something's wrong. Can't you give her something to make her a bit more reasonable?"

"I'll try. But there's a limit to what my herbs can do. She's gotten over the effects of the fire, you know. This trouble started long before that, when she first found out about Tigerstar. She's old and tired, and she thinks she's losing everything she believed in, even StarClan."

"Especially StarClan," Fireheart agreed. "And if she—"

He broke off, realizing that Sandstorm had left Speckletail and was walking toward him. "Finished talking secrets?" she mewed with an edge to her voice. Flicking her tail toward

Speckletail, she added, "She's asleep. I'll leave her to you, Cinderpelt."

"Thanks for your help, Sandstorm."

Both she-cats were being very polite to each other, but somehow Fireheart felt it wouldn't take much for them to unsheathe their claws. He wondered why, then decided he didn't have time to worry about petty squabbles.

"We'll go and eat, then," he meowed.

"And afterward you need to rest," Sandstorm told him. "You've been on your paws since dawn."

She gave him a nudge, propelling him toward the main clearing. Before he had taken more than a couple of paces, Cinderpelt called after him, "Send some fresh-kill for me and Speckletail. If you've got time, that is."

"Of course I've got time." Fireheart felt completely baffled by the tension that had chilled the air. "I'll see to it right away."

"Good." Cinderpelt gave him a curt nod, and Fireheart felt her blue gaze trained on his back all the way across the clearing.

CHAPTER 10

The stars of Silverpelt blazed from a clear sky, and the full moon rode high. Fireheart crouched at the top of the hollow leading down to Fourtrees. Beneath the four great oaks, the ground was carpeted with fallen leaves, glittering in the first frost of leaf-fall. Black shapes of cats moved to and fro against the pale shimmer.

This time Bluestar had insisted on leading her Clan to the Gathering. Fireheart couldn't decide whether that was a good thing or not. True, now he didn't have to invent excuses for her, but he was also worried about what she might say. As ThunderClan's problems piled up, it was becoming more and more difficult to present a strong face to their rival Clans, and his apprehension bit deeper when he admitted to himself that he could no longer trust his leader's judgment.

He edged toward her, out of earshot of Cloudpaw and Mousefur, who were beside him. "Bluestar," he murmured. "What will you—"

As if she hadn't heard him, Bluestar signaled with her tail and the ThunderClan cats sprang to their paws and raced down through the bushes into the hollow. Fireheart had no option but to follow. Before they left the camp, Bluestar had refused to talk about the coming Gathering, and now his last chance to discuss it with her had gone.

Down in the hollow there were fewer cats than Fireheart had expected, and he realized they were all from WindClan and ShadowClan. He spotted Tallstar and Tigerstar seated side by side at the base of the Great Rock. Bluestar walked straight past them, her tail as stiff as if she were advancing on an enemy. Without acknowledging them with so much as the flick of a whisker, she leaped up to the Great Rock and sat there, her gray-blue fur glowing in the moonlight.

Fireheart took a deep breath and tried to calm the fears that welled inside him. Bluestar had already convinced herself that Tallstar was her enemy; to see the WindClan leader talking privately with Tigerstar, the traitor Bluestar feared most, would make her surer that she was right.

As he watched, Fireheart saw Tallstar lean over to Tigerstar and meow something; Tigerstar flicked his tail dismissively. Fireheart wondered if he should creep closer to listen to what they were saying, but before he could move he felt a friendly nudge at his shoulder and looked around to see Onewhisker, a warrior of WindClan.

"Hi, there," Onewhisker meowed. "Do you remember who this is?"

He pushed a young cat forward, a tabby with bright eyes and ears pricked with excitement. "This is Morningflower's kit," Onewhisker explained. "He's my apprentice now—Gorsepaw. Isn't he big now?"

"Morningflower's kit, of course! I saw you at the last Gathering." Fireheart still found it hard to believe that this well-muscled apprentice was the same scrap of fur whom he had carried across the Thunderpath when he and Graystripe brought WindClan home.

"Mother told me about you, Fireheart," Gorsepaw mewed shyly. "How you carried me, and everything."

"Well, I'm glad I don't have to carry you now," Fireheart replied. "If you grow much more, you'll be able to join LionClan!"

Gorsepaw purred happily. Fireheart was sharply aware of the warm friendship that he felt for these cats, which had survived all the skirmishing and disagreements since that long-ago journey.

"We should be starting the meeting," Onewhisker went on. "But there's no sign of RiverClan."

The words were hardly out of his mouth when there was a stir among the bushes at the other side of the clearing. A group of RiverClan cats appeared, padding close together into the open. Stalking proudly at their head was Leopardfur.

"Where's Crookedstar?" Onewhisker wondered out loud.

"I heard he's ill," Fireheart meowed, realizing that he wasn't surprised to see Leopardfur taking her leader's place. From what Graystripe had told him by the river half a moon ago, he hadn't expected the RiverClan leader to be well enough to attend a Gathering.

Leopardfur walked straight toward the base of the Great Rock, where Tallstar and Tigerstar were sitting. She dipped her head courteously and settled down beside them.

Fireheart was too far away to hear what they were saying, and he was distracted a moment later as a familiar gray warrior bounded across the clearing to his side.

"Graystripe!" Fireheart gave a welcoming mew. "I thought you weren't allowed to come to Gatherings."

"I wasn't," replied Graystripe, touching noses with his friend. "But Stonefur said I should have a chance to prove my loyalty."

"Stonefur?" Fireheart echoed. He had noticed both of Bluestar's kits, Stonefur and his sister, Mistyfoot, among the cats who followed Leopardfur. "What's it got to do with him?"

"Stonefur's our new deputy," meowed Graystripe. He frowned. "Oh, of course, you don't know. Crookedstar died two nights ago. Leopardstar is our leader now."

Fireheart was silent for a moment, remembering the dignified old cat who had helped ThunderClan during the fire. The news of Crookedstar's death didn't surprise him, but it still brought a pang of anxiety. Leopardstar would be a strong leader, good for RiverClan, but she had no love for ThunderClan.

"She's already started to reorganize the Clan, even though it's barely a day since she went to the Moonstone to speak with StarClan," Graystripe went on, pulling a face. "Supervising the apprentice training, ordering more patrols. And—" He broke off, his paws working on the ground in front of him.

"Graystripe!" Fireheart was alarmed at his friend's clear

agitation. "What's the matter?"

Graystripe lifted anguished yellow eyes to gaze at his friend. "There's something you ought to know, Fireheart." He took a quick glance around to make sure no RiverClan cats were within earshot. "Ever since the fire, Leopardfur has been planning how to get Sunningrocks back."

"I . . . I don't think you should be telling me that," Fireheart stammered, staring at his friend in dismay. Sunningrocks was a long-disputed territory on the border between ThunderClan and RiverClan. Oakheart and the former ThunderClan deputy, Redtail, had both died in battle over them. For Graystripe to tell Fireheart of his new leader's intentions was an act of betrayal that went completely against the warrior code.

"I know, Fireheart." Graystripe couldn't meet his gaze, and his voice shook with the weight of what he was doing. "I have tried to be a loyal warrior of RiverClan—no cat could have tried harder!" His voice was rising in desperation, but with a huge effort he managed to control himself and go on in a lower voice. "But I can't sit by and do nothing while Leopardstar plans to attack ThunderClan. If it comes to a battle, I don't know what I'll do."

Fireheart moved closer, trying to comfort the gray warrior. He had always known, ever since Graystripe had crossed the river, that sooner or later his friend would have to face the ordeal of fighting against his birth Clan. Now it seemed as if that day had suddenly drawn closer.

"When is this attack going to happen?" he asked.

Graystripe shook his head. "I've no idea. Even if Leopardstar has decided, she wouldn't tell me. I only know about the plan from what the other warriors have said. But I'll see what I can find out, if you like."

For a moment Fireheart was excited by the thought of having a spy in the RiverClan camp. Then he realized what a fearful risk Graystripe would be taking. He couldn't put his friend in that much danger, or add to the pain of his divided loyalties. Unless ThunderClan struck first, without waiting for Leopardstar to attack—which Fireheart didn't want to do—they would just have to deal with the threat when it arose.

"No, it's too dangerous," Fireheart replied. "I'm grateful for the warning, but think what Leopardstar would do to you if she found out. She doesn't exactly like you as it is. I'll tell all the hunting patrols to keep checking Sunningrocks for RiverClan scent, and make sure our scent markings are strong there."

Yowling from the top of the Great Rock interrupted him. He turned to see that the other three leaders had joined Bluestar, who still refused to look at Tigerstar, and were waiting to begin the meeting. When the cats had fallen silent, Tigerstar nodded to Leopardstar, indicating that she should speak first. The golden tabby took a place at the front of the rock and looked down.

"Our former leader, Crookedstar, has gone to join StarClan," she announced. "He was a noble leader and all his Clan mourns his passing. I am leader of RiverClan now, and Stonefur is my deputy. Last night I traveled to Highstones and received my nine lives from StarClan."

"Congratulations," meowed Tigerstar, while Tallstar mewed, "Crookedstar will be missed by all the Clans. But may StarClan grant that RiverClan thrives under your leadership."

Leopardstar thanked them and looked expectantly at Bluestar, but the ThunderClan leader was gazing down into the hollow. There was an expression of pride on her face, and when Fireheart followed her gaze he saw that she was looking at Stonefur. The obvious admiration for her son shocked him, and his heart grew cold when he remembered that Tigerstar knew a pair of ThunderClan kits had once been taken in by RiverClan. Fireheart couldn't help noticing that Tigerstar's gaze was trained on Bluestar, and the massive tabby had a thoughtful look on his face. What would it take for him to guess who the mother of those kits had been?

"I have one more piece of Clan news," Leopardstar meowed, obviously deciding that she had waited long enough for Bluestar to speak. "One of our elders, Graypool, is dead."

Fireheart's ears pricked. He wondered what Mistyfoot and Graystripe had told their leader about Graypool's death, and if he had left any of his own scent on her body. Leopardstar could possibly use that to accuse ThunderClan of killing the old cat, to give her Clan an excuse to attack.

But when Leopardstar went on, it was only to say, "She was a brave warrior and the mother of many kits." She paused to cast a sympathetic glance at Mistyfoot and Stonefur. "Her Clan mourns her," she finished.

Fireheart relaxed, then felt himself tense again as Tigerstar stepped forward. Would the ShadowClan leader announce what he knew about two of Graypool's kits?

To his relief, Tigerstar made no mention of the secret. Instead he gave news of ShadowClan kits that had been made into apprentices and the birth of a new litter—details that showed how ShadowClan was beginning to recover its strength, but nothing that suggested hostility to any other Clan.

Hope flared in Fireheart again. Perhaps there really was no need to keep worrying about a threat from Tigerstar. It would be a relief to forget him and concentrate on the lurking threat of the dog in the forest. Then Fireheart remembered the ShadowClan leader's brutal treatment of Graypool, which had led to her death, and all his suspicions returned.

When Tigerstar had finished speaking, Tallstar moved to take his place, but Bluestar thrust herself in front of the WindClan leader. "*I* will speak next," she growled, giving Tallstar a hard stare.

She stalked to the front of the rock. "Cats of all Clans," she began, her voice coldly angry, "I bring news of theft. Wind-Clan warriors have been hunting in ThunderClan territory."

Fireheart's heart lurched as angry yowling broke out all over the hollow. The WindClan cats sprang to their paws, furiously denying the ThunderClan leader's accusation.

Cloudpaw scrambled around two bigger warriors and came to a halt beside Fireheart, his blue eyes wide with shock and excitement. "*WindClan!*" he meowed. "What's she talking about?"

"Be quiet!" Fireheart snapped. He glanced at Onewhisker, afraid that he might have overheard Cloudpaw's outburst, but the tabby warrior was on his paws, yowling defiance at Bluestar.

"Prove it!" he called, his fur bristling. "Prove that Wind-Clan have taken so much as a mouse!"

"I have proof." Bluestar's eyes blazed cold fire. "Our patrols found remains of rabbit scattered not far from here."

"You call that proof?" Tallstar shouldered his way forward to stand nose-to-nose with Bluestar. "Did you see my cats on your territory? Did your patrols find WindClan scent?"

"I don't need to see or smell thieves to know what they have done," Bluestar retorted. "Every cat knows that only WindClan hunts rabbits."

Fireheart's muscles tensed, and he instinctively unsheathed his claws.

"All this is a pile of mouse dung," Tallstar insisted. His black-and-white fur was fluffed out, and his lips were drawn back in a snarl. "WindClan have lost prey as well. *We* have found rabbit remains on our territory too. And there are far fewer rabbits than usual at this season. I accuse *you*, Bluestar, of letting your warriors hunt on our land and making false accusations to cover up the theft!"

"That seems far more likely," Tigerstar put in, his amber eyes gleaming. "Every cat knows that prey has been scarce on ThunderClan territory since the fire. Your Clan is hungry, Bluestar, and *some* of your warriors know WindClan territory very well."

Fireheart felt the ShadowClan leader's gaze rest on him, and knew Tigerstar meant him and Graystripe.

Bluestar whipped around to face the ShadowClan leader. "Silence!" she hissed. "Stay away from me and my Clan. This is no business of yours."

"It is the business of every cat in the forest," Tigerstar replied calmly. "The Gathering is supposed to be a time of peace. If StarClan are angered, we will all suffer."

"StarClan!" Bluestar spat back at him. "StarClan have turned away from us, and I will fight them if I have to. I care only for feeding my Clan, and I will not stand by while other cats steal our prey."

Her speech was almost drowned by the shocked gasps of the cats listening below. Fireheart couldn't help glancing up to see if StarClan would show their fury by sending a cloud to cover the moon and end the Gathering, as they had done once before. But the sky remained clear. Did that mean StarClan had accepted Bluestar's declaration of war?

Graystripe nudged him. "What's the matter with Bluestar? Does she *want* to pick a fight with WindClan? And what's all this about fighting StarClan?"

"I don't know what she wants," Fireheart muttered.

"I think she's right about the rabbits, and who cares what a stupid old tradition says about keeping the peace at the Gatherings?" meowed Cloudpaw. "Let's face it, StarClan was just thought up by some leader to scare the other cats into being obedient."

Fireheart shot his apprentice a disapproving glance, but

there was no time to discuss his attitude toward their warrior ancestors. His heart thudded as if he were about to leap into battle. There was no way of hiding Bluestar's madness—and ThunderClan's vulnerability—from the other Clans now. Tallstar bristled with fury. So far Leopardstar had not joined in the argument, but she wore the expression of a cat who was about to sink her teeth into a juicy piece of fresh-kill.

When the noise in the hollow had died down, Tallstar made himself heard. "Bluestar, I swear by StarClan that no cat from WindClan has hunted on your territory." His tail lashed from side to side. "But if you insist on fighting with us, we will be ready." He retreated from the edge of the rock and turned his back on Bluestar, a pointed refusal to defend himself any further.

Before Bluestar could retaliate, Leopardstar stepped forward. "The fire was a terrible misfortune," she meowed. "Every cat in the forest knows that, but yours is not the only Clan to suffer recently. Your forest will grow back as rich in prey as it ever was. But Twolegs have invaded our territory and they show no signs of leaving. Last leaf-bare the river was poisoned and cats who ate the fish fell ill. Who can guarantee it won't happen again? I cannot speak for WindClan's needs, but RiverClan needs better hunting ground even more than ThunderClan."

A few RiverClan cats yowled their agreement, and Fireheart's fur bristled with apprehension. He shot a glance at Graystripe, remembering his friend's warning about Sunningrocks. The new RiverClan leader meant to expand her territory, and the logical direction was across the river into ThunderClan land. The gorge cut her off from WindClan territory, and all her other borders were bounded by Twoleg farms.

But Bluestar had not understood the veiled threat. When the RiverClan leader fell silent she dipped her head graciously. "You're right, Leopardstar," she meowed. "RiverClan has endured hard times. Yet your cats are so strong and noble that I know you will survive."

Leopardstar looked taken aback—as well she might, Fireheart thought. The old Bluestar would never have missed the ominous promise in Leopardstar's words.

Tigerstar took a step toward the ThunderClan leader. "Think carefully before you threaten WindClan, Bluestar," he warned. "There will never be peace in the forest if—"

Bluestar bared her teeth and snarled at him, her fur bristling with fury. "Don't talk to me about peace!" she hissed. "I told you to keep out of this. Unless you're allying yourself with that thief over there."

Fireheart watched Tallstar stalk over to Bluestar, and he guessed that the WindClan leader was barely managing not to spring at her throat. "If you want a fight, you'll have one, Bluestar," he growled. Not waiting for a reply, he leaped down from the rock.

Tigerstar exchanged a glance with Leopardstar and both leaders followed, leaving Bluestar alone. Fireheart glanced at the sky again, hardly able to believe there was no sign from StarClan to show that they had seen the Gathering descend into hostility. Did that mean StarClan *wanted* a war between the Clans?

As Bluestar scrambled down from the rock, Fireheart looked around for the other ThunderClan warriors. "Cloudpaw," he instructed urgently, "round up as many of our warriors as you can find and send them to the base of the Great Rock. Bluestar will need an escort."

His apprentice nodded and slipped away into the crowd. Fireheart saw Stonefur thrusting his way through the crowd toward Graystripe.

"Are you ready?" the RiverClan deputy meowed. "Leopardstar wants to leave quickly."

"On my way," Graystripe mewed, springing to his paws. His voice shook as he added, "Good-bye, Fireheart."

"Good-bye," Fireheart replied. There was so much more he wanted to say, but once again he had to face the fact that his best friend belonged to another Clan, and the next time they met could be in battle.

Before the two RiverClan cats turned away, he sought desperately for the right words to speak to Stonefur. "Congratulations," he stammered at last. "I was glad to hear Leopardstar chose you as deputy. ThunderClan don't want trouble, you know."

Stonefur met his eyes. "Nor do I," he meowed. "But sometimes trouble comes anyway."

Fireheart watched them as they headed for the edge of the clearing, and noticed with a jolt that another cat had his gaze fixed on the RiverClan deputy. It was Tigerstar!

Fireheart wondered what his thoughtful look meant. Was the ShadowClan leader sizing up a future ally? Or could he possibly suspect that the tom was one of the kits Graypool had told him of, the kits that came from ThunderClan? After all, it was common knowledge that Stonefur and Mistyfoot had been raised by Graypool. If so, it wouldn't be long before Tigerstar realized who their real mother was. Both Stonefur and Mistyfoot looked very much like Bluestar.

Fireheart was so preoccupied that it was a few moments before he realized that the cat sitting in the shadows beside Tigerstar was Darkstripe. He told himself that it was only natural for Tigerstar's oldest friend to seek him out at a Gathering, but Fireheart didn't like it. He still wasn't sure of Darkstripe's loyalty.

Springing to his paws, he pushed through the cats toward them. As he approached, he heard Tigerstar meow to his companion, "Are my kits well?"

"Very well," the ThunderClan warrior replied warmly. "Growing big and strong—especially young Bramblekit."

"Darkstripe!" Fireheart interrupted him. "The Gathering's over, or hadn't you noticed? Bluestar will want to leave shortly."

"Keep your fur on, Fireheart." Darkstripe's voice was an insolent drawl. "I'm coming."

"Go on, Darkstripe; you mustn't keep your deputy waiting," meowed Tigerstar. He nodded to Fireheart; his amber gaze was carefully neutral.

Fireheart padded across the clearing to join Bluestar with

Darkstripe just behind him. The rest of her warriors were clustered around her, shielding her from the hostile glares and mutterings of WindClan. Her blue eyes still glowed with defiance, and Fireheart realized with a sinking heart that war between the two Clans could not be far away.

CHAPTER 11

❧

The sun was rising over the trees as Fireheart emerged from the warriors' den. Shaking a scrap of dead leaf from his fur, he took a deep breath of the crisp air and extended his forelegs in a long stretch.

After the previous night's Gathering, he was almost surprised to see life in the camp going on as usual: Ashpaw and Cloudpaw were busily patching the outer wall with twigs; Goldenflower and Willowpelt were watching their kits just outside the nursery, where Brightpaw had stopped to play with them; and Whitestorm was padding into the clearing with his jaws full of fresh-kill. Fireheart could sense tension in the air, but so far none of his fears of attack seemed to have come to anything.

He looked around for Sandstorm, who had led the dawn patrol, but she didn't seem to be back yet. She had not been among the cats who had gone to the Gathering, and Fireheart desperately wanted to talk to her about what had happened.

"Fireheart!"

The voice was Bluestar's. Fireheart swung around to see his leader trotting across the clearing from her den.

"Yes, Bluestar, what is it?"

Bluestar jerked her head. "Come to my den. We need to talk."

As Fireheart followed her he noticed her jerky steps and twitching tail. She looked like a cat about to launch herself into battle, yet there was no enemy in sight.

Reaching her den, the blue-gray she-cat padded across to her bedding and sat there facing Fireheart. "You heard that hypocrite Tallstar last night," she hissed. "He refused to admit that his cats have been stealing our prey. So there's only one thing for ThunderClan to do. We must attack!"

Fireheart stared at her, jaws gaping. "But, Bluestar," he stammered, "we can't do that! Our Clan isn't strong enough." He couldn't help remembering that they would have had four extra warriors by now if Bluestar had agreed to promote the apprentices, but he didn't dare mention that to her. "We can't afford to have warriors injured or maybe killed."

Bluestar fixed her eyes on him in a look of fierce hostility. "Are you saying that ThunderClan is too weak to defend itself?"

"Defending ourselves is very different from launching an attack," Fireheart meowed desperately. "Besides, there's no real proof that WindClan stole—"

Bluestar bared her teeth. Her fur bristled as she rose to her paws and took a threatening step toward Fireheart. "Are you questioning me?" she snarled.

With an effort, Fireheart stood his ground. "I don't want needless bloodshed," he told her quietly. "All the signs tell us that there's a dog loose in the forest, and that's what has been taking the rabbits."

"And I tell you that dogs don't wander alone! They come and go with their Twolegs."

"Then where did the dog scent come from?"

"Silence!" Bluestar lashed out with one paw, barely missing Fireheart's nose. He forced himself to stand still. "We will travel tonight and attack WindClan at dawn."

Fireheart's heart lurched. It was an honor for a warrior to fight for his Clan, but never before had he been faced with such an unjust battle. He did not want to shed ThunderClan or WindClan blood for no good reason.

"Did you hear me, Fireheart?" Bluestar demanded. "You will choose the warriors and give them their orders. They must be ready by moonset." Her eyes were blue flames; Fireheart almost felt they could sear him to ash, just as the fire had destroyed the forest.

"Yes, Bluestar, but—" he began.

"Are you afraid of WindClan?" the old leader spat. "Or are you so used to cringing before StarClan that you won't defy them and fight for the rights of your Clan?" She paced to one side of her den, spun around, and paced back again, thrusting out her muzzle toward her deputy. "You disappoint me, you, out of all my warriors. How can I believe you will fight with all your strength when you question my order like this?" she hissed. "You leave me no choice, Fireheart. I will lead this attack myself."

Objections raced through Fireheart's mind. Bluestar was

growing old and losing strength; she was on her last life; she wasn't thinking clearly. But in the face of her fury he could voice none of them. Instead he dipped his head respectfully. "If you wish, Bluestar."

"Then go and do as I ordered." She kept that fiery gaze trained on him as he backed out of the den. "You will come with us, but remember that I will be watching you," she growled after him.

In the clearing outside, Fireheart shivered as if he had just dragged himself out of icy water. His duty was to choose the warriors for the attack on WindClan, and tell them what Bluestar had ordered so that they would be ready to leave after moonset. Yet every hair on his pelt protested against this. A dog had stolen the rabbits, not WindClan. It could *not* be the will of StarClan to attack an innocent Clan! Bluestar was simply wrong.

Fireheart found that his paws were taking him to Cinderpelt's den. Perhaps she could advise him. The medicine cat's wisdom and her special bond with StarClan might help her to see the way forward more clearly than he could. But when he reached Cinderpelt's clearing and called out to her, there was no reply. Fireheart stuck his head a little way into the cleft in the rock and saw that the den was empty, except for the neat piles of herbs stacked along one side.

As he pushed his way out of the fern tunnel, not sure what to do now, he caught sight of Thornpaw padding past with a load of moss for the elders' bedding. The apprentice dropped his burden when he saw the deputy and meowed, "Cinderpelt's out collecting herbs, Fireheart."

"Where?" Fireheart asked. If she was near the camp, he could go and find her.

But Thornpaw shrugged. "Dunno, sorry." He picked up the moss and went on.

Fireheart stood motionless for a few moments, his head spinning with fear and confusion. He could not ask any of the other cats for advice, because a deputy should never question his leader's orders. He could not even talk to Sandstorm, much as he wanted to, because she was bound by the warrior code to obey her leader. There was only one hope left.

Slowly he padded back to the warriors' den, meeting Brindleface on her way out. "I'm going to catch up on some sleep," he explained in answer to her inquiring look. "I want to be fit for a night patrol." He couldn't bring himself to tell her what was really planned for that night.

Brindleface's eyes softened with sympathy. "You do look a bit tired," she meowed. "You're working too hard, Fireheart."

She gave his ear a quick lick and padded off toward the pile of fresh-kill. To Fireheart's relief, no other cats were inside the den, and he did not have to answer any more questions as he curled himself deeply into the moss and fern. If he could just sleep for a while, he might be able to meet with Spottedleaf and ask for her guidance.

Then he remembered his previous dream, when he had searched for Spottedleaf in the dark and fearful forest and failed to find her.

"Oh, Spottedleaf, come to me now," he murmured. "I need you. I have to know what StarClan wants me to do."

Fireheart found himself standing on the border of WindClan territory and looked across the stretch of bare moorland. A stiff breeze rippled over the grass, blowing through his fur. The moor was bounded by an eerie light, hiding the horizon and the land behind Fireheart; he looked back, expecting to see the oaks of Fourtrees, though he could not remember traveling through the forest, but there was nothing there but the pale yellow glow. No cats were in sight.

"Spottedleaf?" he mewed uncertainly.

There was no reply, but he thought he caught a faint trace of the sweet scent that always announced her presence. He stiffened, raising his head and parting his jaws so that he could drink in the beloved smell.

"Spottedleaf!" he repeated. "Please come—I need you so much."

A sudden warmth crept over him. A soft voice murmured, "I am here, Fireheart." He sensed that Spottedleaf was somewhere behind him, and that if he turned his head, he would see her. But he could not move. It was as if cold jaws were gripping him, keeping his gaze fixed on the windswept moorland.

As he stood rigid, Fireheart gradually realized that Spottedleaf was not alone. Another scent wafted over him, painful in its familiarity.

"Yellowfang?" he whispered. "Is that you?"

A faint breath stirred his pelt, and he thought he could hear Yellowfang's rusty purr. "Oh, Yellowfang!" he exclaimed. "I've missed you so much. Are you okay? Have you seen how well Cinderpelt is doing?"

The words spilled out of him in his joy at the reunion with his old friend, but there was no reply, though Fireheart thought the purring grew stronger.

Then Spottedleaf's voice whispered softly into his ear, "I have brought you here for a reason, Fireheart. Look at this place; remember it. This is where a battle will not be fought, and blood will not be spilled."

"Then tell me how to stop it," Fireheart pleaded, knowing that she spoke of Bluestar's planned raid on the WindClan camp.

But there was nothing more, only a gentle sigh that faded and became one with the wind. The paralysis that had gripped Fireheart released him, and he whipped around, but Spottedleaf and Yellowfang had vanished. He drank in the air, desperate for the last trace of their scent, but there was nothing.

"Spottedleaf!" he wailed. "Yellowfang! Don't go!"

The light began to change, became the ordinary sunlight of a morning in leaf-fall, and instead of the moorland Fireheart saw above him a ragged pattern of branches against the sky, the fire-damaged covering of the warriors' den. He lay on his side among the moss, panting.

"Fireheart?" An anxious voice came from just beside him and he turned his head to see Sandstorm. She licked the fur around his ear. "Are you all right?"

"Yes—yes, I'm fine." Fireheart dragged himself into a sitting position and flicked his ears to shake off the clinging moss. "Just a dream, that's all."

"I've been looking for you," Sandstorm went on. "We didn't see anything suspicious on the dawn patrol. Mousefur told me what happened at the Gathering. And the pile of fresh-kill is practically all gone. I thought we could go and hunt."

"I can't, not just now, Sandstorm. I've things to do. But if you could take a patrol out, that would be great."

Sandstorm gazed at him, the sympathetic look in her eyes fading. "Well, okay, if you're too busy." She sounded offended, but Fireheart didn't know how he could explain. "I'll get Brindleface and Brackenfur to come." She rose to her paws and stalked out without looking back at him.

Fireheart licked his paw and rubbed it over his face, clinging to the precious memory of his dream. *A battle will not be fought, and blood will not be spilled*, he repeated to himself. Was Spottedleaf trying to tell him not to worry, that somehow StarClan would stop the fighting? Or did she mean that it was up to him to see that no blood was spilled?

Fireheart was tempted to leave it all in the paws of StarClan. What *could* he do, when his Clan leader had given him her orders? But if he obeyed Bluestar, wouldn't he be going against the will of StarClan? And even more, against all his instincts of what was right for his Clan?

Fireheart made up his mind. Whatever he had to do, ThunderClan must not fight WindClan.

CHAPTER 12

Fireheart padded swiftly out of the camp, hoping no other cats would see him and ask him where he was going. The warrior code said that a Clan leader's orders should be obeyed without question. Until now, Fireheart had always accepted that. He had never imagined that he would ever disobey Bluestar, and yet the time had come when he must challenge her orders or watch the destruction of his Clan. The only way he could see of avoiding the battle was for Tallstar and Bluestar to meet together and talk about the evidence of prey-theft in both their territories. Once Bluestar understood that WindClan was suffering in just the same way as ThunderClan, Fireheart was sure she would call off the attack.

He did not know what Bluestar would do to him afterward, if she realized that he had gone to see Tallstar without her permission. He just hoped she would eventually understand it was for the good of her Clan.

At the entrance to the gorse tunnel Fireheart took a last look around at the camp. For a moment he watched Bright-paw, practicing the hunting crouch all by herself outside the apprentice's den. She crept lightly up on a dead leaf and pounced on it, trapping it with outstretched paws.

"Well done!" Fireheart called.

Brightpaw looked up, her eyes glowing. "Thank you, Fire-heart!"

Fireheart nodded to her, then turned and headed through the gorse tunnel. The short meeting had strengthened his resolve, for the eager young apprentice represented all that was important within the Clan. Fireheart knew that he could not let that be destroyed.

By sunhigh, Fireheart was approaching the stream that lay on the route to Fourtrees. He stopped for a moment to rest. In his confusion and anxiety he had not taken time to eat before he left the camp, and a rustle in the undergrowth reminded him of how hungry he was. He dropped into the hunter's crouch, only to realize a couple of heartbeats later that the sounds were not made by prey. He caught a glimpse of a familiar dark pelt, and breathed in the scent of ThunderClan cats.

Puzzled, Fireheart pressed himself to the ground behind a clump of fern. He hadn't ordered a patrol in this direction, so why were his Clan cats here now? Then the undergrowth parted and Darkstripe emerged, mewing sharply over his shoulder, "Follow me. Try to keep up, can't you?"

Two small shapes appeared out of the bracken. Fireheart's eyes widened in surprise as he recognized Goldenflower's two kits. Bramblekit bounced into the open, batting at a fallen leaf, while Tawnykit followed more slowly.

"I'm tired. My paws ache," the little tabby kit complained.

"What, a strong kit like you?" Darkstripe meowed. "Don't be silly. It's not far now."

What isn't far? Fireheart wondered in alarm. *What are you doing out here, and where are you taking these kits?* He expected to see Goldenflower with them—surely her kits had never been this far from the nursery before?—but she did not appear.

Bramblekit scampered over to his sister and gave her a nudge. "Come on—it'll be worth it!" he urged.

Both kits hurried after Darkstripe to a shallow place where they crossed the stream, squealing in fear and excitement as the water swirled around their paws. On the far side of the stream, Darkstripe veered away from the route that led to Fourtrees, and headed instead along a much narrower path that twisted away under the trees. A burst of outrage shook Fireheart. He knew exactly where that path led. Darkstripe was taking the kits toward the border with ShadowClan.

Fireheart had to wait for them to climb the slope beyond the stream before he dared to emerge from the ferns and follow. By the time he caught up they were approaching the border. The strong reek of ShadowClan reached Fireheart, and he saw the kits stop and start sniffing the air.

"Yuck, what's that?" Tawnykit squealed.

"Is it a fox?" asked Bramblekit.

"No, it's ShadowClan scent," Darkstripe replied. "Come on, we're nearly there." He led the kits across the border, Tawnykit complaining that she was getting the horrid scent all over her paws.

Growing angrier still, Fireheart slid into the shelter of a

hawthorn bush just on the ThunderClan side, where he could watch without being seen.

Close by, Darkstripe had come to a halt. The kits flopped down on the grass, exhausted, only to spring to their paws again a moment later when a clump of bracken rustled and another cat stepped into the open.

The newcomer was Tigerstar. Fireheart froze, though he was hardly surprised. He had guessed that Darkstripe had been hoping to curry favor with Tigerstar by bringing his kits to see him, but the ShadowClan leader's prompt appearance suggested that this meeting had been arranged all along.

Fireheart wondered if Goldenflower knew about this. She was not here with her kits, so perhaps she didn't even know that Darkstripe had taken them away. She might just think they had gone missing. *She must be frantic*, Fireheart thought. He tensed his muscles, ready to leap out and confront Darkstripe, but he stayed in his hiding place and made himself concentrate on what was happening in front of him.

Tigerstar padded forward, the muscles rippling under his dark tabby pelt, until he stood in front of his two kits. For a moment he inspected them, and then bent his head to touch noses, first with Bramblekit and then with Tawnykit. Even though they could never have seen such a massive cat before, both kits stood bravely before him and met his gaze without flinching.

"Do you know who I am?" meowed Tigerstar.

"Darkstripe said he would take us to meet our father," replied Bramblekit.

"Are you our father?" Tawnykit added. "You smell a bit like us."

Tigerstar nodded. "I am."

The kits exchanged a wondering glance as Darkstripe mewed, "This is Tigerstar, the leader of ShadowClan."

Their eyes grew huge, and Bramblekit breathed, "Wow! You're really a Clan leader?"

When Tigerstar dipped his head in agreement, Tawnykit mewed excitedly, "Why can't we come and live with you in your Clan? You must have a really nice den."

Tigerstar shook his head. "Your place is with your mother for now," he told them. "But that doesn't mean I'm not proud of you. They seem fine, strong kits," he meowed to Darkstripe. "When will they be apprenticed?"

"In a moon or so," Darkstripe replied. "It's a pity I have an apprentice already, or I could mentor one of them myself."

Fireheart's claws dug into the ground as a jolt of anger shot through him. *Bluestar and I decide who the mentors will be, not you, Darkstripe!* He almost hissed the words aloud. *And you're the last cat we would choose*, he added silently.

Tigerstar turned his gaze back to his kits. "Can you hunt?" he asked them. "Can you fight? Do you want to be good warriors?"

Both the kits nodded vigorously. "I'm going to be the best warrior in the Clan!" Bramblekit boasted.

Tawnykit refused to be outdone. "And I'll be the best hunter!"

"Good, good." Tigerstar gave each kit a quick lick on the head.

Fireheart couldn't help remembering Graystripe, and how his friend had left the Clan of his birth so that he could stay with the kits he loved. Was it possible that Tigerstar was suffering just as much at being parted from Bramblekit and Tawnykit?

Then Fireheart's blood ran cold as Bramblekit asked, "Please, Tigerstar, why are you the leader of ShadowClan when our mother is a ThunderClan cat?"

"They don't know?" Tigerstar asked Darkstripe. The warrior shook his head. "Well, then," Tigerstar meowed, turning back to the kits, "That's a long story. Sit down and I'll tell you."

Fireheart realized this was the moment when he had to interrupt. The last thing he wanted was for Tigerstar to tell the kits a biased account of how he came to leave ThunderClan. One thing was certain: Tigerstar would never admit that he had been a murderer and a traitor.

Rising to his paws, Fireheart stepped out of the shelter of the hawthorn bush. "Good day, Tigerstar," he meowed. "You're a long way from your camp. And so are you, Darkstripe." His tone sharpened. "What are you doing here with these kits?"

As he padded up to join them, he had the satisfaction of realizing that both Tigerstar and Darkstripe were dumbfounded by his appearance. For a heartbeat they both gaped at him, while the kits bounced across the grass to meet him.

"This is our father!" Tawnykit announced excitedly. "We came all the way from camp to see him."

"Why did no cat tell us he was the leader of a Clan?" Bramblekit piped up.

Fireheart did not want to answer that question. Instead he confronted Darkstripe with his eyes narrowed. "Well?"

"How did you know we were here?" Darkstripe blustered.

"I saw you crossing the stream. You were making enough racket to wake the whole forest."

"Fireheart." Tigerstar dipped his head, the courteous greeting of a leader to the deputy of another Clan. There was no hostility in his tone. "Blame me, not Darkstripe. I wanted to see my kits. You wouldn't deny me that, surely?"

"That's all very well," Fireheart replied in confusion. "But Darkstripe shouldn't have taken them without permission. It's dangerous to let kits wander so far away from their camp." *Especially with that dog loose in the forest*, he added to himself.

"They're not wandering—they're with me," Darkstripe pointed out.

"What if a hawk attacked? There's still little cover in some parts of the forest. Have you forgotten Snowkit?" One of the kits let out a whimper and Fireheart stopped; he didn't want to frighten them. "Take them back to camp, Darkstripe. Now."

Darkstripe exchanged a glance with Tigerstar and shrugged. To the kits, he meowed, "Come on. Fireheart has spoken, and we must obey."

The two kits backed away from their father and followed Darkstripe as he set off back to the camp.

"Say good-bye to your father before you go," Fireheart

meowed, forcing himself to speak in a friendly tone. "You'll see him again when you're apprentices and can go to Gatherings."

Both kits turned to mew good-bye.

"Good-bye," Tigerstar replied. "Work hard, and I shall be proud of you."

He and Fireheart stood side by side as Darkstripe led the kits back down the slope and across the stream. When they had disappeared into the undergrowth, Tigerstar meowed, "Take care of those kits, Fireheart. I'll be keeping an eye on them."

Fireheart's heart was pounding. When he had exposed the former deputy's treachery, Tigerstar had threatened to kill him. Now they were alone once more, with no help nearby for Fireheart if the ShadowClan leader attacked. Fireheart's muscles tensed, but Tigerstar made no move toward him.

"I'll see they're looked after," Fireheart meowed at last. "I'm sure they will be loyal to their Clan. ThunderClan takes care of all its kits."

"Really?" Tigerstar narrowed his amber eyes. "I'm glad to hear it."

Tigerstar knew about the two kits who had been taken to Graypool, Fireheart remembered with a jolt. He waited for the ShadowClan leader to challenge him about them. But Tigerstar did not question him, though his knowing expression chilled Fireheart. It was as though he were well aware that Fireheart could tell him more.

Instead Tigerstar dipped his head again and mewed, "We

shall meet at the next Gathering. I must return to my Clan now." Then he turned and padded away.

Fireheart made sure the ShadowClan leader had really gone before he turned away too, following the border toward Fourtrees. Much as he hated to admit it, he couldn't see that Darkstripe had done any real harm by taking the kits out of the nursery. Fireheart would have had to tell them eventually that their father was the leader of ShadowClan. And Tiger-star himself had behaved with more restraint than Fireheart would have believed possible.

Firmly he put the episode out of his mind. Time was running out. Before sunset, Fireheart knew, he must speak with Tallstar and find another way to solve the dispute over the stolen prey.

CHAPTER 13

Fireheart darted from one clump of gorse to the next as he crossed the moor toward the WindClan camp. He ran with his belly brushing the turf, trying to stay out of sight and longing for the thick undergrowth of his own territory. The last time he had visited the camp, when ThunderClan helped WindClan in a battle against the other two Clans, there had been no need to hide. Now he dared not show himself until he reached Tallstar, or at least met with one of the cats he could call his friends—if any of them were still friendly, after the recent disastrous Gathering. WindClan patrols had attacked him on their territory before; they would be even more hostile now.

The scent of WindClan was all around him, but so far he hadn't seen any cats. The sun had nearly finished crossing the sky. Fireheart tried not to think about that. He came close to panic when he remembered how little time was left before Bluestar would launch her attack.

He was crossing one of the shallow moorland streams, bounding from rock to rock, when a stronger scent of Wind-Clan cats flooded over him, along with the scent of rabbit.

Fireheart's belly growled in complaint, but he had to ignore it. There was no way he could take WindClan's prey now—and it smelled as if there was a hunting patrol not far behind anyway. Diving into a clump of bracken at the water's edge, he peered out cautiously to spot the source of the scent.

Three cats were making their way upstream toward him. At the front of the patrol was his old friend Onewhisker, and Fireheart's heart lifted. Gorsepaw was with his mentor; they were both carrying rabbits. But to Fireheart's dismay, the third cat was Mudclaw, the dark, mottled warrior who had stopped Bluestar when she tried to cross WindClan territory to get to Highstones. This cat would never allow Fireheart to bring his message to Tallstar.

But it seemed that luck—or the favor of StarClan—was on Fireheart's side. With their jaws full of prey, the WindClan cats were unable to pick up his ThunderClan scent, and they passed within a couple of tail-lengths of him. Then Gorsepaw, who was struggling with a rabbit almost as big as he was, stopped to adjust his grip on it and fell behind the others.

Fireheart spotted his chance. "Gorsepaw!"

The young cat raised his head, ears pricked.

"Over here, in the bracken."

Gorsepaw turned, and his eyes stretched wide when he saw Fireheart poking his head out from the rusty fronds. His mouth opened, but Fireheart urgently signaled to him to keep silent.

"Listen, Gorsepaw," he mewed. "I want you to tell Onewhisker I'm here, but don't let Mudclaw know, okay?"

The apprentice hesitated, looking troubled, and Fireheart added urgently, "I have to talk to him. It's important for both our Clans. You've *got* to trust me."

The desperation in his tone reached Gorsepaw, who paused a moment longer and then gave a quick nod. "All right, Fireheart. Wait here."

He picked up his rabbit again and hurried to catch up to the two warriors. Fireheart crept deeper into the bracken and crouched there, waiting. Before long he heard another cat approach his hiding place and murmur, "Fireheart? Is that you?"

To his relief, Fireheart recognized Onewhisker's voice. He peered warily out of the shelter of the bracken, and straightened up when he saw that his friend was alone.

"Thank StarClan!" he exclaimed. "I thought you weren't coming."

"This had better be good, Fireheart," Onewhisker meowed. He gave Fireheart a hard stare, with no trace of his usual friendliness. "It took me a while to get rid of Mudclaw. If he knew you were on our territory, you'd be crowfood, and you know it." He padded up to Fireheart. "I'm sticking my neck out for you," he growled. "I hope it's worth it."

"It is, I promise. I've come to tell you something. I've got to speak to Tallstar. It's important," he added, as Onewhisker went on staring at him.

For a few heartbeats he was afraid that his friend was going to refuse, or even attack him and drive him off WindClan territory.

Then Onewhisker spoke, and to Fireheart's relief he

sounded less hostile, as if he were beginning to realize the urgency of Fireheart's request. "What's it all about? Tallstar will have my fur off if I take a ThunderClan cat into camp without a very good reason."

"I can't tell you, Onewhisker. I can't tell any cat except Tallstar. But believe me, it's for the good of both our Clans."

Once again Onewhisker hesitated. "I wouldn't do this for any cat but you, Fireheart," he meowed at last. Spinning around, he beckoned with his tail and bounded off across the moor.

Fireheart sprang after him. Onewhisker halted at the top of the slope, looking down into the WindClan camp. The rays of the dying sun cast long shadows over the gorse bushes that lined the sides of the hollow. As Fireheart and Onewhisker stood there, a patrol slipped past them. Fireheart was conscious of their stares, where curiosity mingled with antagonism.

"Come on," meowed Onewhisker. He led the way through the tough stems of gorse until they came to a sandy clearing in the middle of the bushes.

As he emerged through a narrow gap in the thorns, Fireheart saw Tallstar crouched at one side of the clearing near a pile of fresh-kill. More WindClan warriors clustered around him. It was the Clan deputy, Deadfoot, who looked up first and then nudged his leader, mewing something rapidly into his ear.

Tallstar rose and padded across the clearing to where Fireheart and Onewhisker waited. Deadfoot hovered at his shoulder, and other cats followed close behind. Fireheart recognized Barkface, the WindClan medicine cat, and Mudclaw, his lips drawn back in a snarl.

"Well, Onewhisker." Tallstar's voice was level, giving nothing away. "Why have you brought Fireheart here?"

Onewhisker dipped his head. "He says he has to talk to you."

"And that means he can just stroll into our camp?" Mudclaw spat. "He's from an enemy Clan!"

Tallstar waved his tail at Mudclaw, a sign for silence, while his eyes looked deep into Fireheart's. "I'm here," he mewed simply. "Talk."

Fireheart glanced around him. The crowd was growing larger, as more WindClan cats heard about the intruder in their midst and came out to see what was going on. "What I have to say is not for all ears, Tallstar," he stammered.

For a heartbeat he thought he heard a faint growl in Tallstar's throat, but then the WindClan leader nodded slowly. "Very well. We will go to my den. Deadfoot, you come with us—and you, Onewhisker." Turning, he stalked toward the rock at the far end of the clearing, his long tail held high, while the two warriors herded Fireheart after him.

The WindClan leader's den was sheltered under a deep overhang in the rock, on the side away from the main camp. Tallstar entered and made himself comfortable in a nest of heather, facing Fireheart. "Well?" he meowed.

Shadows were gathering in the den, and Fireheart could feel rather than see the shapes of the cats who guarded him.

Tension crackled between them, as if they were waiting for the tiniest excuse to attack him. During his journey across the moor he had thought hard about what he would say, but he still didn't know whether he would manage to convince Tallstar that there was a way to avoid Bluestar's attack.

"You know that Bluestar is unhappy about the loss of prey," Fireheart began.

Instantly the fur on the WindClan leader's shoulders began to bristle. "WindClan did *not* steal prey from Thunder-Clan!" he snapped.

"We've found scattered remains too," Deadfoot asserted, limping forward and thrusting his muzzle close to Fireheart's. "Are you sure *ThunderClan* haven't been stealing prey from *us*?"

Fireheart forced himself not to flinch. "No!" he protested. "I don't believe any cats have stolen prey."

"What happened to it, then?" Onewhisker asked.

"I think there's a dog living in the forest. We've smelled it, and found its dung."

"A dog!" Onewhisker echoed. His eyes narrowed thought-fully. "What, loose from its Twolegs?"

"I'm certain of it," Fireheart meowed.

"Could be . . . " mewed Tallstar. To Fireheart's relief, the fur on his shoulders was lying flat again. "We've certainly scented dog in our territory recently, but then, they're always up here with their Twolegs." Sounding more confident, he went on: "Yes, it could be a dog killing the rabbits. I'll see that our patrols keep a lookout."

"But you didn't come all this way to tell us that," Deadfoot meowed. "So what's on your mind, Fireheart?"

Fireheart took a deep breath. He didn't want to betray Bluestar by telling Tallstar of her plans to attack—but he wanted to suggest to the WindClan leader that future battle could be avoided if he would just talk to Bluestar about the prey theft.

"I can't convince Bluestar about the dog," he explained. "She feels threatened by WindClan, and sooner or later this will all end in battle unless we can do something." He could not tell the WindClan warriors how much sooner the battle would take place if he failed now. "Cats will be injured— killed, even—for nothing."

"Then what do you expect me to do?" Tallstar asked testily. "She's your leader, Fireheart. This is your problem."

Fireheart dared to take a couple of steps toward the WindClan leader. "I've come to ask you to hold a meeting with Bluestar. If you could discuss things in private, you might be able to make peace."

"Bluestar wants a meeting?" It was Deadfoot who spoke, sounding disbelieving. "Last time we saw her, she looked as if she would like to claw our throats out."

"This isn't Bluestar's idea—it's mine," Fireheart confessed.

All three WindClan cats stared at him. Finally it was Onewhisker who broke the silence. "Does that mean you're going behind your leader's back?"

"It's for the good of both our Clans," he insisted.

He half expected to be chased out of the camp, but to his relief Tallstar was looking thoughtful. "I'd certainly rather talk than fight," the leader meowed, "but how are we going to arrange it? How willing to listen will she be if she knows that you have talked to us first, without her knowledge?" Not waiting for Fireheart to reply, he went on: "Perhaps it would be best if I sent a messenger to ask her to meet me at Fourtrees—but can you guarantee the safety of a WindClan cat on ThunderClan territory?"

Fireheart was silent, which was answer in itself.

Tallstar shrugged. "I'm sorry, Fireheart. I won't risk one of my warriors. If Bluestar decides that she's willing to talk, she knows where to find us. Onewhisker, you'd better take Fireheart back to Fourtrees. "

"Wait!" Fireheart protested. An idea had just slid into his mind—or perhaps StarClan had sent it to him. "I know what you can do."

Tallstar's eyes gleamed in the gathering darkness. "What?"

"Do you know the cat Ravenpaw? He's a loner who lives on a farm on the edge of your territory, near Highstones. He sheltered us on the journey to bring you home—remember?"

"I know him," meowed Onewhisker. "He's a decent cat, even if he's not a warrior. What about him?"

Fireheart turned to him eagerly. "He could take the message for you. And Bluestar has given him permission to enter ThunderClan territory—as he used to be a ThunderClan cat."

Tallstar shifted in his nest of heather. "That sounds like it might work. What do you think, Deadfoot?"

A reluctant rumble of agreement came from the deputy.

"Then go!" Fireheart urged Onewhisker, realizing once

again how quickly time was running out. "Go now. Tell him to ask Bluestar to meet Tallstar at dawn, at Fourtrees." There was barely enough time for Onewhisker to find Ravenpaw, and for Ravenpaw to carry the message all the way to the ThunderClan camp before Bluestar would be leaving to launch her attack. Fireheart sent a silent prayer to StarClan that Onewhisker would be able to find Ravenpaw easily on the Twoleg farm.

Onewhisker glanced at his leader, who nodded. At once the brown tabby warrior turned around and disappeared into the darkness outside the den.

Tallstar gazed at Fireheart with narrowed eyes. "Why do I think there's something you're not telling me?" he mewed. To Fireheart's relief, he did not press for more answers. "It's time for you to go," he continued. "Deadfoot, escort him off our territory. And Fireheart—I'll be at Fourtrees at dawn, but that's all I can do. If Bluestar wants peace, she must be there."

"Fourtrees at dawn," Fireheart repeated, and followed the deputy out.

Fireheart made good time back to Fourtrees and onto his own territory. He had not eaten since before the Gathering on the previous night; his belly ached with hunger, and he was beginning to feel shaky on his paws, so he forced himself to stop and hunt.

He paused to listen when he reached the stream, and his ears caught the sound of a vole scuffling among the reeds at the water's edge. Lifting his head to taste the air, Fireheart pinpointed the creature more by scent than sight. He pounced, and his claws sank into his prey. Gulping it down, he felt strength flow back into him, and he headed for his own camp with renewed speed. The moon had risen above the trees by the time he slipped down the ravine, reminding Fireheart that he had until moonset to choose warriors for Bluestar's planned attack. His optimism was returning. Tallstar had agreed to talk; surely Bluestar would realize that war with WindClan was unnecessary.

He had almost reached the entrance to the clearing when he heard a cat call his name. He turned to see Whitestorm following him down the ravine at the head of the evening patrol. Brightpaw, Cloudpaw, and Frostfur were with him.

"Everything quiet?" Fireheart asked as Whitestorm came up to him.

"Quiet as a sleeping kit," the white warrior replied. "No sign of the dog. Maybe its Twolegs found it after all."

"Maybe," Fireheart meowed. Suddenly he decided to tell Whitestorm where he had been. He wanted at least one other warrior to share the hope that they might not have to go into battle against WindClan. "Actually, Whitestorm, I wanted a word with you about that. Can you give me a moment?"

"Of course—if you don't mind my eating while I listen."

Whitestorm sent the two apprentices to go take prey for themselves; they bounded over to the pile of fresh-kill and fell into a friendly scuffle over a magpie. Frostfur padded off to the warriors' den with a vole, while Whitestorm chose a squirrel for himself and carried it over to a quiet corner by the newly sprouting nettle patch.

Fireheart followed him. "Whitestorm, Bluestar sent for me this morning. . . ." Quietly he told the older warrior the whole story, from Bluestar's obsessive belief that WindClan had been stealing prey and her order to attack, to Fireheart's decision to ask WindClan for a meeting.

"What?" Whitestorm stared at Fireheart in disbelief. "You went behind Bluestar's back?" His voice failed, and he shook his head in confusion.

Fireheart immediately felt defensive. "What else could I do?"

"You could have consulted me." The fur on Whitestorm's shoulders bristled angrily. "Or some of the other senior warriors. We would have helped you find a solution."

"I'm sorry." Fireheart's heart was pounding. "I didn't want anyone else to get in trouble. I did what I thought was best." It was because of the warrior code that he had acted alone, knowing that he could not ask any other cat to challenge Bluestar's orders like this.

Whitestorm's gaze was intensely thoughtful. "I think we need to tell the other warriors about this," he meowed at last. "They'll need to be ready for Bluestar's attack in case Ravenpaw doesn't get here—and even if Bluestar agrees to meet Tallstar, she might want a patrol behind her. I'd bet a moon's worth of dawn patrols that Tallstar guesses something's up. We can't be sure he won't ambush us."

Fireheart nodded respectfully. "You're right, Whitestorm. I trust them, but we should be prepared."

"I'll find some apprentices to guard the camp," White-storm meowed. "You gather the warriors."

Fireheart ran across the clearing to the warrior's den. Most of them were already there, curled up in their nests, asleep. Fireheart prodded Sandstorm with a paw to rouse her. She blinked up at him. "What is it?"

"Wake the others, please, Sandstorm," Fireheart meowed. "Whitestorm and I have something important to tell everyone."

Sandstorm scrambled to her paws. "What do you mean, something important? It's the middle of the night!"

Fireheart went out again without answering, to look for the remaining warriors. He found Brindleface visiting the queens in the nursery and Mousefur coming into camp with her jaws full of fresh-kill after a late-night patrol. He won-dered whether he ought to call Cinderpelt, but decided it would be better to explain the situation to her individually.

By the time he returned to the warriors' den the other cats were fully awake. A moment later Whitestorm padded under the shelter of the branches and sat down at Fireheart's side.

"What's all this about?" Darkstripe asked bad-temperedly, flicking moss off one ear. "It had better be good."

Fireheart felt his stomach churn with nervousness as he wondered how his Clan mates would react when they heard what he he done. Whitestorm nodded at him, nudging him to speak.

Taking a deep breath, Fireheart began. He explained Bluestar's plan to attack, and how he had tried to work out a peaceful solution instead. His Clan mates listened in stunned silence. Fireheart was acutely conscious of their eyes fixed on him, glowing in the moonlight that filtered through the gaps in the den's roof. In particular he was aware of Sandstorm's pale green gaze, where she sat crouched near the outer branches, but he could not bring himself to look directly at her. He just hoped that the warriors would understand he had done this for the best of reasons, to avoid battle and save lives.

"So Tallstar agreed to meet Bluestar at Fourtrees," he finished. "Ravenpaw should be here anytime now to tell her about the meeting."

He braced himself for an outburst from the other warriors, but no cat seemed to know what to say; they merely looked at each other in bewilderment.

Eventually Mousefur asked, "Whitestorm, do you agree with what Fireheart has done?"

Fireheart waited, his eyes fixed on his paws. He desperately needed Whitestorm's support because of the respect he commanded from the other warriors, but he knew that Whitestorm did not completely approve of his actions, however well-intentioned.

"I wouldn't have done it." Whitestorm spoke with his usual quiet authority. "But I think he's right about not attacking WindClan. I don't believe they have taken any of our prey. There is a dog loose—I've scented it myself."

"So have I, around Snakerocks," confirmed Mousefur.

"At Fourtrees too," meowed Brackenfur. "We can't blame WindClan for that."

"But you're asking us to keep secrets from Bluestar!" Sandstorm rose to her paws, and at last Fireheart had to meet her challenging green stare.

A jolt of dismay ran through Fireheart. He had not expected Sandstorm to be the first cat to object to what he had done. "I'm sorry," he mewed. "I didn't think I had a choice."

"Just what I would expect from a kittypet," growled Darkstripe. "Do you have any idea of what the warrior code means?"

"I know very well what it means," Fireheart defended himself. "It is because of my loyalty to the Clan that I don't want to fight an unnecessary battle. And I respect StarClan as much as any cat. I don't believe it's their will that we attack tonight."

Darkstripe twitched his ears scornfully, but he said no more. Fireheart glanced around, wondering whether he was winning the support of his warriors. When Bluestar gave up her last life and went to join StarClan, he realized uncomfortably, he might have to lead this Clan, and if he could not command their loyalty and respect, the task would be impossible.

"This is what's important," he went on desperately. "WindClan haven't done anything wrong. And we have enough to do, rebuilding the camp and keeping up the patrols, without fighting an unnecessary, dangerous battle. How will we keep ourselves fed and prepare for leaf-bare if we have warriors injured or even killed?"

"He's right." Brindleface spoke up, and the others turned

to look at her. "Our children would be in the battle," she went on quietly. "We don't want them hurt for nothing."

Frostfur added her agreement, but the rest of the warriors were still murmuring among themselves. Again he was aware of Sandstorm, and the distress in her pale green eyes. He could understand how torn she must feel now, between her loyalty to Bluestar and her commitment to him. Right now Fireheart wanted nothing more than to press himself against her flank and forget all this in the sweet scent of her fur, but he had to go on standing in front of his warriors, waiting for their verdict on whether they would support him or not.

"So what do you want us to do?" Longtail meowed at last.

"I'll need a party of warriors ready to go with Bluestar to Fourtrees," Fireheart replied. "If Ravenpaw doesn't come, or if Bluestar doesn't agree to talk, then she'll lead us into battle. And if that happens . . ." His voice failed; he swallowed.

"Yes, what then?" Sandstorm demanded. "Do you want us to disobey Bluestar's direct orders? Turn around and run away? Dustpelt, tell Fireheart what a mouse-brained idea that is!"

Dustpelt's ears pricked in surprise. Fireheart knew very well that part of the brown warrior's antagonism toward him was because Sandstorm so clearly preferred Fireheart now. He braced himself for more criticism, but Dustpelt meowed hesitantly, "I don't know, Sandstorm. Fireheart's right that it's a bad time for a battle, and besides, no cat can seriously believe that WindClan is stealing our prey. If Bluestar thinks so, then . . . well . . . " He broke off, scuffling his paws in confusion.

"It's understandable that Bluestar can't trust WindClan," Fireheart mewed, instinctively defending his leader. "Not since they stopped her going to Highstones. And we've never known dogs loose in the forest before. But there is no evidence at all that WindClan took those rabbits, and plenty of evidence that a dog did."

"So what do you suggest if it comes to battle, Fireheart?" asked Mousefur. "Come back to the camp when Bluestar gives the order to attack?"

"No," Fireheart replied. "Tallstar seemed willing to meet Bluestar in peace, and if we're lucky he'll have only one or two warriors with him. It won't come to a fight."

"That's a pretty big *if*," mewed Mousefur with a skeptical flick of her tail. "What if WindClan assume the same thing, and set an ambush for us? We'd be crowfood." Fireheart winced as she voiced Whitestorm's own doubts about whether they could trust Tallstar.

"I'm not going," Longtail announced loudly. "Let Wind-Clan tear us apart? I'm not mouse-brained!"

Dustpelt, who was sitting next to him, turned his head and gave him a scorching look of contempt. "No, *you're* a coward," he meowed.

"I'm not!" Longtail's protest was shrill. "I'm a loyal ThunderClan cat!"

"Fine, Longtail," Fireheart broke in. "We don't need every warrior to go. You can stay and guard the camp. And that goes for the rest of you," he added. "If you don't want to be part of this, stay here." He waited tensely for his warriors' response, looking around at their troubled faces in the dim light of the den.

"I'll go," meowed Whitestorm at last. "I think we can trust Tallstar not to fight, if there is an alternative."

Fireheart shot him a grateful glance as the other warriors hesitated, murmuring to each other or shifting uncomfortably among the mossy bedding.

"I'll go too." Brackenfur sounded nervous to be the first to speak among so many older warriors.

"So will I," mewed Dustpelt. His tail lashed once in Fireheart's direction. "But if WindClan attack, I'll fight. I'm not going to be clawed apart for any cat."

The rest of the warriors joined in. To Fireheart's surprise, Darkstripe agreed to go, while Mousefur refused.

"I'm sorry, Fireheart," she meowed. "I think you're talking sense, but that's not the point. The warrior code isn't something you stick to just when you feel like it. I don't think I could disobey my leader if she ordered me to attack."

"Well, I *will* go," Brindleface asserted. "I don't want to see my kits torn to pieces in a battle we don't have to fight."

"I'll go too," meowed Frostfur. Her gaze swept over the warriors around her as she added, "We don't raise kits to fight in unjust battles."

At last Fireheart had to face Sandstorm, who so far had said nothing. He could not imagine what he would do if she refused to support him. "Sandstorm?" he mewed hesitantly.

Sandstorm crouched with her head down, not meeting his eyes. "I'll go along with you, Fireheart," she muttered. "I know you're right about the dogs—but I still hate lying to Bluestar."

Fireheart moved to her side and gave her ear a quick lick, wanting to thank her, but she jerked her head away without looking at him.

"What about the apprentices?" Darkstripe asked. "Do you want them to come with us? Fernpaw's too young to get involved."

"I agree," Dustpelt mewed swiftly.

For all his tension Fireheart had to suppress a purr of amusement to hear Dustpelt betraying the soft spot he felt for Darkstripe's apprentice.

"I'd prefer to keep Brightpaw out of it," meowed Whitestorm.

"But won't Bluestar think there's something odd if we don't take any apprentices with us?" asked Brackenfur.

"That's a good point." Fireheart nodded at the young warrior. "Okay, we'll take Swiftpaw and Cloudpaw. But only if Bluestar wants to take that many cats with her, and we'll tell them what's going on *after* we leave. The news will be all around the camp otherwise."

Fireheart realized to his surprise that he had more warriors on his side than he needed. If Ravenpaw made it to the camp on time and Bluestar agreed to go and talk to Tallstar, it would seem odd if a whole fighting patrol of warriors offered to go with her. Besides, he didn't want to leave the camp vulnerable to attack, especially now. "Why don't Frostfur and Brackenfur stay to help guard the camp?" he suggested. "I am grateful for your support, but you may be needed here."

Brackenfur and Frostfur exchanged a glance and then nodded.

"Now the rest of you had better get some sleep," he continued. "We leave at moonset."

He watched the warriors settle down in their bedding, but he did not join them. He knew he had no chance of sleeping, and he wanted to tell Cinderpelt what was going on before she heard it from any other cat. If it weren't for his faith in Spottedleaf, he would have started to doubt long ago that he could stop this battle. There seemed to be so much that could go wrong: Ravenpaw might not bring the message in time; Bluestar might refuse to talk to Tallstar; WindClan might ambush them at Fourtrees. . . .

Giving himself a shake, Fireheart emerged into the clearing. He glanced around for any sign of Ravenpaw, but the camp lay silent in the moonlight. A pair of eyes gleamed from the entrance to the gorse tunnel, and as Fireheart padded closer he made out the pale shape of Ashpaw, on guard.

"Do you know who Ravenpaw is?" he asked, and when the apprentice nodded, he went on: "He hasn't been here tonight, has he?"

Looking puzzled, Ashpaw shook his head.

"If he comes," Fireheart instructed him, "let him in, and take him straight to Bluestar, okay?"

"Okay, Fireheart." Ashpaw was clearly bursting with curiosity, but he didn't ask any questions.

Fireheart nodded to him and went off to find Cinderpelt. Padding up to the medicine cat's den, he saw her sitting outside, deep in conversation with Mousefur.

Both cats looked around at his approach.

"Fireheart?" Cinderpelt meowed, rising slowly to her paws. "What's all this Mousefur is telling me? Why wasn't I invited to the meeting?" Her blue eyes blazed with annoyance.

"It was just for the warriors," Fireheart replied, though the explanation sounded feeble even to him.

"Oh, right," mewed Cinderpelt dryly. "You thought I wouldn't be interested in keeping secrets from Bluestar?"

"It's not like that!" Fireheart protested. "I was coming to tell you now. Mousefur," he added, giving the she-cat a hostile glance, "aren't you supposed to be resting?"

Mousefur returned his glare, then spun around and vanished into the darkness.

"Well?" prompted Cinderpelt.

"It sounds as if Mousefur has told you already. I don't like this situation any more than you, but what choice is there? Do you really think that StarClan want war in the forest—especially an unjust war?"

"StarClan have shown me nothing about any battles," Cinderpelt admitted. "And I don't want bloodshed, but is this the only way to stop it?"

"If you can think of a better idea, tell me."

Cinderpelt shook her head. Moonlight shone on her gray fur, giving her a ghostly appearance, as if she were already halfway into the world of StarClan. "Whatever you do, Fireheart, be careful of Bluestar. Be gentle with her. She was a great leader—and she might be again."

Fireheart wanted so much to believe the medicine cat. But each day Bluestar seemed to slide further into confusion. The wise mentor he had respected when he first came to ThunderClan seemed very far away.

"I'll do my best," he promised. "I don't *want* to deceive her. But that's why I've organized this meeting with Tallstar. I want her to realize we don't have to fight. And she won't listen to me." Tensely, he added, "Do you think I'm wrong?"

"It's not for me to say." Cinderpelt met his gaze steadily. "This is your decision, Fireheart. No cat can make it for you."

CHAPTER 14

❧

When Fireheart returned to the clearing, there was still no sign of Ravenpaw. His belly churned. The moon was high in the sky. Before long, Bluestar would lead her warriors into battle against WindClan, and all hope of a peaceful solution would be lost.

Where was Ravenpaw? Perhaps Onewhisker hadn't been able to find him. Or perhaps he couldn't come—or he was on his way but would arrive too late. Fireheart wanted to dash out into the forest and look for him, but he knew that would serve no purpose.

Then he saw a flicker of movement at the entrance to the camp, and heard a mewed challenge from Ashpaw. Another cat answered, and Fireheart shivered with relief as he recognized Ravenpaw's voice. Springing forward, he bounded across the clearing.

"Okay, Ashpaw," he meowed to the apprentice. "I'll look after Ravenpaw—you stay on guard." He touched noses with the sleek cat who emerged from the gorse tunnel. "It's good to see you, Ravenpaw. How are you?"

Even as he asked the question he could see that the former

apprentice was looking well. His black pelt shone in the moonlight and his strong muscles rippled beneath the fur.

"I'm fine," Ravenpaw replied. He looked around the clearing, his amber eyes very wide. "It seems strange to be here again, Fireheart. I'm sorry to hear you're having trouble with WindClan. Onewhisker told me everything, and he swore they haven't been stealing prey."

"Try convincing Bluestar of that," Fireheart meowed grimly. "Look, I hate to rush you—I know you must have run like the wind to get here so fast—but we don't have much time. Follow me."

He led the way to Bluestar's den. The ThunderClan leader was curled in her nest, but when Fireheart looked closely at her he could see a gleam of moonlight reflected from her narrowed eyes. She was not asleep.

"What's the matter, Fireheart?" she asked, sounding annoyed. "It's not time to go yet. And who's that with you?"

"It's Ravenpaw, Bluestar," the loner meowed, stepping forward. "I've come with a message from Windclan."

"*WindClan!*" Bluestar sprang to her paws. "What does that Clan of thieves want to say to me?"

To Ravenpaw's credit, he didn't flinch, though Fireheart knew he must remember the days when he was a Clan apprentice and Bluestar's anger was something to be feared. "Tallstar wants to meet with you, to discuss the loss of prey," he told her.

"*Does* he?" Briefly Bluestar glared at her deputy, her eyes blazing with blue fire. For a heartbeat Fireheart was sure she had guessed what he had done. There was an ominous pause.

"Bluestar, surely it would be better to talk than fight?" he ventured.

"Don't tell me what to do," Bluestar snapped. Her tail-tip twitched irritably. "Get out of here. Ravenpaw and I will discuss this together."

Fireheart had no choice but to leave the den. He hovered around outside, listening to the murmur of voices but unable to make out what Bluestar and Ravenpaw were saying.

After a while Whitestorm emerged from the warriors' den and padded over to join him. "The moon's going down," the white warrior meowed. "Bluestar will want to leave soon. Is Ravenpaw here yet?"

"Yes, he is," mewed Fireheart. "But I don't know whether—"

He broke off at a movement from inside the den. A heart-beat later, Bluestar stalked out with Ravenpaw behind her. She paced forward until she reached Fireheart, her tail lashing. "Gather a patrol," she ordered. "We go to Fourtrees."

"Does that mean you are going to talk with Tallstar?" Fireheart asked bravely.

His leader's tail lashed again. "I will talk," she meowed. "But if there is no agreement, then we will fight."

The night was still dark when Bluestar led her warriors into the hollow where the four great oaks stood. Fireheart padded at her shoulder; the smallest of rustles told him that the other cats were following. His heart lurched as an owl hooted in the distance. He had barely had a chance to murmur his thanks to Ravenpaw for bringing Tallstar's message before the black cat had slipped away from the ThunderClan warriors. He would follow a different route back to his farmland home, keeping well clear of Fourtrees.

Bluestar paused at the top of the slope. As the other warriors caught up with her, starlight cast a faint sheen on their fur, touching their pricked ears and reflecting from their wide eyes. Fireheart could almost taste their anticipation.

When he looked across the border into WindClan territory, he thought at first that the sweep of moorland was empty, stretching up to the night sky. Wind swept across it and rustled the oak trees in the hollow behind him. Then he caught sight of movement up ahead, and he realized that a line of cats was standing there, with Tallstar at their center. His stomach clenched as Fireheart realized that Tallstar, too, had brought his warriors with him.

"What's that?" Bluestar hissed, turning to glare into his eyes. "So many WindClan cats? I thought I was coming here to talk." Her eyes glared furiously at Fireheart, some sharpened instinct flooding her expression with understanding. "This looks more like an ambush than a meeting of leaders."

At a flick of her tail, the ThunderClan warriors moved up in purposeful silence to form a tight line on either side of their leader, facing the WindClan cats. Fireheart felt the air crackle with tension, and he realized that it would be all too easy for fighting to break out, even if WindClan did not attack first. Would Tallstar keep his word, and try to talk to Bluestar rather than fight?

"Tallstar?" Bluestar meowed coldly. "What have you to say to me?"

Waiting for the WindClan leader's response, Fireheart nervously sheathed and unsheathed his claws. He did not know if the line would hold. If just one cat moved forward, battle could engulf them all. He saw Dustpelt exchange a tense glance with Brindleface, as if both cats were thinking the same as he was. Next to him, Sandstorm kept her gaze fixed on the WindClan cats, her ears flat to her head. Swiftpaw stared nervously at his leader, but he held his place in the line. Cloudpaw, on Fireheart's other side, had dropped into the hunter's crouch, his rump wriggling as if he were about to spring.

"Keep *still*!" Fireheart hissed.

A few fox-lengths away, Tallstar stood a pace or two ahead of his own warriors. As the first pale light of dawn crept into the sky, Fireheart could make him out more clearly. His black-and-white fur was fluffed up, and his tail held erect. Behind him Fireheart spotted Onewhisker and Morningflower, and the young apprentice Gorsepaw. *I don't want to fight these cats*, he thought. He waited, feeling his heart pound like that of a trapped bird.

"No cat is to move," Tallstar ordered his warriors at last, his voice carrying easily in the still air.

"You must be mad!" That was Mudclaw, padding to Tallstar's side. "That's a fighting force she's brought with her. We've got to attack!"

"No." Tallstar took another pace forward, flicking his tail to summon Deadfoot, his deputy, to his side. Looking directly at Bluestar, he dipped his head. "No battle will be fought here today. I said that I would come here to talk, and that's what I intend to do."

Bluestar did not respond. She crouched on the ground, her fur bristling and her teeth bared in a snarl of defiance. Fireheart was suddenly afraid that she had changed her mind, and wondered what would happen if she launched herself at the WindClan leader. He sent up a fervent prayer to Star-Clan that she would not order her warriors to attack.

Meanwhile, Onewhisker came up to Mudclaw and nudged him roughly back into line. For a moment that seemed to Fireheart to last several moons, the two lines of cats faced each other, their fur blowing in the wind, their eyes gleaming with a tension that teetered on the brink of breaking out into squalling, biting rage.

"Bluestar," Tallstar spoke again. "Will you come here to me, between our warriors? Bring your deputy with you, and let us see if we can make peace."

"Peace?" Bluestar spat. "How can I make peace with prey stealers and rogues?"

Yowls of protest rose from the WindClan cats. Mudclaw sprang forward, but Onewhisker leaped after him and bowled him over, holding him writhing on the turf. Fireheart saw Darkstripe lashing his tail to and fro; if Mudclaw attacked, Darkstripe would meet him, and all hope of peace would be over.

"Do as Tallstar says," Fireheart mewed desperately to Bluestar. "That's why we're here. WindClan have suffered from stolen prey, just like ThunderClan."

Bluestar rounded on him, a look of venomous hatred blazing in her blue eyes. "It seems we have no choice," she hissed at him. "But there'll be a reckoning for this, Fireheart. You can be sure of that."

Stiff-legged, her fur bristling, she paced forward until she stood in front of Tallstar, right on the border of WindClan territory. Fireheart followed, murmuring to Sandstorm, "Keep an eye on Darkstripe," as he left the line of warriors.

Tallstar watched Bluestar coolly as she approached. The WindClan leader had never forgiven her, Fireheart knew, for sheltering his old enemy Brokentail, but he had the wisdom not to let his grudge influence him now. "Bluestar," he meowed, "I swear by StarClan that WindClan have not hunted on your territory."

"StarClan!" Bluestar sneered. "What's the worth of an oath by StarClan?"

The black-and-white tom looked taken aback, his gaze flickering to Fireheart as if he were looking for an explanation. "Then I will swear it by anything you hold sacred," he went on. "By our kits, by our hopes for our Clans, by our honor as leaders. WindClan did not do what you accuse us of."

For the first time his words seemed to reach Bluestar. Fireheart saw her fur begin to lie flat. "How can I believe you?" she rasped.

"We have lost prey too," Tallstar told her. "It may be dogs, or rogues. It is not cats from WindClan."

"So you say," meowed Bluestar. She sounded uncertain now. Fireheart thought that perhaps Tallstar was beginning to convince her, but she did not know how to back down without losing dignity.

"Bluestar," Fireheart mewed urgently, "a noble leader doesn't take her warriors into battle without need. If there's the least doubt that—"

"Do you think you know more than I do about how to lead a Clan?" Bluestar interrupted. Her fur had bristled again, but this time it was Fireheart who was the target of her anger. He caught a glimpse of the old, formidable ThunderClan leader, and it was all he could do not to flinch from her.

"Young cats think they know everything," Tallstar meowed. There was a hint of sympathetic humor in his voice, and Fireheart felt a flash of gratitude toward the WindClan leader for his sensitivity to Bluestar's fears. "But sometimes we have to listen to them. There is no need for this battle."

Bluestar's ears twitched irritably. "Very well," she mewed reluctantly. "I accept your word—for now. But if my patrols scent WindClan one tail-length over our border . . ." She whipped around and called to the ThunderClan cats. "Back to camp!" she ordered, leaping ahead of them.

As Fireheart turned to follow her, Tallstar dipped his head to him. "Thank you, Fireheart. You did well, and my Clan honors your courage in averting this battle—but I don't envy you now."

Fireheart shrugged, and followed the rest of his Clan. Just

before he plunged into the hollow at Fourtrees, he glanced over his shoulder to see the WindClan cats racing back across the open moor toward their camp. The turf gleamed pale in the soft dawn light, unstained by the blood of any cat.

"Thank you, Spottedleaf," Fireheart murmured as he turned away.

Bluestar led her warriors back to camp in tense silence. At the entrance to the clearing, Fireheart bounded ahead to talk to Mousefur, who was sitting outside the warriors' den.

"Any problems?" he asked.

Mousefur shook her head. "No trouble at all," she reported. "Frostfur has taken out the dawn patrol with Brackenfur and a couple of the apprentices." Looking him over, she added, "You don't seem to be missing any fur. I suppose the peace talk worked."

"Yes, it did. Thanks for taking care of things here, Mousefur."

Mousefur dipped her head. "I'm going to get some sleep," she meowed. "You'll need to send some cats out to hunt. There's hardly any fresh-kill left."

"I'll lead a hunting party," Fireheart promised.

"No, you won't." Bluestar came padding up behind him. Her eyes were chips of blue ice. "I want to see you in my den, Fireheart. Now." She stalked across the clearing without looking back to see if he was following.

Fireheart's fur prickled with dread. He had expected some sort of recrimination from his leader, but that didn't make it any easier now that it was about to happen.

"I'll see to the hunting party," Whitestorm meowed, giving him a sympathetic look as he came up with Sandstorm and Dustpelt.

Fireheart nodded his thanks and headed toward Bluestar's den. By the time he reached it, his leader was seated on her bedding with her paws tucked under her. The tip of her tail twitched back and forth.

"Fireheart." Her voice was quiet; Fireheart would have been less afraid if she had yowled at him. "Tallstar couldn't have picked a more convenient time to talk to me about the prey theft than if StarClan had told him themselves. That was your doing, wasn't it? You're the only cat who knew that I was planning to attack WindClan. Only you could have betrayed us."

She sounded as if her mind was clearer than it had been for some time, as if the instinct that had sharpened her senses on the moor had settled into hard certainty. She was behaving like the noble leader he had once respected, giving Fireheart an even more agonizing sense of what they had lost. He still believed that he had not betrayed his Clan, but he had given away the advantage of surprise, because Tallstar had been wise enough to realize that battle must be close. Would Bluestar send him into exile? Fireheart shivered at the thought of being forced to live as a rogue, stealing prey and with no Clan to call his own.

He came to stand in front of Bluestar and dipped his head. "I thought it was the right thing to do," he meowed quietly.

"Neither of the Clans needed to fight this battle."

"I trusted you, Fireheart," Bluestar rasped. "You, out of all my warriors."

Fireheart forced himself to meet her flinty gaze. "I did it for the good of the Clan, Bluestar. And I didn't tell him about the attack. I only asked him to try making peace. I thought—"

"Silence!" Bluestar hissed, lashing her tail. "That is no excuse. And why should I care if the whole Clan had been slaughtered? Why should I care what happens to traitors?"

A wild light was growing in her eyes again, and Fireheart realized that the moment's clarity had gone.

"If only I'd kept my kits!" she whispered. "Mistyfoot and Stonefur are noble cats. Far nobler than any of this ragtag bunch in ThunderClan. My children would never have betrayed me."

"Bluestar . . ." Fireheart tried to interrupt, but she ignored him.

"I gave them up to become deputy, and now StarClan are punishing me. Oh, StarClan are clever, Fireheart! They knew the cruelest way to break me. They made me leader and then let my cats betray me! What is it worth, now, to be leader of ThunderClan? Nothing! It's all empty, all . . . " Her paws worked furiously among the moss. Her eyes were glazed, staring at nothing, and her mouth gaped in a soundless wail.

Fireheart shuddered in dismay. "I'll fetch Cinderpelt," he meowed.

"Stay . . . where . . . you . . . are." Each word was rasped out separately. "I need to punish you, Fireheart. Tell me a good punishment for a traitor."

Nearly sick with fear and shock, Fireheart forced himself to reply. "I don't know, Bluestar."

"But I do." Now her voice was a low purr, with a strange note of amusement in it. Her gaze locked with Fireheart's. "I know the best punishment of all. I'll do nothing. I'll let you be deputy still, and leader after me. Oh, that should please StarClan—a traitor leading a Clan of traitors! May they give you joy of it, Fireheart. Now get out of my sight!"

The last words were spat out. Fireheart backed away from her, into the clearing. He felt as if he had been in a battle after all. Bluestar's despair pierced him like sharpened claws. But he couldn't help feeling that Bluestar had let him down too, by not even trying to understand his motives; she had labeled him a traitor without even considering what would have happened if they had fought WindClan.

Head down, Fireheart padded across the clearing, not even aware that another cat had approached him until he heard Sandstorm's voice.

"What happened, Fireheart? Has she sent you away?"

Fireheart looked up. Sandstorm's green eyes were anxious, though she did not move close enough to comfort him with her touch.

"No," he replied. "She didn't do anything."

"Then that's all right." Sandstorm sounded as if she were forcing optimism into her voice. "Why are you looking like that?"

"She's . . . ill." Fireheart couldn't begin to describe what he had just witnessed in Bluestar's den. "I'm going to get Cinderpelt to see her. Then maybe we can eat together."

"No, I . . . I said I'd go hunting with Cloudpaw and Brindleface." Sandstorm scuffled her front paws, not looking at him. "Don't worry about Bluestar, Fireheart. She'll be all right."

"I don't know." Fireheart couldn't repress a shiver. "I thought I could make her understand, but she thinks I betrayed her."

Sandstorm said nothing. Fireheart saw her give him a quick glance and then look away. There was longing in her eyes, but it was mingled with uneasiness, and he remembered how she had resented deceiving Bluestar.

Does Sandstorm think I'm a traitor too? he thought desperately.

After Fireheart had sent Cinderpelt to Bluestar, he headed for the warriors' den. He felt as if his legs could hardly hold him up, and he could think of nothing except sinking into the soft darkness of sleep. His heart sank when he saw Longtail stalking across the clearing toward him.

"I want a word with you, Fireheart," he growled.

Fireheart sat down. "What is it?"

"You ordered *my* apprentice to go with you this morning."

"Yes, and I told you why."

"He didn't like it, but he did his duty," Longtail meowed harshly.

That was true, Fireheart reflected. He had admired the

apprentice's courage in a tough situation, but he wasn't sure why Longtail was making such a fuss now.

"I think it's time he was made a warrior," Longtail went on. "In fact, Fireheart, he should have been a warrior long ago."

"Yes, I know," Fireheart replied. "You're right, Longtail, he should."

Longtail looked taken aback at his ready agreement. "So what are you going to do about it?" he blustered.

"Right now, nothing," Fireheart meowed. "Don't flatten your ears at me, Longtail. Just think, will you? Bluestar is distressed at the moment. She didn't like what happened this morning, and she won't want to think about promoting apprentices. No, wait." He flicked his tail to silence Longtail as the pale warrior opened his mouth to protest. "Leave it with me. Sooner or later Bluestar has to realize that what happened was for the best. Then I'll talk to her about making Swiftpaw a warrior, I promise."

Longtail sniffed. Fireheart could see he wasn't happy, but he couldn't think of any reason to object. "All right," the pale tabby warrior mewed. "But it had better be soon."

He stalked off again, leaving Fireheart to head for his nest. As he curled into the soft moss, shutting his eyes tight against the early morning light, he couldn't help worrying about the four older apprentices. Cloudpaw, Brightpaw, and Thornpaw all deserved to be warriors as well as Swiftpaw. And the Clan desperately needed them to take on full warrior duties. But in her present mood, convinced that she was surrounded by traitors, Bluestar would never agree to give them warrior status.

Fireheart's dreams were dark and confused, and he woke to find that a cat was nudging him. A voice meowed, "Wake up, Fireheart!"

Blinking, he focused his eyes on Cinderpelt's face. Her gray fur was ruffled and her eyes wide with anxiety; Fireheart was awake in a heartbeat.

"What's the matter?"

"It's Bluestar," Cinderpelt replied. "I can't find her anywhere!"

CHAPTER 15

♣

Fireheart sprang to his paws. "*Tell* me what happened."

"When I saw her earlier this morning, I took her poppy seeds to calm her down," Cinderpelt explained. "But when I went to her den just now, she wasn't there, and she hadn't eaten the poppy seeds. I tried the elders' den and the nursery, but she isn't there either. She isn't anywhere in camp, Fireheart."

"Did anyone see her leave?"

"I haven't asked yet. I came to tell you first."

"Then I'll get the apprentices to search, and find out if—"

"Bluestar's not a kit, you know." The interruption came from Whitestorm, who had padded into the warriors' den in time to hear Cinderpelt's news. "She might have gone on patrol. For all you know, other cats are with her." He spoke calmly as he bared his teeth in a yawn and settled into his nest.

Fireheart nodded uncertainly. What Whitestorm said was sensible, but he would have liked to be sure. After the state Bluestar had been in that morning, she could be anywhere in the forest. She might even have gone to RiverClan in search of her kits.

"There's probably no need to worry," Fireheart reassured Cinderpelt, hoping he sounded more confident than he felt. "But we'll look anyway, and find out if any cat has seen her."

Leaving the den, he spotted Fernpaw and Ashpaw sharing tongues near the blackened remains of the tree stump outside the apprentices' den. Quickly Fireheart explained that he had a message for Bluestar, but he wasn't sure where she was. The two apprentices dashed off willingly to look for her.

"You go and ask if any cat has seen her," he suggested to Cinderpelt, who had followed him out of the den. "I'll go up the ravine and see if I can pick up her scent. I might be able to track her."

Privately he didn't have much hope. While he had slept, clouds had covered the sky and a thin rain was drizzling down. It was not good weather for following scent. Before he could leave, Fireheart noticed that Sandstorm was just returning to camp, along with Cloudpaw and Brindleface. All three of them carried fresh-kill, which they went over to drop on the pile.

Fireheart raced up to them, with Cinderpelt limping behind. "Sandstorm," he meowed, "have you seen Bluestar?"

Sandstorm swiped her tongue around her mouth to remove the prey juices. "No. Why?"

"She isn't here," mewed Cinderpelt.

Sandstorm's eyes widened. "Are you surprised? After what happened this morning? She must feel like she's losing control of her Clan."

That was so close to the truth that Fireheart didn't know how to answer.

"We're going out again," meowed Cloudpaw. "We'll keep a lookout for her."

"Okay, thanks." Fireheart blinked gratefully at his apprentice.

The young white tom raced off again, with the two warriors following more slowly. Brindleface paused to meow, "I'm sure she'll be fine, Fireheart," as she left, but Sandstorm didn't look back.

Fireheart's problems were about to overwhelm him, but then he felt Cinderpelt's breath soft against his ear. "Don't worry, Fireheart," she murmured. "Sandstorm's still your friend. You need to accept that she doesn't always see things the way you do."

"You don't either." Fireheart sighed.

Cinderpelt let out an affectionate purr. "I'm still your friend too," she told him. "And I know you've done what you believe to be right. Now, let's see what we can do to find Bluestar."

By the time the sun set, Bluestar was still missing. Fireheart had tracked her as far as the top of the ravine, but after that, with the rain coming down more heavily, the scent was lost among the tang of charred branches and the musty smell of fallen leaves.

Too anxious to sleep, Fireheart put himself on watch. The

night was far gone, and the moon was setting when he spotted movement by the camp entrance. The last rays of moonlight picked out a silver-gray coat as Bluestar limped back into the camp. Her fur was soaked, plastered to her body, and her head was low. She looked old, exhausted, defeated.

Fireheart hurried across to her. "Bluestar, where have you been?"

The Clan leader raised her head and looked at him. A jolt ran through Fireheart; her eyes, faintly glowing in the dim light, were clear and bright in spite of her exhaustion. "You sound like a queen scolding her kit," she rasped, an edge of humor in her voice. She jerked her head in the direction of her den. "Come with me."

Fireheart obeyed, pausing only to snatch a vole from the pile of fresh-kill. Bluestar needed to eat, wherever she had been. When he reached Bluestar's den, his leader was seated in her mossy nest, washing herself with long, careful strokes. Fireheart would have liked to sit beside her and share tongues with her, but after their last encounter he did not dare. Instead he dropped the vole in front of her and respectfully dipped his head. "What happened, Bluestar?" he asked.

Bluestar stretched her neck to sniff the vole, half turned away from it, and then began to gulp it down as if she had suddenly realized how hungry she was. She did not answer until she had finished it.

"I went to speak with StarClan," she announced, flicking the last traces of vole from her whiskers.

Fireheart stared. "To Highstones? On your own?"

"Of course. Which of this pack of traitors could I ask to escort me?"

Fireheart swallowed. Gently he meowed, "Your Clan are loyal, Bluestar. All of us."

Bluestar shook her head stubbornly. "I went to Highstones, and I spoke with StarClan."

"But why?" Fireheart was feeling more and more confused. "I thought you no longer wanted to share tongues with StarClan."

The old cat drew herself up. "I do not. I went to challenge them. I wanted to ask how they could justify what they have done to me, when I have served them all my life and tried to do their will. And to demand an explanation for the things that are happening in the forest."

Fireheart gazed at her in disbelief, amazed that his leader had dared to challenge the spirits of their warrior ancestors.

"I lay beside the Moonstone and StarClan came to me," Bluestar went on. "They did not justify themselves—how could they? There is *no* justification for what they have done to me. But they told me something. . . . "

Fireheart leaned closer. "What?"

"They said that there is evil loose in the forest. They spoke of a 'pack.' They told me that it will bring more death and destruction than the forest has ever seen before."

"What did they mean?" Fireheart whispered. Surely there had been enough death and destruction already, with the fire and the floods?

Bluestar lowered her head. "I don't know."

"But we *must* find out!" Fireheart exclaimed, his mind whirling. "Perhaps they mean the dog—but a dog couldn't do damage on that scale. And what about 'pack'? Maybe . . . yes, maybe they were talking about ShadowClan. You know how Tigerstar vowed to take revenge on us. Maybe he's planning an attack. Or Leopardstar," he added, still trying to cling to his hope that Tigerstar had lost interest in harming his old Clan.

Bluestar shrugged. "Maybe."

Fireheart narrowed his eyes. He couldn't understand why she didn't want to work out the meaning of what StarClan had told her and make plans to stop the attack if it came. "We have to do something," he insisted. "We could set a watch on the borders, and we should increase the patrols." He wasn't sure how he was going to that with so few warriors. "We need to make sure there's always a guard on the camp when . . ."

His voice trailed off as he realized Bluestar wasn't listening. She crouched motionless, her eyes fixed on her paws. "Bluestar?"

The ThunderClan leader looked up at him, her eyes bottomless pools of despair. "What is the point?" she rasped. "StarClan have decreed that death will come. A dark force walks this forest, and even StarClan themselves cannot control it. Or *will* not. There is nothing we can do."

A shudder went through Fireheart. Was Bluestar right that StarClan were not powerful enough to avert the doom that was coming? For a few heartbeats he almost shared his leader's despair.

Then he raised his head. He felt as though he were clawing his way up from the depths of black water. "No," he growled. "I won't believe that. There is always something that a cat can do, as long as he has courage and loyalty."

"Courage? Loyalty? In ThunderClan?"

"*Yes*, Bluestar." Fireheart tried to put all the force of his belief into his reply. "No cat but Tigerstar has ever wanted to betray you."

Bluestar held his gaze for a moment before looking away. Her tail flicked wearily. "Do what you want, Fireheart. It won't make any difference. Nothing will. Now leave me."

Fireheart murmured a farewell. Backing away, he noticed the poppy seeds Cinderpelt had left earlier, still lying neatly on a leaf. He nodded toward them. "Eat your poppy seeds, Bluestar," he mewed. "You need to rest. Tomorrow everything will look better."

He took the leaf between his teeth and carefully moved it into Bluestar's reach. Bluestar gave a disdainful sniff, but as Fireheart left the den he glanced back to see her bend over and lick up the seeds.

Outside, he gave his pelt a shake, trying to get rid of the creeping horror he had felt as Bluestar revealed the message of StarClan. His paws carried him instinctively in the direction of Cinderpelt's den. He would have to tell the medicine cat that Bluestar was back, and he wanted to discuss what his leader had told him.

Only then did he remember that more than a moon ago, Cinderpelt had told him of a dream in which she heard the words *pack, pack*, and *kill, kill*.

CHAPTER 16

Cinderpelt could tell Fireheart nothing more, nor suggest what the evil in the forest might be.

"StarClan wouldn't repeat the warning if it weren't important," she meowed, her troubled blue gaze resting on Fireheart. "All we can do is keep watch."

"At least Bluestar is back safely." Fireheart tried to encourage her, but it was a poor effort. Both cats were aware of the shapeless, voiceless threat hanging over the Clan they loved.

In the days that followed, Fireheart did his best to set up a system of patrols that would give the Clan ample warning if ShadowClan or RiverClan decided to attack. There were barely enough warriors for the regular patrols and sentry duties, and Fireheart felt his fur grow thin with worry as the season moved on. The rain gave way to crisp, dry weather, but there was a thin rime of frost on the ground each morning and the remaining leaves dropped steadily from the trees. The brief recovery of the forest was over, and prey became scarce again.

One morning, about half a moon after the confrontation with WindClan, Fireheart was about to lead out the dawn patrol with Brackenfur and Cloudpaw when Bluestar came padding from her den. "I'll lead the patrol this morning," she meowed, and went to wait by the entrance to the camp.

"Bluestar leading a patrol?" muttered Cloudpaw. "That ought to go well. Watch out for flying hedgehogs!"

Fireheart aimed a cuff at the side of his head, but he couldn't help feeling as surprised as his apprentice that Bluestar should start taking up Clan duties again. "Show some respect," he ordered. "She's your leader, and she's been ill."

Cloudpaw grunted. Fireheart was about to join his leader when an idea struck him. "Listen, Cloudpaw, you want to be a warrior, don't you?" The white cat nodded eagerly. "Well, then, this is your chance to impress Bluestar. We'll take another apprentice as well. Go and find Swiftpaw."

Cloudpaw's eyes lit up with excitement, and he dashed off toward the apprentices' den.

Fireheart watched him go, then turned to Brackenfur. "Can you get Longtail?" He knew the pale tabby warrior would be pleased to have a chance to show off his apprentice's skills. "He's due to go out on hunting patrol—you don't mind swapping duties with him, do you?"

"No, that's fine, Fireheart."

Brackenfur disappeared into the warriors' den, and a moment later Longtail appeared. The two apprentices joined their mentors, and all four cats padded over to where Bluestar was waiting.

Her tail twitched. "Sure you've got the right cats, Fireheart?" she inquired acidly. Without waiting for a reply she led the way out of the camp and up the ravine.

As he followed the blue-gray she-cat toward the River-Clan border, Fireheart could almost imagine that the last few seasons had never happened, and he was still a young warrior going out on patrol without any of the responsibilities that troubled him now. But the fire-scarred forest reminded him that there was no going back.

The frost was beginning to melt as the sun rose over the river, though the leaves still crackled beneath the cats' paws as they padded through the shadows. As they went, Fireheart tested the two apprentices on what they could see and scent, hoping to demonstrate their hunting abilities to their leader. They answered confidently, but Bluestar gave no sign that she had heard.

The ThunderClan leader paused when they came within sight of the river and stood gazing at the opposite bank. "I wonder where they are," she murmured, almost too quietly for Fireheart to hear. "What are they doing now?"

Fireheart did not need to see the sadness in her eyes to know that she was thinking of Mistyfoot and Stonefur. He glanced uneasily at the other cats to see if they had noticed, but Swiftpaw and Cloudpaw were sniffing at an old water-vole hole, while Longtail was watching the movements of a squirrel high in the branches of a tree.

After a few moments Bluestar turned and followed the border upstream toward Sunningrocks. Fireheart noticed that she kept casting glances into RiverClan territory. But everything was quiet. They saw no RiverClan cats at all.

Eventually Sunningrocks came within sight. The smoothly sloping boulders seemed deserted. Then, as Fireheart watched, a cat climbed up from the opposite side and stood silhouetted against the sky.

Fireheart stopped dead, his fur prickling with the sense of danger. Though he could not make out the color of her fur, there was no mistaking that aggressive stance, the arrogant tilt of her head, and her long, winding tail. It was Leopardstar.

A couple of other cats had joined Leopardstar, and as the ThunderClan patrol drew closer, Fireheart recognized Stonefur, the RiverClan deputy, and the warrior Blackclaw. "Bluestar!" he hissed. "What are RiverClan doing on Sunningrocks?" But Fireheart felt his heart sink with dread when he saw the way that Bluestar was looking at the RiverClan deputy—not the challenging glare of a leader faced with enemy cats on her territory, but the admiring gaze of a queen who has seen her beloved kit become a noble warrior.

Bluestar padded forward until she reached the base of the rock where Leopardstar waited. Fireheart followed.

"What do they think they're doing?" Cloudpaw muttered indignantly behind him. "Sunningrocks is *ours*!"

Fireheart shot him a warning glance to keep silent, and the apprentice dropped back beside Swiftpaw and Longtail, while Fireheart went to stand at Bluestar's shoulder.

"Good day, Bluestar," Leopardstar meowed, her voice confident. "I've been waiting since moonset to see ThunderClan cats, but I never hoped that one of them would be you."

There was an edge of mockery in her tone, and Fireheart winced that the head of his Clan could be scorned so openly by other leaders.

"What are you doing here?" Bluestar asked. "Sunningrocks belongs to ThunderClan." But her voice was low and unchallenging, as if she did not really believe what she was saying—or did not care.

"Sunningrocks has always belonged to RiverClan," Leopardstar retorted, "even though we allowed Thunder-Clan to hunt here for a while. But ThunderClan stands in our debt after the help we gave you at the time of the fire. Today we claim that debt, Bluestar. We are taking Sunning-rocks back."

Fireheart's fur bristled with fury. If Leopardstar thought she could stroll onto Sunningrocks without a fight, she was mistaken! Whipping around, he hissed, "Swiftpaw, you're fastest. Run back to camp and fetch reinforcements."

"But I want to fight!" Swiftpaw protested.

"Then get back here *fast*!"

The apprentice dashed off into the trees. Leopardstar tracked him with narrowed eyes, and Fireheart knew she must realize why he had gone. It was essential to hold off the battle for as long as possible. "Keep her talking," he murmured to Bluestar. "Swiftpaw's gone for help."

He was not sure if Bluestar had heard him. She was staring at Stonefur again.

"Well, Bluestar?" Leopardstar challenged. "Do you agree? Do you allow RiverClan the right to Sunningrocks?"

For a few heartbeats Bluestar did not reply. As the silence stretched out, more RiverClan cats crept up to the top of the rock and emerged to stand beside their leader. Fireheart's heart lurched when he saw that one of them was Graystripe. His gaze locked with his friend's, and he saw in Graystripe's appalled face a message as clear as if the gray warrior had yowled it to the skies. *I don't want to fight you!*

"No." Bluestar spoke at last, and to Fireheart's relief her voice was firm. "Sunningrocks belongs to ThunderClan."

"Then you'll have to fight us for it," growled Leopardstar.

Fireheart heard Longtail whisper at his shoulder, "They'll make crowfood of us!"

At the same moment, Leopardstar uttered a bloodcurdling yowl and launched herself down the face of the rock at Bluestar. The two cats crashed to the ground, spitting and clawing. Fireheart sprang forward to help his leader, but before he reached her a warrior crashed into his side, bowling him over and sinking his teeth into Fireheart's shoulder. Fireheart scrabbled against the RiverClan cat's belly with his hind paws, desperate to break his grip, and slashed his claws at his enemy's throat. The tabby warrior let go and backed off, yowling.

Fireheart spun around, looking for Bluestar, but she was nowhere to be seen. He spotted Longtail in the midst of a heaving mass of cats, but before he could do anything to help he caught a glimpse of Blackclaw springing toward him. He managed to avoid the warrior's outstretched claws, and as the RiverClan cat fell awkwardly Fireheart sprang on him and bit hard into his ear.

Blackclaw scrabbled on the ground, trying to escape Fireheart's grip. Fireheart raked his claws across his back, only to lose his hold as another cat barreled into him from the side. He went down and felt teeth meet in his tail.

Longtail was right, he thought despairingly. *They'll tear us into strips!*

The ThunderClan cats were hopelessly outnumbered, and there had been no time for Swiftpaw to reach the camp and return with help. Long before reinforcements could arrive, the patrol would have been driven off or killed, and Sunningrocks would belong to RiverClan again.

Fireheart writhed helplessly, struggling for enough space to use teeth and claws. Suddenly the weight lifted as the cat lying across his legs was yanked away. He sprang to his paws to see Cloudpaw perched on Blackclaw's back, his claws fastened deep in the warrior's black fur and the wild light of battle in his eyes. Blackclaw reared up on his hind legs, but he couldn't shake the apprentice off.

"See, Fireheart!" Cloudpaw yelled. "Do it this way—it's easy!"

There was no time for Fireheart to answer. He spat an insult after the other warrior, who vanished wailing among the rocks, and threw himself into the whirling mass of cats around Longtail. Fireheart dragged one warrior off him, and suddenly came face-to-face with Brackenfur as the younger warrior burst out of the trees.

He gasped with surprise and gave fervent thanks to Star-Clan. Swiftpaw must have met the hunting patrol scouting near Sunningrocks, as Fireheart had ordered after Gray-stripe's warning—and sent them along, bringing help long before Fireheart had dared to hope for it.

"Where's Bluestar?" Brackenfur called.

"Don't know."

In the moment's respite, Fireheart looked around for his leader. There was still no sign of her, though he caught sight of Leopardstar facing up to Whitestorm on top of a rock a few fox-lengths away.

Longtail staggered to his paws, panting for breath as he leaned against the rock face. Blood trickled from a gash on his forehead and he had lost a strip of fur along his flank, but his lips were still drawn back in a snarl, and he followed Brackenfur willingly as the ginger warrior leaped into the battle.

Fireheart was about to join them when he heard a voice calling out urgently above the noise of the fighting: "Fireheart! Fireheart!"

He spun around to see Graystripe crouched on top of the nearest rock, a look of anguish on his broad face. "Fireheart, come here!" he yowled.

For a heartbeat Fireheart wondered if this was a trap, and then felt ashamed of himself. His friend had avoided fighting him face-to-face; he would never snare him with a trick.

Fireheart bounded up the smooth slope of the rock to Graystripe's side. "What is it?"

Graystripe pointed with his muzzle toward the other side of the rock. "Look."

Fireheart peered over the edge. The rock sloped down more steeply there into a narrow gully. Bluestar was crouching almost directly below him. Her fur was ruffled, and she was bleeding from one shoulder. Coming along the gully on either side, cutting off any possible escape, were Mistyfoot and Stonefur.

The RiverClan deputy slashed his claws at Bluestar without touching her. "Defend yourself!" snarled the gray tom. "Or I swear by StarClan I'll kill you."

On Bluestar's other side, Mistyfoot crept closer, her belly flat to the ground. "Are you scared to fight us?" she hissed.

Bluestar did not move, except to turn her head from one to the other. Fireheart could not see her expression from his vantage point, but he knew she would never be able to attack her own kits.

"I had to tell you," Graystripe whispered beside Fireheart. "They'll call me a traitor—but I couldn't let them kill Bluestar."

Fireheart shot his friend a look of gratitude. Graystripe had no idea of the real relationship between Bluestar and these two RiverClan cats. His only motive was loyalty to his former leader.

But Fireheart had no time to think for long about Graystripe's tangled loyalties. He had to save Bluestar. The RiverClan cats had advanced until they were almost touching her, their fur bristling and their teeth bared in a snarl.

"Call yourself a leader?" Stonefur sneered. "Why won't you fight?"

He drew back a paw to bring it raking down over Bluestar's shoulder. At the same instant, Fireheart launched himself down the rock face. He landed hard in the gully, practically on top of Stonefur, forcing him away from Bluestar. On the Clan leader's other side, Mistyfoot let out a screech of defiance and unsheathed her claws.

"Stop!" Fireheart yowled. "You can't harm Bluestar—she's your mother!"

CHAPTER 17

♣

The RiverClan warriors froze, their blue eyes wide with shock.

"What do you mean?" Stonefur rasped. "Graypool was our mother."

"No, listen . . ." Fireheart bundled Bluestar against the rock face and stood in front of her. He could still hear the yowls and spitting of the battle on the other side of the rock, but suddenly it seemed to have nothing to do with the confrontation in this gully.

"Bluestar gave birth to you in ThunderClan," he meowed desperately. "But she couldn't keep you. Your father, Oakheart, brought you to RiverClan."

"I don't believe you!" Stonefur drew his lips back in a vicious snarl. "It's a trick."

"No, wait," mewed Mistyfoot. "Fireheart doesn't lie."

"How would you know?" her brother demanded. "He's a ThunderClan cat. Why should we trust him?"

He advanced on Fireheart, claws out, and the ThunderClan warrior braced himself for the attack, but before Stonefur could spring, Bluestar slipped out from behind him and faced the two RiverClan cats.

"My kits, oh, my kits . . ." Bluestar's voice was warm, and when she turned her head Fireheart saw that her eyes were blazing with admiration. "You're such fine warriors now. I'm so proud of you."

Stonefur glanced at Mistyfoot, uncertainty showing in his twitching ears.

"Leave Bluestar alone," Fireheart urged quietly.

A sudden yowling interrupted him. "Fireheart! Watch out!" The voice was Graystripe's.

Fireheart looked up in time to see Leopardstar plunging down the rock toward him. Graystripe's warning gave him just enough time to scramble backward, so that her outstretched claws only raked his shoulder. Spitting, she flung herself at him, driving the breath out of his body as she hurled him to the ground.

Fireheart gripped the RiverClan leader's neck with his front paws and felt her powerful hind paws raking at his belly. Pain stabbed through him, and he slashed out blindly, feeling his claws score through fur. For a few heartbeats all he could see was Leopardstar's spotted pelt; his face was pressed into it, half smothering him, and he struggled to breathe.

Suddenly Leopardstar jerked her head back, and Fireheart lost his hold on her neck. Her stifling weight was lifted off him. Scrambling to his paws, he backed against the rock, ready for her to spring at him again. His head whirled with exhaustion, and he could feel blood pulsing out of a wound on his leg. Suddenly he wasn't sure that this was a battle he could win.

He looked around for Bluestar, but she had disappeared,

and so had Mistyfoot and Stonefur. The RiverClan leader crouched on the ground in front of him, breathing hard, bleeding from her neck and side. To Fireheart's astonishment, Graystripe stood over her, pinning her down with his front paws.

"I had him," Leopardstar panted, almost incoherent with fury. "I heard you just now. You *warned* him."

Graystripe released his leader so she could stagger to her paws again. "I'm sorry, Leopardstar, but Fireheart's my friend."

Leopardstar shook drops of blood from her golden tabby fur and glared at the gray warrior. "I was right about you all along," she hissed. "You were never loyal to RiverClan. All right, you've got a choice. Attack your *friend* for me now, or leave my Clan for good."

Graystripe stared at her in dismay. Fireheart's breath caught in his chest. Was Leopardstar going to force him to fight his former Clan mate? He knew that he didn't have the strength to beat a cat who was still relatively fresh—and much more than that, how could he lift a claw against his best friend?

"Well?" snarled Leopardstar. "What are you waiting for?"

Graystripe glanced at Fireheart, his amber eyes filled with anguish. Then he bowed his head. "I'm sorry, Leopardstar. I can't do it. Punish me if you want."

"Punish you?" Leopardstar's face was contorted in fury. "I'll claw your eyes out; I'll set you loose in the forest for the foxes to track down. Traitor! I'll—"

A chorus of yowling drowned her threats. Fireheart

looked up, almost despairing at the thought of more enemies to fight. He could hardly believe what he saw. A wave of ThunderClan cats was streaming over the rock and down into the gully. He spotted Mousefur, Darkstripe, Sandstorm, and Dustpelt, and Swiftpaw leading the other apprentices. His message had gotten through, and help had come at last!

Leopardstar took one look and fled. The ThunderClan warriors gave chase at once with furious yowls. Fireheart and Graystripe were left looking at each other.

"Thank you," Fireheart mewed after a few moments.

Graystripe shrugged and padded over to him. He was limping slightly, and his fur was torn and thick with dust. "There was no choice," he whispered. "I couldn't hurt you, could I?"

Fireheart drew himself up. As his head cleared, he realized that the sounds of battle were fading and a heavy silence was gathering over Sunningrocks, filled with the reek of blood. "Come on. I've got to see what's happening."

He turned and padded along the gully, aware that Graystripe was following close behind. Coming to the open ground beyond the rocks, he saw the RiverClan warriors retreating down the slope that led to the river. At the head of the patrol, Blackclaw launched himself into the river and began swimming toward the opposite bank.

Brackenfur and Sandstorm stood nearby, and more ThunderClan cats crouched on top of Sunningrocks, watching their enemies depart. Cloudpaw raised his head and let out a yowl of pure triumph.

Bluestar padded after the retreating cats as far as the RiverClan border, her ears pricked with determination. Fireheart saw with a twinge of distress that she was following Mistyfoot and Stonefur. "Now that you know the truth, we must talk," she called after them. "You will be welcome in the ThunderClan camp. I will tell my warriors to bring you to my den whenever you want to see me."

But both warriors turned away from her and stalked down to the edge of the water. Stonefur glanced back before he waded out into the river. "Leave us alone," he growled. "You're no mother of ours, whatever you say."

Leopardstar was the last cat to retreat across the border. "Look there!" she snapped at her warriors, flicking her tail toward Graystripe, who was standing beside Fireheart. "If it weren't for that traitor, Sunningrocks would be ours again. He's no longer a member of RiverClan. If you catch him on our territory, kill him."

Without waiting for any response, she spun around and limped rapidly toward the river.

Graystripe said nothing. He stood as motionless as the rocks behind him, with his head hanging.

Sandstorm padded across to Fireheart. "What happened?" she asked. She was bleeding from a scratch on her shoulder, but her eyes were clear and questioning.

Fireheart longed to go back to camp and curl up in the warriors' den to share tongues with her, but he knew he had too much to do. "Graystripe saved my life," he explained. "He pulled Leopardstar off me."

"So that's why he can't go back." The pale ginger she-cat turned her head to watch the last of the RiverClan cats plunging into the river. Then she looked back at Graystripe, her eyes huge with concern. "What is he going to do, then?" she murmured.

Sudden joy stabbed through Fireheart. Whatever Graystripe felt for his kits, if he could not go back to RiverClan, he could come home. Then the joy faded and anxiety twisted Fireheart's belly. That decision wasn't his to make. Would Bluestar now allow the gray warrior to come back to the Clan he had left? And how would the other warriors react?

Looking around for his leader, Fireheart saw her padding wearily up the slope, and went to meet her. "Bluestar . . ."

She raised her head, and he saw that her eyes were puzzled. "They hate me, Fireheart."

Sorrow flooded over Fireheart. With his own worries about Graystripe, he had almost forgotten what his leader must be suffering. "I'm sorry, Bluestar," he murmured. "Perhaps I shouldn't have told them. But I couldn't think of what else to do."

"That's all right, Fireheart." To his amazement Bluestar reached out and gave his shoulder a swift lick. "I always wanted them to know. But I didn't think they would hate me for what I did." She let out a long sigh. "Let's go back to camp."

She showed no sense of triumph that ThunderClan had succeeded in defending their claim to Sunningrocks. When she reached the place where her warriors were gathered, she said nothing about the victory, not even to congratulate them for fighting so well. Her mind still seemed fixed on her kits.

Fireheart fell in beside his leader as she padded up the slope. "Well done," he meowed to Cloudpaw as his apprentice leaped off the rock and landed neatly at his side. "You fought like a warrior. So did all of you," he added, raising his voice as he glanced around, hoping to make up for their leader's indifference. "Bluestar and I are both proud of you."

"Thank StarClan we managed to beat RiverClan off," mewed Brackenfur.

"No, thank *us*," Cloudpaw put in. "*We* did all the fighting. I didn't notice any StarClan warriors on our side."

Bluestar turned her head at that and fixed an intent gaze on the white apprentice, her eyes narrowed. Fireheart expected her to rebuke him, but her expression showed interest rather than anger. She gave a little nod but said nothing.

As the warriors began to move off toward their camp, Fireheart went to stand beside Graystripe. "Bluestar," he mewed nervously, "Graystripe's here."

Bluestar's gaze flickered vaguely over the gray warrior. For a moment Fireheart was afraid that her mind was drifting again, and she wouldn't even remember that Graystripe had ever left ThunderClan.

Then Darkstripe shouldered his way forward. "Get off our territory!" he spat at Graystripe, adding to Bluestar, "I'll drive him off, if you want."

"Wait," Bluestar ordered with a touch of her old authority. "Fireheart, explain what's going on."

He told her how Graystripe had warned him about Leopardstar's attack and pulled her away when Fireheart was losing their fight. "He brought me to help you when Mistyfoot and Stonefur were attacking you," he explained. "And I owe him my life. Bluestar, please let him come back into ThunderClan."

Graystripe looked at his former leader with a glimmer of hope in his amber eyes. But before Bluestar could reply, Darkstripe broke in roughly. "He left ThunderClan of his own free will. Why should we let him come crawling back now?"

"I'm not crawling to you or any cat," Graystripe retorted. He turned to face the gray she-cat again. "But I'd like to come back, if you'll have me, Bluestar."

"You can't take back a traitor!" Darkstripe spat. "He just betrayed his leader—how do you know he won't betray you the first chance he gets?"

"He did it for Fireheart!" Sandstorm protested.

Darkstripe snorted contemptuously.

Bluestar fixed a cold look on him. "If Graystripe is a traitor," she meowed, with all the ice of leaf-bare in her voice, "then he's just the same as the rest of you. The Clan is full of traitors, so one more won't make any difference." She whirled on Fireheart, power and strength seeming to flow back into her body. "You should have let Mistyfoot and Stonefur kill me!" she spat. "Better a quick death at the claws of noble warriors than a life dragged out in a Clan I can't trust—a Clan doomed to destruction by StarClan!"

There were gasps from the other cats as she spoke, and Fireheart realized that few of the Clan had any idea how distrustful and despairing Bluestar had become. He knew there was no point in trying to argue with her now. "Does that mean Graystripe can stay?" he asked.

"Stay or go, whatever he likes," Bluestar responded indifferently. Her flash of strength ebbed, leaving her looking more exhausted than ever. Slowly, not meeting the troubled gazes of any of her warriors, she padded away in the direction of the camp.

CHAPTER 18

❧

As Fireheart wearily pushed his way through the entrance to the camp he spotted Bramblekit dashing toward him, almost falling over his paws in his eagerness to greet the returning warriors. "Did we win?" he asked. He stopped and stared round-eyed at Graystripe. "Who's this? Is he a prisoner?"

"No, he's a ThunderClan cat," Fireheart replied. "It's a long story, Bramblekit, and I'm too tired to explain now. Get your mother to tell you."

Bramblekit took a step back, looking slightly crestfallen. Though he wouldn't remember it, Fireheart reflected, he had suckled side by side with Graystripe's two kits. Goldenflower had cared for them in the few days they had spent in ThunderClan after Silverstream's death.

The dark tabby kit eyed Graystripe suspiciously as the two warriors padded past him, and then turned to Tawnykit as she came bounding up. "Look!" he mewed. "There's a new cat in the Clan."

"Who is he?" Tawnykit wondered.

"A traitor," Darkstripe spat as he stalked past on his way to the warriors' den. "But then, we're all traitors, according to Bluestar."

The two kits stared at him with total bewilderment in their faces. Fireheart fought down his fury; there was no time to start an argument with Darkstripe, but the warrior had no business letting his anger spill over onto the kits. Feeling an unusual pang of sympathy for Bramblekit, he turned back and meowed, "Yes, we did win. We keep Sunningrocks."

Bramblekit gave a little joyous bounce. "Great! I'm going to tell the elders." He scurried off with Tawnykit hard on his paws.

"Those are Tigerstar's kits, aren't they?" asked Graystripe curiously, watching them go.

"Yes." Fireheart didn't want to discuss them now. "Let's go see Cinderpelt and get patched up."

Graystripe looked around as the two warriors crossed the burned-out clearing. "It's never going to be the same," he muttered despondently.

"Next newleaf, you'll see," Fireheart replied, trying to cheer him up. He hoped Graystripe was only referring to the damage caused by the fire, and not a sense that he could never recover his old place within the Clan. "Everything will grow back stronger than before."

Graystripe didn't reply. He didn't look as happy as Fireheart had expected him to be, as if he were beginning to doubt that the rest of his birth Clan would accept him. And Fireheart could see pain in his eyes that suggested he was already beginning to miss the kits he had given up. After all, he hadn't even had a chance to say good-bye.

The returning warriors were gathering in Cinderpelt's clearing. As Fireheart and Graystripe approached, the medicine cat looked up from pressing cobwebs against a wound in Cloudpaw's side. "Here's Fireheart now," she mewed, and added, "Great StarClan, you look as if you've been fighting monsters on the Thunderpath."

"It feels like it." Fireheart grunted. Settling down to wait for Cinderpelt to check him over, he realized how much his wounds hurt. The one in the leg that Leopardstar had given him was still bleeding, and he bent his head to lick it.

"What are you thinking, bringing *him* back again?" Fireheart looked up to see Dustpelt glaring at Graystripe. "We don't want him here."

"Who's 'we'?" Fireheart asked, gritting his teeth. "*I* think he belongs here—and so does Sandstorm, and—" He broke off as Dustpelt pointedly turned his back.

Graystripe shot an apologetic look at Fireheart. "They won't accept me," he mewed. "It's true; I left the Clan, and now . . ."

"Give it time," Fireheart tried to encourage him. "They'll come around."

Privately, he wished he could believe it. Thanks to Bluestar's indifference, some of the ThunderClan cats would have no qualms about objecting to Graystripe's return. One more problem, Fireheart thought, to add to his worries about what was really going on in the forest. How could the Clan hope to survive the destruction StarClan had prophesied, unless they were united?

Fireheart wondered if Graystripe knew about the dark threat in the forest from RiverClan's medicine cat the "pack" that StarClan had warned them of. Though Fireheart's fur prickled with dread, there was some comfort in knowing that Graystripe was back, and he would have his friend to rely on, whatever lay ahead. Fireheart began to lick his wound again, wishing that he could just enjoy the gray warrior's return for a few moments.

"That's right, get it clean," Cinderpelt meowed as she came up to him. She sniffed at the leg wound and then rapidly checked his other injuries. "You'll be fine," she reassured him. "I'll give you some cobwebs for the bleeding, but apart from that you just need to rest."

"Have you seen Bluestar?" Fireheart asked as Cinderpelt brought the cobwebs and laid them over the wound. "Is she badly hurt?"

"A bite on her shoulder," replied the medicine cat. "I gave her a poultice of herbs, and she went back to her den."

Fireheart struggled to his paws. "I'd better go and see her."

"Okay, but if she's asleep, don't wake her. Clan business, whatever it is, can wait. And while Fireheart does that," she added to Graystripe, "I'll have a look at you." She gave his ear a quick lick. "It's good to have you back."

At least some cats would welcome Graystripe, Fireheart told himself as he padded across the clearing. The others would change their minds; Graystripe just needed time to prove that he would to be a loyal member of ThunderClan again.

"Fireheart!" Sandstorm hailed him as he approached Bluestar's den. "Mousefur and I are going out to hunt."

"Thanks," Fireheart mewed gratefully.

"Are you all right?" Sandstorm drew closer, her eyes narrowing. "I thought you'd be pleased—we won the battle, and Graystripe has come home."

Fireheart pressed his muzzle briefly against her flank. He felt a pang of relief that the ginger she-cat seemed to have forgiven him for going behind Bluestar's back to arrange the talk with WindClan. "I know—but I'm not sure that all the cats will accept Graystripe. They'll find it hard to forget that he loved a cat from another Clan, and then left us altogether."

Sandstorm shrugged. "That's in the past. He's here now, isn't he? They'll just have to put up with it."

"That's not the point!" Pain and weariness made Fireheart more irritable than he intended. "We can't afford quarrels just now. Can't you see that?"

Sandstorm stared at him, anger flaring in her pale green eyes. "Sorry, I'm sure," she spat. "I was only trying to help."

"Sandstorm, don't . . ." Fireheart began, realizing too late that he'd said the wrong thing. But Sandstorm had already turned away and was stalking back toward the warriors' den, where Mousefur was waiting for her.

Feeling even more despondent than before, Fireheart went on to Bluestar's den. When he looked through the entrance he thought she was asleep, curled up in her nest, but almost at once her blue eyes blinked open and she raised her head.

"Fireheart." Her voice was dull. "What do you want?"

"Just reporting, Bluestar." Fireheart slipped into the den and stood in front of his leader. "All the cats are back. There are no serious injuries, as far as I can see."

"Good." Sounding a little more interested, she added, "Your apprentice fought well today."

"Yes, he did." Fireheart felt a rush of pride in his kin. Whatever problems there had been with Cloudpaw in the past, no one could question his courage.

"I think it's time he became a warrior," Bluestar went on. "We'll hold his naming ceremony at sunset."

Hope flared in Fireheart's chest. Had Bluestar finally accepted the need to make new warriors?

But his optimism ebbed away like water into sand when Bluestar's lips curled into a sneer, and she added, "There must be a ceremony, I suppose. It means nothing to me, but these cats are so gullible they'll never accept Cloudpaw without one."

And how much meaning does the ceremony have for Cloudpaw? Fireheart asked himself. *Does he really care about the warrior code?* If not, he reflected, then the young cat didn't deserve to become a warrior, no matter how well he fought.

But Bluestar had made up her mind, and Fireheart wouldn't try to change it. Instead he suggested, "Swiftpaw should be a warrior too. He did well today."

"Swiftpaw carried a message back to the camp. That's apprentice work. He's not ready to become a warrior yet."

"But he came back to the battle," Fireheart objected.

"*No!*" Bluestar's tail lashed in anger. "I cannot trust Swiftpaw. Cloudpaw is stronger and braver—and besides, he doesn't grovel to StarClan like the rest of you. The Clan needs more warriors like that."

Fireheart wanted to say that Cloudpaw's lack of respect for the warrior code was the last thing ThunderClan needed, but he did not dare. Instead he dipped his head and backed away. "I'll see you at sunset," he meowed, and went to break the news to Cloudpaw.

His apprentice, as Fireheart had guessed, was delighted at the news that he was to become a warrior at last. Fireheart instructed him on what he had to do in the ceremony, and then headed for the warriors' den and some much-needed sleep. His heart sank right to his paws when he spotted Longtail sitting with the apprentices outside their den. There was one more thing he had to do before he could rest.

Padding toward Longtail, he jerked his muzzle for the tabby warrior to join him, out of earshot of the apprentices. "Longtail," he began, searching for the right words. "I'm sorry, I've got some bad news. Bluestar has agreed to make Cloudpaw a warrior, but—"

"But not Swiftpaw?" Longtail finished angrily. "That's what you're going to say, isn't it?"

"I'm sorry, Longtail," he meowed. "I tried to persuade

Bluestar, but she wouldn't agree."

"So you say." The pale warrior sneered. "But it's strange that *your* apprentice is chosen, and mine is ignored. *Swiftpaw* never went off to live with Twolegs!"

"I'm not going into all that again," Fireheart retorted. Cloudpaw had never intended to leave the Clan, but every cat knew that he had visited the Twoleg nest regularly for food before the Twolegs captured him and shut him in. "Bluestar said she's making Cloudpaw a warrior because he fought well, while Swiftpaw . . . "

"Took a message." Longtail's tabby fur bristled with fury. "And who made him take it? He would have stayed to fight if you hadn't sent him away!"

"I know that," Fireheart mewed wearily. "I'm just as disappointed as you are. I'll do my best to get Swiftpaw made a warrior soon, I promise."

"If I believed that, I'd believe anything!" Longtail spat. He turned his back on Fireheart, scraped angrily at the ground as if he were covering his dirt, and stalked back to the apprentices.

The sun was sinking behind the wall of the camp when Fireheart emerged from the warriors' den with Graystripe close behind him. Sleep had restored his body, and he tried to feel optimistic about the coming ceremony, even though he was not looking forward to it.

Shadows were stretching across the camp, and Fireheart saw that Bluestar had emerged from her den. To his relief she was moving easily, and the shoulder wound she had taken in the battle didn't seem to be bothering her as she sprang up onto the Highrock.

"Let all cats old enough to catch their own prey join beneath the Highrock for a Clan meeting," she called.

Graystripe gave Fireheart a friendly nudge. "You've done well with Cloudpaw," he meowed. "I never thought that pest of a kit would grow up into such a fine warrior!"

Fireheart acknowledged his friend's praise by pressing his muzzle against the gray warrior's shoulder. His friend remember how upset he had been when Cinderpelt had her accident, and knew how much it meant to Fireheart to have an apprentice ready to be made a warrior at last. Graystripe had seen his own apprentice, Brackenpaw, made a warrior long ago.

Many of the cats were already in the clearing. News of Cloudpaw's warrior ceremony must have spread around the camp. Cinderpelt appeared from her den and took her place near the base of the rock, while Goldenflower brought her two kits to sit at the front of the gathering crowd. Willowpelt's litter stayed with their mother near the entrance to the nursery.

Fireheart couldn't help noticing that the other apprentices were the last to join the circle around the rock. He saw Brightpaw nudging Swiftpaw out of their den. Even when the black-and-white cat had crossed the clearing, he stayed on the very edge of the crowd, and the other apprentices settled down around him.

A pang of dismay shot through Fireheart. It wasn't Cloudpaw's fault that Bluestar had chosen him and none of the others. It would be hard for him not to have the good wishes of his friends when he became a warrior.

But Cloudpaw didn't seem bothered. He strolled out of the elders' den and padded across to Fireheart with his tail waving in the air, his eyes shining with excitement.

Fireheart murmured into his ear, "I'm very proud of you, Cloudpaw. Tomorrow you can take a hunting patrol over to Twolegplace and tell Princess."

Cloudpaw shot him a delighted look, but before he could say anything, Bluestar spoke. "Cloudpaw, you fought well against RiverClan this morning, and I have decided that the time has come for you to take your place as a warrior in ThunderClan."

The white tom turned to face the Highrock and gazed up at his leader as she began to speak the ritual words. "I, Bluestar, leader of ThunderClan, call upon my warrior ancestors to look down on this apprentice. He has trained hard to understand the ways of your noble code, and I commend him to you as a warrior in his turn."

Her voice was harsh, and Fireheart thought that it was obvious that she was merely going through the motions of a ritual that had ceased to have meaning for her. Uneasily he wondered whether StarClan would be willing to watch over Cloudpaw when neither he nor his leader had any respect for their warrior ancestors.

"Cloudpaw," Bluestar continued, "do you promise to

uphold the warrior code and to protect and defend this Clan, even at the cost of your life?"

"I do," Cloudpaw meowed fervently.

Did he understand what he was promising? Fireheart wondered. He was sure that Cloudpaw would do his best to protect the Clan, because these cats were his friends, but he knew that the young cat wouldn't be prompted to act by any sense of loyalty to the warrior code.

"Then by the powers of StarClan, I give you your warrior name," Bluestar went on, each word dragged out of her like thorns. "Cloudpaw, from this moment you will be known as Cloudtail. StarClan honors your courage and your independence, and we welcome you as a full warrior of ThunderClan."

Leaping down from the Highrock, she padded over to Cloudtail and rested her muzzle on his head. Cloudtail gave her shoulder a respectful lick, then went over to stand beside Fireheart.

This was the moment at which the Clan should have greeted the new warrior by chanting his name, but now there was only silence. Fireheart heard uneasy murmurs start up around him, as if the cats had sensed Bluestar's lack of conviction when she recited the ritual. Flicking a glance at the apprentices at the edge of the crowd, Fireheart saw that they were all looking at their paws, and Swiftpaw had turned his back on his old den mate.

Cloudtail was beginning to look a little crestfallen when Brindleface, who had suckled him as a tiny kit, padded up and pressed her tabby muzzle against his. "Well done, Cloudtail!"

she exclaimed. "I'm so proud of you!"

As if she had given a signal, Cinderpelt and Graystripe came up, and then at last the other cats began to crowd around, greeting Cloudtail by his new name and congratulating him. Fireheart breathed a sigh of relief that the awkward moment was over. But he couldn't help noticing that Longtail was nowhere to be seen, and the apprentices waited until the very end to come up, led by Brightpaw, each mewing a few quick, subdued words before slipping away again. Swiftpaw was not among them.

"You're keeping vigil tonight," Fireheart reminded his former apprentice, trying to sound as if this were like any other warrior naming ceremony. "Remember, you have to stay silent until dawn."

Cloudtail nodded and padded off to take up a position in the center of the clearing. His head and tail were raised proudly, but Fireheart knew that the ceremony had been shadowed by the jealousy of the other apprentices, and by Bluestar's transparent loss of faith.

How long could the Clan survive, Fireheart wondered, when their leader no longer honored StarClan?

CHAPTER 19

Next morning, Fireheart watched the dawn patrol leave before going to relieve Cloudtail from his vigil. His injured leg felt stiff, but the bleeding had stopped.

"All quiet?" he meowed. "Do you want to sleep now, or are you up to going hunting? We could go through Tallpines, if you like, and see Princess."

Cloudtail stretched his jaws in an enormous yawn, but a heartbeat later he had sprung to his paws. "Let's hunt!"

"Okay," Fireheart mewed. "We'll take Sandstorm with us. She has met Princess too."

Fireheart knew that his closeness to Sandstorm had been trickling away ever since he had stopped the battle with WindClan. He desperately wanted to restore their previous bond, and inviting her to go hunting might be a good way of doing that.

Glancing around to see if she had emerged from the den, he spotted Dustpelt padding toward him, with Fernpaw following. As they drew closer, Fireheart could see that the light brown warrior looked worried.

"There's something you ought to know," Dustpelt

announced. "Fernpaw, tell Fireheart what you just told me."

Fernpaw's head was lowered, and she scuffled in the dust with her front paws. Her hesitation gave Fireheart time to wonder what was troubling her, and why she had chosen to confide in Dustpelt instead of her mentor, Darkstripe.

The second question was answered as Dustpelt bent his head and gave her ear a couple of licks. Fireheart had never seen the prickly young warrior so gentle. "It's okay," Dustpelt mewed. "There's nothing to be scared of. Fireheart won't be angry with you." The glare he gave Fireheart, unseen by Fernpaw, said, *He'd better not!*

"Come on, Fernpaw." Fireheart tried to sound encouraging. "Tell me what is the matter."

Fernpaw's green eyes flickered toward him and away again. "It's Swiftpaw," she mewed. "He . . ." She hesitated, this time with a glance at Cloudtail, and then went on: "He was really angry that Bluestar wouldn't make him into a warrior. Last night he got all us apprentices together in the den. He said we'd never be warriors unless we did something so brave that Bluestar *couldn't* go on ignoring us anymore."

She paused again, and Dustpelt murmured, "Go on."

"He said we ought to find out who has been killing prey in the forest," mewed Fernpaw, her voice shaking. "He said you didn't seem bothered about finding our enemy. He wanted us to go to Snakerocks because that's where most of the scraps of prey have been found. Swiftpaw thought we might pick up a trail."

"What a mouse-brained idea!" Cloudtail burst out.

"And what did the rest of the apprentices think about this?" Fireheart asked, shooting a warning glance at Cloudtail and trying to ignore the cold lump of apprehension that was gathering in his belly.

"We didn't know. We want to be warriors, but we all knew we shouldn't do something like that without orders, and without at least one warrior with us. In the end, only Swiftpaw and Brightpaw went."

"Did you see them go when you were on vigil?" Fireheart demanded, turning to look at Cloudtail.

Beginning to look worried, Cloudtail shook his head.

"Swiftpaw said Cloudtail wouldn't notice a Twoleg monster roaring through the camp," Fernpaw mumbled. "He and Brightpaw sneaked out through the ferns behind the elders' den."

"When was this?" Fireheart demanded.

"I'm not sure—before dawn." Fernpaw's voice rose as if she were about to start wailing like a tiny kit. "I didn't know what to do. I *knew* it was wrong, but I didn't want to give them away. Only I've been feeling worse and worse, and so when I saw Dustpelt, I went to tell him." She gave the brown tabby warrior a grateful glance, and he pressed his muzzle against her speckled gray flank.

"We'll have to go after them," Fireheart decided.

"I'm coming," Cloudtail meowed instantly, startling Fireheart by the blaze in his blue eyes. "Brightpaw's out there. If anything's hurt her, I'll . . . I'll *shred* it!"

"Okay," Fireheart agreed, surprised to realize that the

young warrior cared so transparently for his former den mate. "Go and fetch a couple more cats to come with us."

As the new warrior shot off, Dustpelt meowed, "We'll come too."

"I don't want the apprentices involved," Fireheart replied. "Fernpaw is upset enough as it is. Why don't you take her hunting? Take Ashpaw and Darkstripe as well. The Clan needs fresh-kill."

Dustpelt gave him a long look. Then he nodded. "Okay."

Fireheart wondered whether he ought to tell Bluestar what was going on before they left, but he was reluctant to get Swiftpaw into trouble and give the Clan leader another excuse why the young cat shouldn't become a warrior. *If we can fetch them back, Bluestar need never know*, he told himself.

Besides, Fireheart didn't want to waste a single moment. Cloudtail was already returning with Sandstorm and Graystripe hard behind him. *Just the cats I'd have chosen*, Fireheart thought. He couldn't ignore the warm feeling at the thought that Graystripe was home again, and they could hunt and fight together as they used to. The gray warrior's eyes were shining as he fell into his accustomed place at Fireheart's side. Fireheart wished he could have had Whitestorm, too; he was Brightpaw's mentor, but he had gone out with the dawn patrol.

Sandstorm looked her usual self, alert and focused on their mission. "Cloudtail told us," she meowed briskly. "Let's go."

Fireheart took the lead out of the camp and up to the top of the ravine. Almost at once he picked up Swiftpaw's and

Brightpaw's scent leading directly toward Snakerocks. There was no need to spend time trying to track them; all they had to do was get to Snakerocks as soon as possible.

But we'll be too late, he thought. *If they meet whatever's out there . . .*

He raced through the forest, his paws scattering fallen leaves. The stiffness in his injured leg was forgotten. Graystripe ran close beside him, and Fireheart recognized the comfort of facing danger with his friend by his side once again, even though so much had changed.

As they approached Snakerocks, Fireheart slowed down and signaled with his tail for the other cats to do the same. If they dashed straight in without knowing what they had to face, they would be no help to the apprentices. They had to treat this threat, whatever it was, like any other enemy. But something inside Fireheart screamed that it was unpredictable, far beyond the reach of any Clan code, and that he was in more danger than he had ever been in before. Was this how mice and rabbits felt, he wondered, knowing that death could be stalking through the undergrowth?

Everything was still. Fireheart did not want to risk calling to the apprentices in case he alerted whatever was lurking up ahead. Swiftpaw must be right, he realized; this was the center of the darkness that had poisoned the forest, but he began to doubt his theories about what the threat was. Could one dog really cause so much destruction and fear in the forest?

As cautiously as if he were stalking prey, Fireheart slid through the undergrowth until the smooth, sand-colored sides of Snakerocks came into sight. For a few heartbeats he stood and tasted the air. A mixture of scents reached him: Swiftpaw's and Brightpaw's, still fresh; the staler scent of other ThunderClan cats; dog, as Fireheart had expected; but over it all the stench of newly spilled blood.

Sandstorm turned to look at him, her eyes huge with fear. "Something terrible has happened."

Terror coursed through Fireheart. He was about to confront the source of the fear that had stalked him for more than a moon, the faceless enemy that had invaded their forest. He was barely able to make himself go on.

With a twitch of his tail he gestured for his companions to move forward again; now they crept with their bellies close to the ground, intent on seeing without being seen, until the rocks were only a few fox-lengths away.

A fallen tree barred their way. Scrambling onto the trunk, Fireheart looked out over an open space carpeted with dead leaves. Foul-tasting bile rose into his throat as he took in the scene in front of him. The leaves had been churned up by massive paws, and clots of earth sprayed upward to catch in the branches of the tree. In the middle of the clearing Swiftpaw's black-and-white body lay motionless, and just beyond him, Brightpaw.

"Oh, no," whispered Sandstorm, as she drew herself up to crouch on the trunk beside Fireheart.

"Brightpaw!" yowled Cloudtail. Without waiting for Fireheart's order he launched himself across the clearing toward her.

Fireheart tensed, waiting for whatever had hunted down these apprentices to emerge from the trees and attack, but nothing stirred. Feeling as if his legs hardly belonged to him, he sprang down and stumbled across to Swiftpaw.

The apprentice lay on his side, his legs splayed out. His black-and-white fur was torn, and his body was covered with dreadful wounds, ripped by teeth far bigger than any cat's. His jaws still snarled and his eyes glared. He was dead, and Fireheart could see that he had died fighting.

"Great StarClan, what did this to him?" he whispered. For moons he had been afraid, and now it was far worse than he ever could have imagined. Swiftpaw had been slaughtered like prey. The hunters in the forest had become the hunted. Something had happened in the forest, the balance of life had changed, and for a moment Fireheart felt the ground beneath his paws shift.

Graystripe and Sandstorm stared down at Swiftpaw's body, too stunned to reply. Fireheart knew that Graystripe was remembering another bloodstained body, all his grief for Silverstream reawakening.

"What a waste," Fireheart murmured sadly. "If only Bluestar had made him a warrior. If only I'd let him fight, instead of sending him—"

He was interrupted by a screech from Cloudtail. "Fireheart! Fireheart, Brightpaw isn't dead!"

Fireheart spun around and raced across the clearing to crouch beside Brightpaw. Her white-and-ginger fur, which she had always kept so neatly groomed, was spiky with drying blood. On one side of her face the fur was torn away, and there was blood where her eye should have been. One ear had been shredded, and there were huge claw marks scored across her muzzle.

Fireheart heard a choking sound as Sandstorm came up behind him. "No . . ." the ginger she-cat whispered. "Oh, StarClan, no!"

At first Fireheart thought Cloudtail was wrong and that Brightpaw must be dead, until he saw the very faint rise and fall of her breathing, and the blood bubbling in her nostrils. "Fetch Cinderpelt," he ordered.

Sandstorm dashed off while Graystripe stood beside Swiftpaw's body, all his senses alert in case their fearsome enemy should return. Fireheart went on looking down at the injured Brightpaw. Somehow his fear had drained away. He felt nothing but an icy calm, and a stern, ferocious determination to avenge the young apprentices. He asked StarClan to be with him and to give him the strength to unleash all their fury on whatever had dared to wreak such havoc.

Cloudtail curled himself close to the motionless apprentice and began licking her face and the fur around her ears. "Don't die, Brightpaw," he begged. "I'm with you now. Cinderpelt's coming. Hold on just a bit longer."

Fireheart had never heard him sound so distraught. He hoped the white cat would not have to suffer the pain he had felt when Spottedleaf died, or Graystripe's when he lost Silverstream.

One of Brightpaw's ears twitched under Cloudtail's gentle

tongue. Her remaining eye opened a slit and closed again.

"Brightpaw." Fireheart leaned close to her and spoke urgently. "Brightpaw, can you tell us what did this to you?"

Brightpaw's eye opened wider and she fixed a cloudy gaze on Fireheart.

"What happened?" he repeated. "What did this?"

A thin wailing came from Brightpaw, which gradually formed into words. Fireheart stared at her in horror as he made out what she was trying to say.

"Pack, pack," she whispered. "Kill, kill."

CHAPTER 20

"Will she live?" Fireheart asked anxiously.

Cinderpelt let out a weary sigh. She had come to Snakerocks as fast as her uneven legs could run and done her best to patch up the worst of Brightpaw's injuries with cobwebs to stop the bleeding and poppy seeds for the pain. At last the apprentice had recovered enough to be dragged back through the forest to the camp, and now she lay unconscious in a nest among the ferns near Cinderpelt's den.

"I don't know," Cinderpelt admitted. "I've done the best I can. She's in the paws of StarClan now."

"She's a strong cat," Fireheart meowed, trying to reassure himself. When he looked at Brightpaw now, curled among the ferns, she looked anything but strong. She seemed smaller than a kit, no more than a scrap of fur. Fireheart half expected each shallow breath to be her last.

"Even if she recovers, she'll be hideously scarred," Cinderpelt warned him. "I couldn't save her ear or eye. I don't know that she'll ever be a warrior."

Fireheart nodded. He felt sick as he forced himself to look at the side of Brightpaw's face, now swathed in cobwebs. All this reminded him of Cinderpelt's accident, when Yellowfang had told him that the young she-cat's leg would never heal properly.

"She said something about the 'pack,'" he murmured. "I wonder what it was she really saw."

Cinderpelt shook her head. "It's what we've been afraid of all along. There's something in the forest hunting us down. I heard it in my dream."

"I know." Fireheart's muscles tensed with regret. "I should have done something long ago. StarClan sent that warning to Bluestar too."

"But Bluestar has no respect for StarClan anymore. I'm surprised she even listened to them."

"Do you think that's why this happened?" Fireheart spun around and faced the medicine cat.

"No." Cinderpelt's voice was strained as she moved closer to Fireheart and pressed herself against him. "StarClan did not send the evil; I'm sure of that."

As she spoke, a rustling in the fern tunnel announced the arrival of Cloudtail.

"I thought I told you to get some rest," Cinderpelt meowed.

"I couldn't sleep." The white cat padded over to settle himself in the ferns beside his friend. "I want to be with Brightpaw." He bent his head to give her shoulder a gentle lick. "Sleep well, Brightpaw. You're still beautiful," he murmured. "Come back to us. I don't know where you are now, but you have to come back."

He went on licking her for a moment more and then

looked up to fix a hostile glare on Fireheart. "This is all your fault!" he burst out. "She and Swiftpaw should have been made warriors, and then they wouldn't have gone off on their own."

Fireheart met his kin's gaze steadily. "Yes, I know," he mewed. "I tried, believe me."

He broke off as he heard the soft pawsteps of another cat, and turned to see that Bluestar was approaching. Fireheart had sent Sandstorm to fetch her, and the ginger warrior followed her into the medicine cat's clearing.

The Clan leader stood and looked down at Brightpaw in silence. Cloudtail raised his head challengingly, and for a heartbeat Fireheart thought he was going to accuse Bluestar of being responsible for Brightpaw's terrible injuries as well, but Cloudtail stayed silent.

Bluestar blinked a couple of times and asked, "Is she dying?"

"That's up to StarClan," Cinderpelt told her, catching Fireheart's eye.

"And what mercy can we expect from them?" Bluestar growled. "If it's up to StarClan, Brightpaw will die."

"Without ever being a warrior," mewed Cloudtail; his voice was quiet and sorrowful, and he bent his head again to lick Brightpaw's shoulder.

"Not necessarily." Bluestar spoke reluctantly. "There is a ritual—thankfully little used—if a dying apprentice is worthy, she can be made into a warrior so that she may take a warrior name to StarClan." She hesitated.

Fireheart held his breath in disbelief. Would Bluestar really put aside her anger at their ancestors to acknowledge the importance of StarClan in a warrior's life? Was she about to admit that Brightpaw had been denied the warrior status she deserved?

Cloudtail looked up at the gray she-cat again. "Then do it," he growled.

Bluestar did not react to being ordered around by her newest warrior. As Fireheart and Cinderpelt looked on, pelts touching for comfort, and Sandstorm approached to bear silent witness, the Clan leader dipped her head and began to speak. "I ask my warrior ancestors to look down on this apprentice. She has learned the warrior code and has given up her life in the service of her Clan. Let StarClan receive her as a warrior." Then she paused, and her eyes blazed with anger that burned like cold fire. "She will be known as Lostface, so that every cat knows what StarClan did to take her from us," she growled.

Fireheart stared at his leader in horror. How could she use this terribly wounded apprentice in her war against her warrior ancestors?

"But that's a cruel name!" Cloudtail protested. "What if she lives?"

"Then we will have all the more reason to remember what StarClan have brought us to," Bluestar replied, her voice barely more than a whisper. "They will have this warrior as Lostface, or not at all."

Cloudtail held her gaze for a moment longer, the light of

challenge in his blue eyes, and then dipped his head as if he knew there was no point in arguing.

"Let StarClan receive her by the name of Lostface," Bluestar finished. She bent her head and lightly touched her nose to Lostface's head. "There, it is done," she murmured.

As if the touch had roused her, Lostface's eyes opened and a look of terrible fear flooded into them. For a moment she struggled back to wakefulness. "Pack, pack!" She gasped. "Kill, kill!"

Bluestar recoiled, her fur bristling. "What? What does she mean?" she demanded.

But Lostface had sunk into unconsciousness again. Bluestar looked wildly from Cinderpelt to Fireheart and back again. "What did she mean?" she repeated.

"I don't know," Cinderpelt mewed uneasily. "That's all she will say."

"But, Fireheart, I told you . . ." Bluestar was struggling to speak. "StarClan showed me an evil in the forest, and they called it 'pack.' Is it the pack that has done this?"

Cinderpelt avoided her eyes, going instead to check on Lostface. Fireheart sought for an answer that would satisfy his leader. He did not want Bluestar to know that her cats were being hunted down as if they were prey for some nameless, faceless enemy. But he knew that she would not be satisfied by empty reassurances.

"No cat knows," he replied at last. "I'll warn the patrols to be on their guard, but—"

"But if StarClan has abandoned us, *patrols* will not help us,"

Bluestar finished scornfully. "Perhaps they have even sent this pack to punish me."

"No!" Cinderpelt faced her leader. "StarClan did not send the pack. Our ancestors care for us, and they would never disrupt the life of the forest or destroy a whole Clan for a single grudge. Bluestar, you *must* believe this."

Bluestar ignored her. She padded over to Lostface and stood looking down at her. "Forgive me," she meowed. "I have brought down the wrath of StarClan on you." Then she turned away toward her den.

Almost as soon as she had gone, an agonizing wail broke out in the main clearing. Fireheart raced through the ferns to see that Longtail and Graystripe were bringing Swiftpaw's body back for burial. When the limp black-and-white shape had been laid in the center of the clearing, his mentor crouched beside him, touching his nose to his fur in the ritual position of mourning. Swiftpaw's mother, Goldenflower, sat next to him, while Bramblekit and Tawnykit, Swiftpaw's half brother and half sister, looked on with wide, scared eyes.

A fresh wave of grief flooded through Fireheart. Longtail had been a good mentor to Swiftpaw. He did not deserve the pain he was going through now.

Returning to Cinderpelt's clearing, he saw that Sandstorm had padded over to stand beside the medicine cat, who was pressing fresh cobwebs onto the blood-soaked dressings. "Maybe she'll pull through," she mewed. "If any cat can help her, you can, Cinderpelt."

Cinderpelt looked up and blinked gratefully. "Thanks,

Sandstorm. But healing herbs can only do so much. And if Lostface lives, she might not thank me." She caught Fireheart's eye, and he saw in her face a fear that the injured cat would be unable to cope with her horrifically changed appearance. What future lay ahead for a cat whose scars would remind her forever of this living nightmare?

"I'll still look after her," vowed Cloudtail, glancing up from his gentle licking.

Fireheart felt a burst of pride. If only his former apprentice could show the same unquestioning loyalty to the warrior code, he would be one of the finest warriors in ThunderClan.

Sandstorm gently nosed Lostface and then drew away. "I'll fetch some fresh-kill for you and Cloudtail," she meowed to Cinderpelt. "And a piece for Lostface too. She might want something if she wakes up." Determinedly optimistic, she padded out into the clearing.

"I don't want anything to eat," mewed Cloudtail. His voice was dull and exhausted. "I feel sick."

"You need to sleep," Cinderpelt told him. "I'll give you some poppy seeds."

"I don't want poppy seeds either. I want to stay with Lostface."

"I'm not asking you what you want; I'm telling you what you need," Cinderpelt retorted. "You kept vigil last night, remember?" More gently, she added, "I promise I'll wake you if there's any change."

While she went to fetch the seeds, Fireheart gave his kin a sympathetic glance. "She's the medicine cat," he pointed out. "She knows what's best."

Cloudtail didn't reply, but when Cinderpelt came back carrying a dried poppy head and shook a few seeds out in front of him, he licked them up without complaining. Exhausted, he curled himself close to Lostface and was asleep within a few heartbeats.

"I never thought he would care for another cat as much as that," Fireheart murmured.

"You didn't notice?" For all her anxiety, there was a glint of amusement in Cinderpelt's blue eyes. "He's been padding after Brightpaw—Lostface—for a season now. He really loves her, you know."

Seeing the two young cats curled up together, Fireheart could believe it.

Fireheart headed toward the pile of fresh-kill. It was almost sunhigh, but though the rays poured down brightly into the clearing there was little warmth in them. Leaf-bare had come to the forest.

Days had passed since Swiftpaw had been killed and Lostface injured. Fireheart had just been to check on her, and she still clung to life. Cinderpelt began to be cautiously optimistic that she would survive. Cloudtail spent nearly every moment with her; Fireheart had excused him temporarily from warrior duties so that he could care for the injured cat.

As Fireheart crossed the clearing, he saw Graystripe emerge from the warriors' den and approach the fresh-kill pile. Darkstripe overtook him before he reached it and shouldered him aside to snatch up a rabbit. Dustpelt, already choosing his own meal, gave Graystripe a hostile glare and the gray warrior hesitated, unwilling to go any closer until the other two warriors had withdrawn to the nettle patch to eat.

Quickening his pace, Fireheart came up beside his friend. "Ignore them," he muttered. "They keep their brains in their tails."

Graystripe flashed him a grateful glance before picking a magpie out of the pile.

"Let's eat together," Fireheart suggested, choosing a vole and leading the way to a sunny patch of ground near the warriors' den. "And don't let those two worry you," he added. "They can't stay hostile forever."

Graystripe did not look convinced, but he said nothing more, and the two warriors settled down to eat. Across the clearing, Tawnykit and Bramblekit were playing with Willowpelt's three kits. Fireheart felt a pang of grief as he remembered how Lostface had sometimes played with them, as if she were looking forward to having kits herself. Would she ever mother her own litter now?

"I can't get over how much that kit looks like his father," meowed Graystripe after watching them for a moment.

"Just so long as he doesn't *behave* like his father," Fireheart replied. He stiffened when he saw Bramblekit bowl over one of Willowpelt's much smaller kits, but relaxed again as the tiny tortoiseshell sprang up and hurled herself joyfully on Bramblekit.

"It must be time he was apprenticed," remarked Graystripe.

"He and Tawnykit are older than—" He broke off, and a distant, sorrowful expression clouded his amber eyes.

Fireheart knew that he was thinking of his own kits, left behind in RiverClan. "Yes, it's time I was thinking about mentors," he agreed, hoping to distract his friend from his bittersweet memories. "I'll ask Bluestar if I can mentor Bramblekit myself. Who do you think would—"

"You'll mentor Bramblekit?" Graystripe stared at him. "Is that a good idea?"

"Why shouldn't I?" Fireheart asked, feeling his fur start to prickle. "I haven't an apprentice, now that Cloudtail has been made a warrior."

"Because you don't like Bramblekit," retorted Graystripe. "I don't blame you, but wouldn't he be better off with a mentor who trusts him?"

Fireheart hesitated. There was some truth in what Graystripe said, but Fireheart knew that he couldn't give the task to any other cat. He *had* to have Bramblekit under his own guidance to make sure he stayed loyal to ThunderClan.

"My mind's made up," he mewed curtly. "I wanted to ask you who you think would be good for Tawnykit."

Graystripe paused, as if he wanted to go on arguing, then shrugged. "I'm surprised you have to ask. There's an obvious choice." When Fireheart didn't speak, he added, "Sandstorm, you mouse-brain!"

Fireheart took a mouthful of vole to give himself time to think of an answer. Sandstorm was an experienced warrior. She had been an apprentice along with Fireheart himself,

Graystripe, and Dustpelt, and she was the only one of the four never to have had an apprentice of her own. Yet something made him reluctant to give Tawnykit to her.

Swallowing the vole, he meowed, "I more or less promised Snowkit to Brackenfur. It's only fair I should ask Bluestar if he can mentor Tawnykit, seeing as he was disappointed so recently. Besides, he's a fine warrior, and he'll do a good job."

Graystripe's eyes glowed briefly with pride; Brackenfur had been his apprentice, and he was clearly delighted to hear how well the young warrior was doing. Then he twitched his ears disbelievingly. "Come on, Fireheart. That's not the real reason, and you know it."

"What do you mean?"

"You don't want to give Tawnykit to Sandstorm because you're afraid of what Tigerstar might do."

Staring at his friend, Fireheart knew that the gray warrior was right. The reason had been there in his mind, but he had refused to admit it, even to himself.

"You want to protect her," Graystripe went on, when Fireheart didn't speak.

"And what's wrong with that?" Fireheart demanded. "Tigerstar already encouraged Darkstripe to take the kits out of camp to visit him. Do you think that will be the end of it? Do you think he'll be content just to see them at Gatherings?"

"No, I don't." Graystripe gave an exasperated snort. "But what will Sandstorm think? She's not some pretty little kitty-pet, hiding behind big, strong warriors. She can take care of herself."

Fireheart shrugged uncomfortably. "Sandstorm will just have to accept the decision. I'm sure Bluestar will agree to let Brackenfur have Tawnykit."

Graystripe's amber eyes gleamed in anticipation of trouble ahead. "You're the deputy. But Sandstorm isn't going to like it," he predicted.

"You want to mentor Bramblekit?" asked Bluestar.

Fireheart stood in her den. He had just raised the question of the new apprentices, suggesting that they should hold the naming ceremony at sunset.

"Yes," he mewed. "And Brackenfur to mentor Tawnykit."

Bluestar gazed at him with narrowed eyes. "A traitor to mentor the son of a traitor," she rasped. Clearly she had no interest in who should mentor Tawnykit. "How suitable."

"Bluestar, there are no traitors in the Clan now," Fireheart tried to assure her, pushing down his misgivings about Bramblekit.

Bluestar gave a disdainful sniff. "Do what you want, Fireheart. Why should I care what happens to this nest of rogues?"

Fireheart gave up his attempt to reason with her. Backing out of the den, he returned to the clearing. The sun was already going down, and the Clan had begun to gather in anticipation of the ceremony. Fireheart spotted Brackenfur and called him over.

"I think you're ready for an apprentice," he announced. "How would you like to mentor Tawnykit?"

Brackenfur's eyes glowed. "Do you really mean it?" he

stammered. "That would be great!"

"You'll do a fine job," Fireheart meowed. "Do you know what to do in the ceremony?"

He paused as Sandstorm appeared from the warriors' den and began walking toward him. "Hang on, Brackenfur," he muttered hastily. "I'll be back in a moment." Then he went to meet the pale ginger warrior.

"What's this Graystripe tells me?" Sandstorm demanded as soon as he was in earshot. "Is it true that you asked Bluestar if Brackenfur could mentor Tawnykit?"

Fireheart swallowed. Her green eyes were blazing with anger, and the fur on her shoulders bristled. "Yes, it's true," he began.

"But I'm more experienced than he is!"

Fireheart resisted the urge to tell her the truth, so that Sandstorm knew he was doing it for her sake and for no other reason. But telling her that she wasn't going to mentor Tawnykit because he wanted to protect her from possible trouble with Tigerstar would make her even more furious. She would only think that he had judged her too weak to deal with the threat posed by the ShadowClan leader.

"Well?" Sandstorm insisted. "Don't you think I'm capable of being a good mentor?"

"It's not that at all," Fireheart protested.

"Then what? Give me one good reason why I shouldn't mentor Tawnykit!"

"Because I . . . " Fireheart cast around desperately for something he could tell her. "Because I want you to lead extra hunting patrols. You're a *brilliant* hunter, Sandstorm—the best. And with leaf-bare here, prey will be scarce again. We're really going to need you." As he spoke, he realized that what he said was true. Extra hunting patrols led by Sandstorm would be one way to solve the problem of feeding the Clan through the bitter moons of leaf-bare.

Sandstorm, however, was not impressed. "You're just making excuses," she meowed scornfully. "There's no reason why I shouldn't lead hunting patrols *and* mentor Tawnykit. She's bright and fast, and I bet she turns out to be a *brilliant* hunter, too."

"I'm sorry," Fireheart mewed. "I've already asked Brackenfur to take Tawnykit. I'll ask Bluestar to give you one of Willowpelt's kits when the worst of leaf-bare is over. Okay?"

"No, it's not okay," Sandstorm hissed. "I haven't done anything to be passed over like this. I won't forget this in a hurry, Fireheart."

She turned away and went to join Frostfur and Brindleface. Fireheart took a step after her and then stopped. There was nothing he could say, and besides, Bluestar had just appeared from her den to call the Clan to the meeting.

As the Clan assembled, Fireheart noticed Graystripe crouching alone not far from the Highrock. Mousefur stalked pointedly past him on her way to sit with the other she-cats. Frustrated at the way some of the Clan still refused to accept Graystripe, Fireheart wanted to go over to reassure him, but he had to stay where he was, ready for his part in the ceremony. A moment later Cloudtail and Whitestorm appeared from the fern tunnel leading to Cinderpelt's den and settled down alongside the gray warrior, to Fireheart's relief.

Cinderpelt followed them out of the ferns and limped hurriedly over to Fireheart. As she drew closer he saw that her blue eyes were sparkling. "Good news, Fireheart," she announced. "Lostface just woke up and managed to eat some fresh-kill. I think she's going to be okay."

Fireheart let out a delighted purr. "That's great, Cinderpelt." But for all his relief at the news, he couldn't help wondering how Lostface would cope when she learned that her face was so terribly injured.

"She's already sitting up and trying to groom herself," Cinderpelt went on, "but she's still very shaky. She'll need to stay in my den for a few days yet."

"Has she said anything about what attacked her?"

Cinderpelt shook her head. "I tried to ask her, but it upsets her too much to think about it. She still cries out 'pack' and 'kill' in her nightmares."

"The Clan needs to know," Fireheart reminded her.

"Then the Clan will have to wait," Cinderpelt assured sharply. "Lostface needs peace and quiet if she's going to get better."

Fireheart wanted to ask her when she thought Lostface would be fit to talk to him, but he had to pay attention to the ceremony as Goldenflower came out of the nursery, flanked by her two kits. Fireheart could see she had groomed both of them especially carefully. Tawnykit's ginger fur glowed like a flame in the dying sun, and Bramblekit's dark tabby pelt had a glossy sheen. As they approached the Highrock, Tawnykit bounced around with excitement, but Bramblekit seemed calm, padding forward with his head and tail held high.

Fireheart wondered if this was what Tigerstar had looked like when he had first been made an apprentice. Had he shown the same promise of courage and a long life in the service of his Clan? Had his Clan leader and his mentor had any idea of what he was destined to become?

Bluestar called both kits forward to stand beside her at the foot of the Highrock. Fireheart noticed that she was looking more alert than usual, as if even she could not be indifferent to the prospect of more warriors to fight for her Clan.

"Brackenfur," she began, "Fireheart tells me that you are ready for your first apprentice. You will be mentor to Tawnypaw."

Looking nearly as excited as his new apprentice, Brackenfur stepped forward, and Tawnypaw ran up to meet him.

"Brackenfur," Bluestar continued, "you have shown yourself to be a warrior of loyalty and forethought. Do your best to pass on these qualities to Tawnypaw."

Brackenfur and Tawnypaw touched noses and withdrew to the side of the clearing, while Bluestar turned to Fireheart.

"Now that Cloudtail is a warrior," she went on, "you are free to take on another apprentice. You will be mentor to Bramblepaw."

Her eyes glittered as she gazed at Fireheart, and he realized with a flash of horror that she was suspicious of his motives in offering to train Tigerstar's son. Fireheart tried to meet his leader's icy gaze steadily. Whatever Bluestar thought, he *knew* that he was motivated by loyalty to his Clan.

Bramblepaw padded toward his mentor, and Fireheart went to meet him in the middle of the circle of cats. Looking down into the young cat's eyes, he felt both stirred and challenged by the blaze of enthusiasm there.

What a warrior he'll make! Fireheart thought, and then added silently, *If only he weren't Tigerstar's son!*

"Fireheart, you have shown yourself to be a warrior of rare courage and quick thinking," meowed Bluestar, her eyes narrowed. "I'm sure that you will pass on all you know to this young apprentice."

Fireheart bent his head to touch noses with Bramblepaw. As he led the new apprentice back to the side of the clearing, Bramblepaw asked, "What do we do now, Fireheart? I want to learn *everything*—fighting and hunting and all about the other Clans. . . ."

In spite of his misgivings, Fireheart had to admit that Bramblepaw clearly knew nothing about the old hostility between his mentor and his father. That was thanks to Goldenflower, who sat looking at them with an unreadable expression. Fireheart guessed she wouldn't be too pleased that he had chosen to train Tigerstar's son himself. And what would happen when Tigerstar found out? He could feel Darkstripe watching him closely and knew that the dark warrior would take the news to Tigerstar at the next Gathering, if not before.

"All in good time," Fireheart promised the eager apprentice. "Tomorrow we'll go with Brackenfur and your sister to tour the territory. Then you'll learn where the borders are and how to recognize the scents of the other Clans."

"Great!" Bramblepaw let out an excited squeak.

"But for now," Fireheart went on as Bluestar drew the meeting to a close, "you can go and get to know the other apprentices. Don't forget you sleep in their den tonight."

He flicked his tail in dismissal, and Bramblepaw dashed off to his sister's side as the other cats started to crowd around, congratulating the two new apprentices and calling them by their new names.

Watching them, Fireheart saw Graystripe get up and come toward him, passing Sandstorm on the way. He heard the ginger she-cat meow, "Graystripe, aren't you sorry you weren't given an apprentice?"

"In a way," Graystripe replied. He sounded awkward, shooting Fireheart a sideways glance as he spoke. "I can't expect one for a while, though. Half the Clan haven't accepted me yet."

"Then half the Clan are stupid furballs," asserted Sandstorm, giving the gray warrior's ear a lick.

Graystripe shrugged. "I know I'll have to prove my loyalty before I can mentor an apprentice again. And you'll have one soon," he added, as if he could read her mind, "when Willowpelt's kits are ready."

An annoyed look flashed across Sandstorm's face. Fireheart wondered whether he ought to try talking to her again, but as she spotted his hesitant approach she turned to Graystripe and meowed loudly, "Come on; let's see if there's any fresh-kill left."

Fireheart halted and watched miserably as Sandstorm got to her paws and led the way over to the pile of prey. Graystripe followed her, casting a worried glance at Fireheart as he went.

Seeing Sandstorm turn her back on him, Fireheart felt bitter disappointment welling up inside him. However hard he tried, all his attempts to rekindle the old bond between him and Sandstorm seemed to be failing, and he missed her with a loneliness that could not be comforted by any of the other cats that thronged around him.

CHAPTER 21

❧

"Keep well back," Brackenfur warned. *"This* is a dangerous place."

He and Fireheart, with their two apprentices, were standing at the edge of the Thunderpath. Bramblepaw and Tawnypaw wrinkled their noses against its bitter smell.

"It doesn't look dangerous to me," meowed Bramblepaw. Tentatively he reached out one paw to place it on the dark, stony surface.

At the same moment, Fireheart felt the ground tremble with the roar of an approaching monster. "Get back!" he snarled.

Bramblepaw leaped back into the safety of the verge as the monster flashed past, buffeting his fur with hot, stinking wind. He was quivering with shock.

Tawnypaw's eyes were wide with astonishment. "What *was* that?" she mewed.

"A monster," Fireheart explained. "They carry Twolegs in their belly. But they never leave the Thunderpath, so you're quite safe—as long as you stay away from it." He fixed Bramblepaw with a stern gaze. "When a warrior tells you to do something, you do it. Ask questions if you like, but *afterward*."

Bramblepaw nodded, scuffling his paws. "Sorry, Fireheart."

He was already recovering from the shock; Fireheart had to admit that many more experienced cats would have been terrified to find themselves so close to a monster. Since they had left camp that morning, Bramblepaw had shown himself to be brave, curious, and eager to learn.

Sandstorm, Graystripe, and Whitestorm had gone out on the dawn patrol, while Fireheart and Brackenfur gave their apprentices the tour of the territory. Fireheart had found himself moving with extra stealth along the once-familiar trails, haunted by shadows and afraid at any moment that he would come face-to-face with the dark presence in the forest.

He had kept well away from Snakerocks, unwilling to risk that accursed place with two new apprentices. Soon, he knew, he would have to do something about the threat that lurked there, but he was waiting until Lostface was well enough to tell them exactly what had attacked her. And deep down Fireheart couldn't help wondering if, even when they knew, his warriors would be able to deal with it.

"What's over there?" Tawnypaw flicked her tail at the part of the forest on the other side of the Thunderpath.

"That's ShadowClan territory," Brackenfur told her. "Can you smell their scent?"

A chill breeze was carrying the scent of ShadowClan toward them. Bramblepaw and Tawnypaw opened their mouths to taste it.

"We've smelled that before," announced Tawnypaw.

"Oh?" Brackenfur shot a startled glance at Fireheart.

"When Darkstripe brought us to the border to meet our father," explained Bramblepaw.

"I spotted them." Fireheart wanted Brackenfur to know that this wasn't news to him. "I suppose we can't blame Tigerstar for wanting to see them," he added, forcing himself to be charitable.

Brackenfur didn't reply, but he looked faintly worried, as if he shared Fireheart's misgivings about Tigerstar's relationship with these ThunderClan kits.

"Can we go over there now and see our father?" Tawnypaw asked eagerly.

"No!" Brackenfur sounded shocked. "Clan cats don't go into each other's territory. If a patrol caught us, there would be big trouble."

"Not if we told them Tigerstar's our father," Bramblepaw insisted. "He wanted to see us last time."

"Brackenfur told you no," Fireheart snapped. "And if I catch either of you setting one paw across the border, I'll have your tails off!"

Tawnypaw jumped back as if she thought he was going to carry out the threat there and then.

Bramblepaw's amber eyes searched Fireheart's face for several heartbeats. "Fireheart," he meowed hesitantly, "there's something else, isn't there? Why will no cat talk to us about our father? Why did he leave ThunderClan?"

Fireheart stared down at his apprentice. He couldn't see any way of avoiding such a direct question. Long ago, he had promised Goldenflower that he would tell her kits the truth, but he had hoped for a bit more time to think out exactly what he would say.

He exchanged a quick glance with Brackenfur, and the younger warrior murmured, "If you don't tell them, some other cat will."

He was right, Fireheart realized. The time had come for him to fulfill his promise to Goldenflower. Clearing his throat, he meowed, "All right. Let's find a place to rest and I'll tell you."

He retreated several rabbit-hops from the Thunderpath until he came to a dip in the ground sheltered by a few clumps of fern, brown and broken now in the frosts of leaf-bare. The two apprentices followed, their eyes wide and curious.

Fireheart checked that there was no smell of dog before settling down in a patch of dry grass, tucking his paws under his chest. Brackenfur remained at the top of the slope, keeping watch for danger, from the dog or from ShadowClan territory so close by.

"Before I tell you about your father," Fireheart began, "I want you to remember that ThunderClan is proud of you. You'll both make fine warriors. What I'm going to say now won't make any difference to that."

The apprentices' curiosity changed to uneasiness as they listened. Fireheart knew they must be wondering what was coming next.

"Tigerstar is a great warrior," he went on. "And he always wanted to be leader of a Clan. Before he left ThunderClan, he was deputy."

Bramblepaw's eyes glowed excitedly. "When I'm a warrior, I'd like to be deputy too."

Fireheart's fur prickled at this evidence of his apprentice's ambition, so like Tigerstar's. "Be quiet and listen."

Bramblepaw dipped his head obediently.

"As I said, Tigerstar has always been a great warrior," Fireheart continued, forcing each word into the cold air. "But there was a fight with RiverClan over Sunningrocks, and Tigerstar used the battle to kill Redtail, who was the ThunderClan deputy then. He blamed a RiverClan warrior, but we found out what really happened."

He paused. Both apprentices were staring at him with disbelief and horror in their eyes.

"You mean . . . he *killed* a cat of his own Clan?" Tawnypaw faltered.

"I don't believe it!" Bramblepaw let out a desperate cry.

"It's true," Fireheart meowed, feeling sick with the effort of telling these kits the truth about their father's treachery in a way that was loyal to their mother's insistence that the account be unbiased, and would not alienate the kits from their birth-clan. "He hoped he would be made deputy in Redtail's place, but Bluestar chose a cat called Lionheart instead."

"Tigerstar didn't kill Lionheart as well?" asked Bramblepaw, his voice quavering.

"No, he didn't. Lionheart died in a battle with ShadowClan. Tigerstar became deputy then, but that wasn't enough for him. He wanted to be leader."

He paused again, wondering how much to say. No need to burden these apprentices, he decided, with the tale of how Cinderpelt had been injured in a trap set by Tigerstar for Bluestar, or Tigerstar's attempts to murder Fireheart himself.

"He gathered a band of rogues from the forest," he continued. "They attacked ThunderClan, and Tigerstar tried to kill Bluestar."

"Kill *Bluestar!*" Tawnypaw gasped. "But she's our *leader!*"

"Tigerstar thought that he could make himself leader in her place," Fireheart explained, keeping his voice carefully neutral. "The Clan sent him into exile, and that's when he joined ShadowClan and became their leader."

The two apprentices looked at each other. "So our father was a traitor?" mewed Bramblepaw softly.

"Well, yes," Fireheart replied. "But I know it's hard to think about that. Just remember that both of you can be proud to belong to ThunderClan. And the Clan are proud of you, just as I said. You're not responsible for what your father did. You can be great warriors, completely loyal to your Clan and the warrior code."

"But our father wasn't loyal," Tawnypaw mewed. "Does that mean he's our enemy now?"

Fireheart met her scared gaze. "All cats from other Clans have to have their own interests at heart," he told her gently. "That's what Clan loyalty means. Your father is loyal to ShadowClan now, just as it is your duty to be loyal to ThunderClan."

There was silence for a few heartbeats, and then Tawnypaw drew herself up and gave her chest fur a few quick licks.

"Thank you for telling us, Fireheart. Is it . . . is it really true that the rest of the Clan are proud of us?"

"It really is," Fireheart assured her. "Don't forget, the Clan discovered all this when you two were only newborns. And they've never wanted to punish you, have they?"

Tawnypaw blinked gratefully at him. Glancing at Bramblepaw, Fireheart saw that he was gazing up at the sky between the arching fronds of fern. There was no reading the emotion in his amber eyes.

"Bramblepaw?" Fireheart meowed uneasily. The young cat did not respond. Wanting to reassure him, Fireheart went on, "Work hard and be loyal to your Clan, and no cat will blame you for what your father did."

Bramblepaw's head whipped around; his eyes glared at his mentor with all the hostility that Fireheart had once seen in Tigerstar. He had never looked more like his father. "But that's not true, is it?" he hissed. "*You* blame us. I don't care what you're saying now. I've seen the way you look at me. You think I'll be a traitor just like he was. You'll never trust me, whatever I do!"

Fireheart stared at him, unable to deny the young cat's accusations. For a few heartbeats he had no idea what to say. While he hesitated, Bramblepaw sprang to his paws and blundered through the ferns to the top of the hollow, where Brackenfur was waiting. Tawnypaw cast one scared look at Fireheart and scurried after her brother.

Fireheart heard Brackenfur meow, "Ready to go? Let's head along the border up to Fourtrees." He paused and called out, "Fireheart, are you ready?"

"Coming," Fireheart replied. His heart was heavy as he rose and followed the apprentices. Had he managed to explain to them the true meaning of loyalty, or had he simply succeeded in pushing them further away from ThunderClan, and from him?

As he and Brackenfur led the apprentices back through their territory, Fireheart kept watch for any signs of the mysterious evil in the forest. He saw nothing; there were no unusual scents, and no signs of scattered prey. The evil, whatever it was, had gone to ground again, and somehow that made Fireheart more afraid. What was it that could wreak such terrible damage, and then fade into the depths of the forest as if it had never been?

I must talk to Lostface as soon as I can, he decided. The cats were still being hunted, he was sure of that, and it was only a matter of time before another one was caught.

Early the next morning, Fireheart emerged into the clearing to find the dawn patrol getting ready to leave. Graystripe and Sandstorm were waiting beside the entrance to the gorse tunnel, while Dustpelt was calling Ashpaw from the apprentices' den. Fireheart hurried toward the entrance, but before he reached it he heard Sandstorm meow loudly to Graystripe, "I'm tired of hanging about. I'll meet you at the top of the ravine." Without looking at Fireheart she whipped around and disappeared.

Sadness almost overwhelmed Fireheart, and he halted at

the mouth of the gorse tunnel, tasting the last of Sandstorm's scent as she retreated.

"Give her time," Graystripe meowed, touching his nose to Fireheart's shoulder. "She'll come around."

"I don't know. Ever since the meeting with WindClan . . ."

He stopped as Dustpelt and Ashpaw hurried up, and stood back to let the rest of the patrol follow Sandstorm. At least, Fireheart told himself, Dustpelt seemed to be reconciled to Graystripe's return, to the extent of going on patrol with him. Perhaps time was all his friend would need to truly be part of the Clan again.

Fireheart padded across the clearing to Cinderpelt's den. Lostface was seated in a patch of sunlight with Cloudtail beside her, gently washing her. The wounds along her sides were healing cleanly, and her ginger-and-white fur was beginning to grow back, and as he approached Fireheart thought for a single heartbeat that she was almost back to normal. Then she lifted her head, and for the first time he saw the damaged side of her face without its covering of cobwebs.

Freshly healed scars were stretched across Lostface's cheek, bare flesh where no fur would ever grow. Her eye was gone, and her ear was reduced to a few shreds. Fireheart realized how dreadfully apt the name Lostface was, and remembered her as she had been before, bright and lively. Anger burned deep in his belly. Somehow he must drive this evil out of the forest!

Lostface let out a faint whimper as Fireheart approached, and shrank closer to Cloudtail.

"It's okay," Cloudtail mewed softly. "It's only Fireheart." Looking up at his former mentor, he explained, "You came up on her blind side. She's scared when cats do that, but she's getting better every day."

"That's right," agreed Cinderpelt, emerging from her den. Limping over to Fireheart so she could speak to him without Lostface overhearing, she went on, "To be honest, there's not much more I can do for her. She just needs time to get strong."

"How long?" Fireheart asked. "I need to talk to her—and it's time Cloudtail was going back to his warrior duties. I know Sandstorm wants him for her hunting patrol." He gave his kin a sympathetic glance, still admiring him for his loyalty to Lostface.

Cinderpelt shrugged. "I'll have to let Lostface decide when she feels ready to leave my den. Have you thought about what's going to happen to her now?"

Fireheart shook his head. "Officially she's a warrior. . . ."

"And you think she'd be happy among you ruffians in the warriors' den?" Cinderpelt let out a mew of exasperation. "She still needs someone to look after her."

"I think she could go and live with the elders, at least while she's still getting stronger." It was Cloudtail who spoke; he had padded over to join Fireheart and the medicine cat. "Speckletail is still grieving in the elders' den for Snowkit. It would do her good to have another cat to care for."

"That's a brilliant idea," Fireheart meowed warmly.

"I'm not sure," Cinderpelt objected. "What's Speckletail going to think? You know how prickly and proud she is. She wouldn't like the idea that you were doing her a favor by trying to distract her from Snowkit's death."

"Leave Speckletail to me," Fireheart meowed. "I'll tell her that *she's* doing *me* a favor by looking after Lostface."

"That might work," agreed Cinderpelt. "And when Lostface is a bit better, she could help the elders and free up the apprentices for other duties."

"Let's ask her," meowed Cloudtail. He bounded back to Lostface's side and pressed close to her. "Lostface, Fireheart wants to talk to you."

Fireheart followed. "Lostface, it's Fireheart." Her ravaged face turned slowly toward him. "Would you like to go and stay with the elders for a while?" he suggested. "It would be a load off my mind if you could help look after them—the apprentices have too much to do as it is."

Lostface gave a nervous start and looked at Cloudtail with her one good eye. "I don't have to, do I? I'm *not* an elder."

Cloudtail pressed his muzzle against her wounded face. "No one will make you do anything you don't want to."

"But you'd be doing me a favor," Fireheart added quickly. "Speckletail's still grieving for Snowkit, and it will do her good to have a young, energetic cat around." As Lostface still hesitated, he went on: "It's just until you get your strength back."

"And when you're strong again, I'll help you train," Cloudtail added. "I'm sure you'll be able to hunt with your good eye and ear. It'll just take a bit of practice."

Lostface's eye began to glow with hope, and she nodded

slowly. "All right, Fireheart. If that's the best way I can be useful."

"It is, I promise. And Lostface"—Fireheart crouched down beside her and gave her a reassuring lick—"is there anything you can tell me about that day in the forest? Did you see what attacked you?"

Lostface's flicker of confidence died, and she shrank back against Cloudtail again. "I don't remember," she whimpered. "I'm sorry, Fireheart; I don't remember."

Cloudtail licked her head comfortingly. "It's all right; you don't have to think about it now."

Fireheart tried to hide his disappointment. "Never mind. If you do think of anything, tell me right away."

"*I'll* tell you one thing," Cloudtail growled. "When we find out who did this to her, I'll make crowfood of them. I promise you that."

CHAPTER 22

❧

A full moon crossed the sky behind thin wisps of cloud as Bluestar led her warriors to the Gathering. Fireheart was already uneasy. In spite of her declaration of war against StarClan, Bluestar had insisted on going. "How can I trust you to lead the Clan?" she had spat at her deputy when he had asked her which warriors he should take. Fireheart had simply bowed his head in obedience, but he could still feel the pain of knowing that his leader was convinced he was a traitor.

He also had his doubts about including Graystripe, but his friend had begged desperately to be allowed to come. "Please, Fireheart! I'll be able to get news of Featherkit and Stormkit," he had meowed. Fireheart knew that Graystripe was inviting hostility from RiverClan by appearing so soon after the battle at Sunningrocks, and had half hoped that Bluestar would refuse. But the ThunderClan leader had merely flicked her tail dismissively. "Let him come. You're all traitors, so what does it matter?"

Now Fireheart bunched together with the other ThunderClan warriors to follow Bluestar down the slope. As they emerged into the hollow, the first thing he saw was

Tigerstar and Leopardstar sitting side by side, watching approvingly as a group of their apprentices scuffled playfully with eachother. Fireheart's fur crawled as he saw those two together. He still had no evidence that Tigerstar was plotting revenge on his former Clan, but Leopardstar would certainly be feeling hostile after her Clan's defeat at Sunningrocks.

"You've done a good job there," meowed Leopardstar to her companion. "Those are strong young cats, and they've learned their fighting moves well."

A purr rumbled in Tigerstar's chest. "We've made some progress," he agreed. "But there's a long way to go yet."

A pair of tumbling apprentices rolled right up to their leaders' paws and Leopardstar shifted backwards to give them more room. The young ShadowClan cats were certainly muscular and well fed, Fireheart thought; he could hardly believe they were the same scrawny creatures who had almost died when the sickness swept through their Clan. He exchanged an uneasy glance with Graystripe; sooner or later, he was sure, ThunderClan would have to meet these skilled fighters in battle.

At a word from Tigerstar the apprentices stopped their playful skirmish and sat up, licking their ruffled fur. The two leaders began to make their way toward the Great Rock. Fireheart spotted Bluestar already waiting at its base, but he couldn't see Tallstar, the WindClan leader.

As the ThunderClan cats dispersed to meet with warriors in other Clans, he noticed Graystripe hurrying up to a plump bracken-colored she-cat, and caught the scent of RiverClan from her. Fireheart felt a pang of anxiety as he watched his friend. He trusted Graystripe absolutely, even though he would always have one paw in RiverClan while his kits were there. But several ThunderClan warriors would doubt his loyalty if they saw him so eager to talk to a RiverClan cat.

"Mosspelt, how are you?" Graystripe greeted the she-cat. "How are Featherkit and Stormkit?"

"Featherpaw and Stormpaw now," replied Mosspelt proudly. "They've just been apprenticed."

"That's great!" Graystripe's yellow eyes were glowing as he turned to Fireheart. "Did you hear what Mosspelt said? My kits are apprentices now." He glanced around. "They're not here, are they?"

Mosspelt shook her head. "They're too newly apprenticed for that. Maybe next time. I'll tell them you were asking after them, Graystripe."

"Thanks." Graystripe's excitement faded and was replaced by anxiety. "What did they think when I didn't come back from the battle?"

"Once they knew you weren't dead, they coped well," replied Mosspelt. "Come on, Graystripe; it wasn't much of a shock. Every cat in RiverClan knew you would go back eventually."

Graystripe blinked in surprise. "Really?"

"Really. All the time you used to spend mooning around on the border or looking across the river. All the stories you told those kits about what you and Fireheart used to get up to when you were apprentices . . . It wasn't hard to see that your heart had never left ThunderClan."

Graystripe blinked again. "I'm sorry, Mosspelt."

"Nothing to be sorry for," retorted Mosspelt briskly. "And you can be sure that your kits will be well cared for. I'll keep an eye on them, and Mistyfoot and Stonefur are mentoring them."

"They are?" Graystripe's eyes lit up again. "That's great!"

Fireheart felt a pang of misgiving. Mistyfoot and Stonefur were both fine warriors, but he wondered why they had agreed to mentor Graystripe's kits. Mistyfoot had been a good friend to their mother, Silverstream, and so she might be expected to take an interest. But she and her brother had reacted with such hostility when he told them that Bluestar was their mother that Fireheart was surprised they wanted anything to do with kits who were half ThunderClan. Or was it possible that they wanted to teach the kits to be especially hostile toward their father's Clan?

"You'll tell them how proud I am, won't you?" Graystripe meowed urgently to Mosspelt. "And remind them to do what their mentors tell them?"

"Of course I will." Mosspelt let out a reassuring purr. "And I know Mistyfoot will help you keep in touch with them. Leopardstar might not like it, but . . . well, what she doesn't know won't hurt her."

Fireheart had his doubts; after her rejection of Bluestar, Mistyfoot might not want anything more to do with ThunderClan. He suspected she would feel more loyal than ever to RiverClan and Graypool, the cat she had always loved as her mother.

"Thanks, Mosspelt," mewed Graystripe. "I won't forget all you've done." He looked around as yowling sounded from the top of the Great Rock to signal the start of the meeting.

Turning, Fireheart saw that all four leaders were now assembled, their pelts shining in the moonlight as they stood looking down at the cats below. He paid little attention as the leaders formally opened the meeting. Instead, he wondered whether Bluestar would mention the terrible assault on Swiftpaw and Brightpaw, and whether any of the other leaders had similar news. Fireheart almost hoped that they had, because that would prove that the dark force in the forest was not a threat to ThunderClan alone, and so had not been sent by StarClan to punish Bluestar's challenge to them. Fireheart couldn't help thinking it was something greater even than that, a huge shadow that encompassed the whole forest; something that did not know the warrior code and regarded the cats merely as its prey.

When Tallstar had finished, Tigerstar stepped forward. He gave a quick summary of how ShadowClan's training program was progressing, that another new litter of kits had been born, and that three apprentices had been made into warriors. "ShadowClan grows strong again," he finished. "We are ready to take a full part in the life of the forest."

Fireheart wondered if that meant *ready to attack our neighbors*. He waited with a sinking heart for Tigerstar to make a case for expanding his territory. The ShadowClan leader had paused and was gazing down at the assembled cats as if he had something particularly important to say.

"I have a request to make," he began. "Many of you know that when I left ThunderClan, two kits of mine were in the nursery. They were too young then to travel, and I am grateful to ThunderClan for the care they have given them. But now it's time for them to join me in the Clan where they rightfully belong. Bluestar, I ask that you give me Bramblepaw and Tawnypaw."

Yowls of protest from ThunderClan warriors broke out before Tigerstar had finished speaking. Fireheart was too stunned to join in. He had been concerned all along that meeting with his kits at Gatherings would not be enough for Tigerstar, but he had never expected a public demand for the kits to be handed over to ShadowClan.

Bluestar drew herself up and waited for the noise to die away before she replied. "Certainly not," she meowed. "These are ThunderClan kits. They are apprenticed now, and they will stay where they belong."

"In ThunderClan?" Tigerstar challenged her. "I think not, Bluestar. The kits belong with me, and *my* warriors will take care of their apprentice training."

By that argument, Fireheart thought, Graystripe's kits should be returned to ThunderClan, although he guessed that Bluestar wouldn't want to reopen that debate with RiverClan. He was relieved to see that Bluestar was not going to back down easily. "Your concern is natural, Tigerstar. But you can be sure that the kits will receive the best possible training in ThunderClan."

Tigerstar paused again, his gaze sweeping around the

clearing, and when he spoke again it was not just to Bluestar but to the whole audience of cats. "The ThunderClan leader tells me how well my kits will be trained under her guidance—but ThunderClan have a poor record in looking after their young cats. One kit carried off by a hawk. One apprentice savaged to death and another permanently crippled when they were sent out alone without a warrior. Does any cat wonder that I'm concerned about the safety of my kits?"

Gasps of horror came from all around the clearing. Fireheart gaped up at the ShadowClan leader. How had Tigerstar learned about Swiftpaw and Brightpaw? It was too soon for news to have traveled to ShadowClan, except . . . *Darkstripe!* Fireheart thought, flexing his claws in anger. That treacherous warrior must have gone straight to Tigerstar and blurted out everything!

In his fury Fireheart missed Bluestar's reply, and when he made himself concentrate Tigerstar was speaking again. "I don't see what's so difficult," he meowed smoothly. "After all, it won't be the first time that ThunderClan has handed over kits to other Clans. Will it, Bluestar?"

Fear clenched in Fireheart's belly. Tigerstar was referring obliquely to Mistyfoot and Stonefur. Graypool had told Tigerstar that they had been born in ThunderClan. Fireheart thanked StarClan that Tigerstar did not know the names of the kits or who their mother was. But what little he knew was more than the rest of ThunderClan.

Fireheart glanced sideways at Stonefur, sitting only a couple of tail-lengths away. The blue-gray tom had drawn himself up, his head erect, and he was staring up at the Great Rock. His gaze was not fixed on Tigerstar, Fireheart noticed, but on Bluestar, and the expression in his eyes was one of pure hatred.

Digging his claws into the ground, Fireheart waited for the ThunderClan leader's response. He could see how shaken she was, and when she managed to reply every word seemed to catch in her throat like thorns. "The past is the past. We must judge each situation on its own merits. I will think carefully about what you say, Tigerstar, and give you my answer at the next Gathering."

Fireheart doubted that Tigerstar would consent to wait for a whole moon, but to his surprise the ShadowClan leader dipped his head and stepped back a pace. "Very well," he agreed. "One more moon—but no longer."

CHAPTER 23

♣

Fireheart padded warily through Tallpines toward the Twolegplace. Heavy rain had fallen the night before, so that wet ash and burned debris clung to his paws. All his senses were alert, not for prey, but for any sign that the dark threat in the forest would emerge to attack his small group of cats as it had attacked Swiftpaw and Lostface.

The injured she-cat was following Fireheart now, with Cloudtail at her side, while Graystripe brought up the rear, watchful for anything that might come upon them from behind. They were on their way to visit Cloudtail's mother, Princess. The young warrior had insisted on bringing Lostface with them.

"You have to leave camp sooner or later," he had meowed. "We're not going anywhere near Snakerocks. I'll make sure you're safe."

Fireheart was amazed at how much Lostface trusted Cloudtail. She was obviously terrified by the thought of venturing outside the shelter of the camp. She jumped at every sound, every crackle of leaves under her paws, yet she kept going, and Fireheart thought he saw in her a return of the courage she had shown when she was Brightpaw.

When they came in sight of the fence at the end of the Twoleg gardens, Fireheart signaled with his tail for his companions to stop. He could not see Princess, but when he opened his mouth to taste the air, he caught her scent.

"Wait here," he told the others. "Keep a lookout and call me if there's trouble."

Checking again to make sure there were no fresh scents of dogs or Twolegs, he raced across the stretch of open ground and leaped up to the top of Princess's fence. A flash of white among the bushes in her garden alerted him, and a moment later his sister appeared, picking her way fastidiously across the wet grass.

"Princess!" he called softly.

Princess halted and looked up. As soon as she saw Fireheart she bounded over to the fence and scrambled up to sit beside him.

"Fireheart!" she purred, pressing herself against him. "It's so good to see you! How are you?"

"I'm fine," Fireheart replied. "I've brought you some visitors—look."

He pointed with his tail to where the other three cats were crouching on the edge of the trees.

"There's Cloudpaw!" Princess exclaimed delightedly. "But who are the others?"

"That big gray tom is my friend Graystripe," Fireheart told her. "You don't need to worry—he's much gentler than he looks. And the other cat"— he flinched—"is called Lostface."

"Lostface!" Princess echoed, opening her eyes wide. "What a horrible name! Why did they call her that?"

"You'll see," Fireheart mewed grimly. "She's been badly hurt, so be kind to her."

He jumped down from the fence, and after a moment's hesitation Princess followed him and padded across to where the three cats waited.

Cloudtail ran out to meet his mother, leaving Graystripe with Lostface, and touched noses with her.

"Cloudpaw, it's ages since I've seen you," Princess purred. "You're looking wonderful, and haven't you grown?"

"You've got to call me Cloudtail now," her son announced. "I'm a warrior."

Princess let out a little trill of joy. "A warrior already? Cloudtail, I'm so proud of you!"

While the tabby queen eagerly questioned her son about his life in the Clan, Fireheart did not forget that danger might be near. "We can't stay long," he meowed. "Princess, have you heard anything about a dog loose in the forest?"

Princess turned to him, her eyes wide and scared. "A dog? No, I don't know anything about that."

"I think that might have been what the Twolegs were looking for that day Sandstorm and I met you in Tallpines," Fireheart went on. "I don't think you should come into the forest alone anymore, not for the time being, anyway. It's too dangerous."

"Then you're in danger all the time," mewed Princess. Her voice rose in distress. "Oh, Fireheart . . . !"

"There's nothing for you to worry about." Fireheart tried to sound confident. "Just stay in your garden. The dog won't bother you there."

"But I worry about you, Fireheart, and Cloudtail. You haven't got a nest to—Oh!"

Princess had just caught sight of Lostface's damaged side and could not restrain a squeak of horror. Lostface heard her and crouched closer to the ground, uneasiness showing in her bristling fur.

"Come and meet Lostface," Cloudtail meowed, giving his mother a hard stare.

Nervously Princess took the few paces that brought her to where Graystripe and Lostface waited. Graystripe nodded to her in greeting, and Lostface gazed up at her with her one good eye.

"Oh, my goodness, whatever happened to you?" Princess blurted out, her paws working on the ground.

"Lostface went out to tackle the dog," Cloudtail answered. "She was very brave."

"And it did that to you? Oh, you poor thing!" Princess's eyes were huger still as she took in the full horror of Lostface's injuries—the ravaged face, the lost eye, and the shredded ear. "And the same thing could happen to any of you. . . ."

Fireheart gritted his teeth. His sister was saying all the wrong things, and Lostface was gazing at her with deep sadness in her remaining eye. Cloudtail pressed his flank against her and nosed her comfortingly.

"It's time we were going," Fireheart decided. "Cloudtail

just wanted to give you his news. You'd better get back into your garden."

"Yes—yes, I will." Princess backed away, her eyes still fixed on Lostface. "You'll come and see me again, Fireheart?"

"As soon as I can," he promised, and added silently, *alone*.

Princess retreated another pace or two, then turned and dashed for her fence, swarming up it and pausing briefly on the top to meow, "Good-bye!" before vanishing into the safety of her garden.

Cloudtail let out a long breath. "That went well," he meowed bitterly.

"You can't blame Princess," Fireheart told him. "She doesn't really understand what Clan life is all about. She's just seen some of the worst of it, and she doesn't like it."

Graystripe grunted. "What can you expect from a kittypet? Let's get home."

Cloudtail gently nosed Lostface. As she got to her paws, the young cat mewed timidly, "Cloudtail, Princess looked as if she were scared of me. I want—" She broke off, swallowed, and began again. "I want to see myself. Is there a puddle nearby I can look into?"

Fireheart felt a pang of sorrow for the young she-cat, and admiration at her courage in facing what she had become. He turned his eyes to Cloudtail, willing to be guided by the younger cat on what they should do next.

Cloudtail looked around for a moment, then pressed his muzzle against Lostface's shoulder. "Come with me," he meowed. He led her to where some of the previous night's rain still lay in a puddle among the roots of a tree, and nudged the ginger-and-white she-cat to the edge of the shining water. Together they stood looking down. Cloudtail did not flinch away from what he saw reflected there, and Fireheart felt another rush of warmth toward his former apprentice.

Lostface stood rigid for several heartbeats, gazing into the water. Her body stiffened and her single eye opened wide. "Now I see," she mewed quietly. "I'm sorry if the other cats feel upset when they look at me."

Fireheart watched as Cloudtail turned her away from the terrible sight and covered the injured side of her face with slow, gentle licks. "You're still beautiful to me," he told her. "You always will be."

Fireheart felt almost overwhelmed by his pity for the young she-cat, and his pride in Cloudtail for being so faithful to her. Padding over to them, he meowed, "Lostface, it doesn't matter what you look like. We're still your friends."

Lostface dipped her head to him gratefully.

"Lostface!" Cloudtail spat suddenly. The venom in his voice startled Fireheart. "I hate that name," he hissed. "What right does Bluestar have to remind her of what happened every time a cat speaks to her? Well, I'm not going to use it again. And if Bluestar objects, she can . . . she can go and eat snails!"

Fireheart knew he ought to rebuke the young warrior for his disrespectful words, but he said nothing. He had a good deal of sympathy for Cloudtail's point of view. Lostface *was* a cruel name, a symbol of Bluestar's continuing war with

StarClan, given without any thought for the cat who bore it. But the name had been given to the ginger-and-white she-cat in a formal ceremony watched by StarClan, and there was nothing Fireheart could do about it now.

"Are we standing about here all day?" Graystripe asked.

Fireheart heaved a deep sigh. "No, let's go." The time was coming when he and his warriors would have to confront whatever had turned them into prey in their own territory.

Fireheart dreamed he was padding through a forest clearing in newleaf. Sunlight streamed through the trees, making dappled patterns of light and shade that shifted as the leaves stirred in the breeze. He paused and opened his mouth so that he could taste the air. Very faintly he made out a familiar sweet scent, and a quiver of happiness ran through him.

"Spottedleaf?" he whispered. "Spottedleaf, are you there?"

For a moment he thought he could see bright eyes shining at him from the depths of a clump of ferns. Warm breath caressed his ear, and a voice murmured, "Fireheart, remember the enemy that never sleeps."

Then the vision faded, and he woke to find himself in the warrior's den with the cold light of a day in leaf-bare striking him through the branches.

Still clutching at the last sheds of his dream, Fireheart stretched and shook scraps of moss from his fur. It was several moons since Spottedleaf had first warned him to beware of the enemy that never slept. That had been shortly before Tigerstar attacked the ThunderClan camp with his band of rogues—just when Fireheart had hoped that the treacherous deputy's exile had sent him away for good.

The thought of Tigerstar reminded Fireheart of the most recent Gathering. There was no doubt now that the former deputy wanted Bramblepaw and Tawnypaw, and in spite of what he said to Bluestar, Fireheart was sure that he would not be prepared to wait. Even though Fireheart was not surprised at Tigerstar's demand, there could be no question of handing them over. Part of Fireheart would have been relieved to see them go, to put an end to his own feelings of mistrust and guilt, but these were *ThunderClan* kits, and the warrior code demanded that the Clan should do everything to keep them.

A rustle in the bedding behind him told Fireheart that Sandstorm was waking up. He cast an uneasy glance at her. "Sandstorm . . . " he began.

The ginger she-cat glared at him as she shook herself and stood up. "I'm going hunting," she spat. "That's what you want, isn't it?" Without waiting for a reply, she padded across the den and prodded Dustpelt. "Come on, you lazy furball," she meowed. "All the prey will die of old age before you get out there."

"I'll find Cloudtail for you," Fireheart offered hastily, and slipped out of the den. Sandstorm clearly wasn't going to welcome any attempt to be friendly.

The day was gray and cold, and as he paused to taste the air a drop of rain stung him in the face. On the far side of the clearing Bramblepaw and Tawnypaw were sitting with the other apprentices outside their den. "Bramblepaw,

I'll take you hunting later!" Fireheart called.

His apprentice got to his paws, dipped his head in acknowledgment, and sat down again with his back to Fireheart. Fireheart sighed. Sometimes it felt as if every cat in the Clan had a reason to dislike him.

He headed for the elders' den, guessing that Cloudtail would be with Lostface. Even though the injured cat had been in the elders' den for a few days now, Cloudtail still spent all his spare time with her. When Fireheart reached the burned-out shell of the fallen tree where the elders lived, he saw the white tom seated near the entrance to the den. His tail was curled around his paws while he watched Lostface gently examining Dappletail's pelt for ticks.

"Is she okay?" Fireheart murmured, his voice low so that Lostface would not hear him.

"Of course she's okay," another voice snapped.

Fireheart turned to see Speckletail. The desolate look that she had worn since Snowkit's death had vanished. Her temper clearly hadn't softened, but her eyes glowed with affection as she looked at Lostface. "She's a fine young cat. Have you found out what hurt her?"

Fireheart shook his head. "It's a real help that you can look after her, Speckletail," he meowed.

Speckletail sniffed. "Hmmm. I sometimes get the feeling that she thinks *she* has to look after *me*." She looked sharply at Fireheart, and he was saved from having to answer by One-eye.

"Did you want something, Fireheart?" asked the elderly pale gray she-cat, looking up from her washing.

"I was looking for Cloudtail. Sandstorm's ready to go out hunting."

"What?" Cloudtail sprang to his paws. "Why didn't you say so? She'll claw my ears off if I keep her waiting!" He dashed off.

"Mouse-brain," muttered Speckletail, but Fireheart suspected that she was as fond of the young warrior as all the elders.

Saying good-bye to Lostface and One-eye, he padded into the clearing in time to see Sandstorm leaving at the head of her hunting patrol. Brindleface was saying good-bye to them, gazing proudly at her foster kit.

"You will be careful, won't you?" she mewed anxiously. "None of us know what's out there."

"Don't worry." Cloudtail flicked her affectionately with his tail. "If we meet the dog, I'll bring it back for fresh-kill."

At the entrance to the camp the patrol passed Longtail on his way in. The pale warrior was shaking as if with cold, and his eyes were staring. Instantly alarmed, Fireheart crossed the clearing to meet him.

"What's happened?" he asked.

Longtail shuddered. "Fireheart, there's something I have to tell you."

"What's the problem?"

As he drew closer, Fireheart caught an unexpected scent on Longtail's fur—the stench of the Thunderpath. The acrid scent was unmistakable, and Fireheart's alarm turned to suspicion.

"Where have you been?" he growled. "To ShadowClan, maybe, to see Tigerstar? Don't try to deny it; your fur stinks of the Thunderpath!"

"Fireheart, it's not what you think." Longtail sounded worried. "Okay, I did go that way, but I didn't go anywhere near ShadowClan. I went to Snakerocks."

"Snakerocks? What for?" Fireheart wasn't sure that he could believe anything the pale warrior told him.

"I've scented Tigerstar there," Longtail explained. "Two or three times lately."

"And you didn't report it?" Fireheart felt his fur bristle with fury. "A cat from another Clan on our territory—a murderer and a traitor, what's more—and you didn't report it?"

"I . . . I thought . . ." stammered Longtail.

"I know what you thought," Fireheart snarled. "You thought, 'This is Tigerstar. He can do what he likes.' Don't lie to me. You and Darkstripe were his allies when he was in ThunderClan, and you're still his allies now. It was you or Darkstripe who told him about Swiftpaw and Lostface— don't try to deny it."

"It was Darkstripe." Longtail scuffled the dry earth with his paws.

"So that traitor could accuse Bluestar of negligence in front of the entire Gathering," Fireheart concluded grimly. "So you could help him steal a couple of apprentices from this Clan. That's it, isn't it? You're plotting with Tigerstar to steal his kits."

"No—no, you've got it wrong," meowed Longtail. "I don't

know anything about that. Darkstripe and Tigerstar often meet together on the border by the Thunderpath, but they don't tell me what it's about." He glared resentfully. "Anyway, this isn't about the kits at all. I went to Snakerocks to find out what Tigerstar was doing there. And I found something that you need to see."

Fireheart stared at him. "You want me to come with you, to Snakerocks—where you admit you've scented Tigerstar? Do you think I'm quite mad?"

"But, Fireheart—"

"Silence!" Fireheart hissed. "You and Darkstripe were always Tigerstar's allies. Why should I trust what you say now?"

He turned and stalked away. He was convinced that Longtail and Darkstripe were setting a trap for him, just as Tigerstar had once set a trap for Bluestar beside the Thunderpath. If he were mouse-brained enough to go with Longtail to Snakerocks, he might never come back.

He found that his paws had taken him to the medicine cat's clearing. As he brushed through the ferns, Cinderpelt put her head out of the cleft in the rock.

"Who—Fireheart! What's the matter?"

Fireheart halted, trying to get his anger under control.

Cinderpelt's blue eyes widened in consternation; she padded to his side and pressed her gray flank against him. "Steady, Fireheart. What got you worked up like this?"

"It's just . . ." Fireheart flicked his tail toward the main clearing. "Longtail. I'm convinced he and Darkstripe are plotting against the Clan."

Cinderpelt narrowed her eyes. "What makes you think that?"

"Longtail wants to lure me out to Snakerocks. He told me he scented Tigerstar there. I think they're setting a trap for me."

Dismay spread over the medicine cat's face, but when she spoke her words were not what Fireheart had expected.

"Fireheart—do you know how much you sound like Bluestar?"

Fireheart opened his mouth to reply, and could not. What did Cinderpelt mean? He was *nothing* like Bluestar, with her irrational fears that every cat in the Clan was trying to betray her. Or was he? He forced himself to relax, letting the fur on his shoulders lie flat again.

"Come on, Fireheart," Cinderpelt urged. "If he meant to lead you into a trap with Tigerstar, would he *tell* you he'd scented him? Even Longtail isn't as mouse-brained as that!"

"I . . . suppose not," Fireheart admitted reluctantly.

"Then why don't you go and ask him what it's all about?" As he hesitated, she added, "I know he and Darkstripe were Tigerstar's friends when he was here, but Longtail at least seems to be loyal to the Clan now. Besides, if he *is* tempted to betray the Clan, you won't help by refusing to listen when he tries to tell you something. That's just pushing him into Tigerstar's paws."

"I know." Fireheart sighed. "I'm sorry, Cinderpelt."

Cinderpelt let out a little purr and touched her nose to his. "Go and talk to him. I'll come with you."

Bracing himself, Fireheart headed out into the clearing again, looking around for Longtail. A chill ran through him as he realized that he might have already driven the pale warrior out in search of Tigerstar, but when he checked the warriors' den he was there, crouched in a huddle with Whitestorm.

"Whitestorm, you've got to listen to me," Longtail was meowing as Fireheart and Cinderpelt entered. There was real fear in his voice. "Fireheart thinks I'm a traitor, and he won't have anything to do with me."

"Well, it seems like you've been meeting Tigerstar and telling him our news," Whitestorm pointed out reasonably.

"Not *me*—Darkstripe," Longtail protested.

Whitestorm shrugged, as if he weren't interested in arguing. "All right, go on. What's the problem?"

"There are dogs living at Snakerocks," Longtail blurted out.

"Dogs? Have you seen them?" Fireheart interrupted. Both his warriors looked up as he padded over to them, with Cinderpelt just behind.

"You're sure you want to hear?" Longtail said accusingly. "You're not going to charge me with plotting again, are you?"

"I'm sorry about that," Fireheart mewed. "Tell me about the dog."

"*Dogs*, Fireheart," meowed Longtail. "A whole pack of them." Fireheart's blood turned to ice at the word *pack*, but he said nothing, and Longtail went on. "I told you I scented Tigerstar over at Snakerocks. I . . . I thought I should warn him about the danger there—and I wanted to know what he was doing so far into ThunderClan territory. Well, I found out." He shuddered.

"Go on," Fireheart urged. He realized how wrong he had been; Longtail really did have important news to report.

"You know the caves?" Longtail meowed. "I was just coming up to them when I saw Tigerstar, but he didn't see me. I thought he was stealing prey at first because he was dragging a dead rabbit along, but he left it on the ground just outside the cave entrance." He broke off, his eyes clouding with terror as he saw again something unseen by the other cats.

"And then?" Whitestorm prompted.

"Then this . . . this creature appeared out of the cave. I swear it was the biggest dog I've ever seen. Forget the stupid things that come with Twolegs. This was *huge*. I only saw its front paws and its head . . . enormous slavering jaws, and you've never seen such teeth." Longtail's eyes were wide with the memory of fear.

"It snatched the rabbit and dragged it into the cave," he continued. "And then the howling and barking started. It sounded as if there were more dogs in there, all fighting over the rabbit. It was hard to understand what they were saying, but I think they were saying 'pack, pack' and 'kill, kill.'"

Fireheart stiffened, every limb locked in terror, and Cinderpelt mewed quietly, "Those were the words in my dream."

"And what Lostface said," Fireheart added. He knew at last what terrible creatures had attacked the young she-cat. He remembered that StarClan had warned Bluestar about a pack. Longtail had discovered the true nature of the evil in the forest, the force that had turned the cats into prey, the hunters into hunted. Not a single dog, separated from its Twolegs, but a whole pack of savage creatures. Fireheart could not imagine where they had come from, but he knew that StarClan would *never* have unleashed such destruction and risked the balance of life in the whole forest. "And you say Tigerstar *fed* these dogs?" he questioned Longtail. "What does he think he's doing?"

"I don't know," the pale warrior admitted. "When he dropped the rabbit, he jumped on top of the rock. I don't think the first dog saw him. Then he went away."

"You didn't speak to him?"

"*No*, Fireheart, I didn't. He never knew I was there. I'll swear by anything you like—by StarClan, by the life of Bluestar—I don't know what Tigerstar is doing."

His fear convinced Fireheart. He had been expecting an attempt by Tigerstar to steal the kits, but this was something far more complicated. How could he ever have imagined that the ShadowClan leader would give up his grudge against ThunderClan? He realized that he should have been more afraid of Tigerstar all along. Somehow he was linked to the dark force in the forest. Yet Fireheart didn't know what Tigerstar wanted with the dogs, or what advantage he could gain by feeding them.

"What do you think?" he asked Whitestorm.

"I think we need to investigate," meowed the older warrior

grimly. "And I'm just wondering how much Darkstripe knows about all this."

"So am I," agreed Fireheart. "But I'm not going to ask him. If he *is* in league with Tigerstar, he won't tell us anything useful." Rounding on Longtail, he added, "Don't you *dare* say a word to Darkstripe about this. Stay away from him."

"I . . . I will, Fireheart," the pale warrior stammered.

"We still need to know why Tigerstar is taking such an enormous risk, feeding fresh-kill to these dogs," Whitestorm went on. "If you want to lead a patrol up to Snakerocks, I'll come with you."

Fireheart looked upward, judging the light. "It's too late today," he decided. "By the time we reached Snakerocks, it would be getting dark. But we'll go at dawn tomorrow. I'll find out what Tigerstar thinks he's up to, if it's the last thing I do."

CHAPTER 24

Fireheart emerged from the warriors' den and paused. He gazed across the clearing to where Sandstorm was crouched by the nettle patch, gulping down a piece of fresh-kill. He had chosen some of the warriors he wanted to come with him to Snakerocks, but so far he had not spoken to Sandstorm. He was reluctant to risk her life on this dangerous mission, and afraid that she would refuse to come if it meant following his orders. Yet he knew that he could not imagine going without her.

Taking a deep breath, he padded over to the nettle patch and sat down beside her.

Sandstorm swallowed the last mouthful of squirrel. "Fireheart? What is it?"

Quietly Fireheart told her what Longtail had discovered at Snakerocks. "I want you to come with us," he told her. "You're fast and brave, and the Clan needs you."

The she-cat turned her green gaze on him, but Fireheart could not read the expression there.

"I need you," he blurted out, afraid she was about to refuse. "For Bluestar's sake, as well as the Clan's. I know things haven't been right between us ever since I stopped the battle with WindClan. But I trust you. Whatever you think about me, do it for the Clan."

Sandstorm nodded slowly. She was looking thoughtful, and a small seed of hope began to grow in Fireheart's heart. "I know why you didn't want to fight WindClan," she began. "In a way, I thought you were right. But it was hard to know you had gone behind Bluestar's back without telling the rest of us."

"I know, but—"

"But you're the deputy," Sandstorm interrupted, reaching one paw toward him for silence. "You have responsibilities the rest of us can't understand. And I can see how torn you must have felt—between loyalty to Bluestar and loyalty to the Clan." Hesitating, staring down at her paws, she added, "I was torn too. I wanted to be loyal to the warrior code, and I wanted to be loyal to you, Fireheart."

Fireheart felt too full of emotion to answer. He stretched out his head to press against her flank, and to his delight she did not move away. Instead she looked up at him again, and he felt as if he were drowning in the depths of her green gaze. "I'm sorry, Sandstorm," he murmured. "I never meant to hurt you." His voice barely more than a whisper, he added, "I love you."

Sandstorm's eyes glowed. "I love you too, Fireheart," she whispered. "That's why it hurt so much when you asked Bluestar if Brackenfur could mentor Tawnypaw. I thought you didn't respect me."

"I made a mistake." Fireheart's voice shook. "I don't know

how I could have been so mouse-brained."

Sandstorm let out a purr and touched her nose to his.

"I want you beside me always." Fireheart breathed in her scent, rejoicing in the warmth of her body. He suddenly felt that he would always be happy if he could stay like that forever.

But he knew that he could not. "Sandstorm," he told her, lifting his head. "I know what we're going to face out there. It's more dangerous than I ever imagined. I'm not ordering you to come, but I still want you with me."

Sandstorm's purr grew deeper, a vibration that filled her whole body. "Of course I'm coming, you stupid furball," she mewed.

Fireheart set a double watch on the camp that night and kept vigil himself in the center of the clearing. A growing sense of horror crept over him as he listened to the wind sighing through the bare trees. It seemed to carry Spotted-leaf's voice to him, murmuring about the enemy that never slept: Tigerstar, the dogs—or both. The enemy was about to unleash its fury, and no cat was safe. The next day, Fireheart knew, could see the final destruction of his Clan.

As he watched the moon above him, barely waning from the full, Cinderpelt emerged from her den and padded across the clearing to sit beside him.

"If you're leading a patrol tomorrow, you should get some sleep," she advised. "You'll need your strength."

"I know," Fireheart agreed. "But I don't think I could sleep." He raised his eyes to the moon again and the glittering stars of Silverpelt. "It looks so peaceful up there. But down here . . ."

"Yes," murmured Cinderpelt. "Down here I can feel the evil growing. The forest is dark with it, and StarClan cannot help us. It's up to us."

"So you really don't believe that StarClan has sent this pack to punish us?"

Cinderpelt met his gaze, her eyes shining with the reflected light of the moon. "No, Fireheart, I don't." She leaned toward him and let her muzzle brush lightly against the side of his face. "You're not alone, Fireheart," she promised. "I'm with you. And so is the rest of the Clan."

Fireheart hoped she was right. The Clan would survive only if it united and faced this dark threat together. They had supported him in the battle that wasn't fought against WindClan, but would they join him in facing the pack?

After a few moments Cinderpelt asked, "What will you tell Bluestar?"

"Nothing," Fireheart replied. "Not until we've had a look around, at least. There's no point in upsetting her. She doesn't have the strength to cope with this—not now."

Cinderpelt murmured agreement. She kept watch with him in silence until the moon began to set. Then she meowed, "Fireheart, I'm telling you as your medicine cat that you need to rest. What happens tomorrow could determine the very future of this Clan, and we need all our warriors to be at full strength."

Reluctantly Fireheart had to admit that she was right. Giving Cinderpelt's ear a farewell lick, he got to his paws, padded off to the warriors' den, and curled himself into the moss beside Sandstorm. But his sleep was broken, and his dreams were dark. Once he thought he saw Spottedleaf bounding toward him, and his heart lifted in joy, but before she reached him she turned into a huge dog with gaping jaws and eyes like flames. Fireheart woke, shuddering, to see that the first light of dawn was beginning to seep into the sky. *This could be the last dawn I'll ever see*, he thought. *Death waits for us out there.*

Then as he raised his head he saw that Sandstorm was sitting beside him, watching over him while he slept. As he saw the love in her eyes he felt new strength flowing through his limbs. He sat up and gave the she-cat's ear a gentle lick. "It's time," he meowed.

Bracing himself, he roused the cats he had chosen the evening before for his patrol to Snakerocks. Cloudtail almost leaped out of his nest, his tail lashing fiercely at the thought of confronting the creatures who had injured Lostface.

Brindleface, who had been sleeping close to the young warrior, awoke with him and followed him to the edge of the den. "May StarClan go with you," she mewed, grooming the scraps of moss out of his fur.

Cloudtail pressed his muzzle against hers. "Don't worry,"

he assured his foster mother. "I'll tell you all about it when I come back."

Fireheart woke Whitestorm and then padded across the den to where Graystripe lay curled up in a pile of heather. Prodding him with one paw, he murmured, "Come on."

Graystripe blinked and sat up. "This is just like the old days," he mewed, in a vain attempt to sound cheerful. "You and me, charging into danger again." He pushed his forehead against Fireheart's shoulder. "Thanks for choosing me, Fireheart. I'm scared stiff, but I'll prove that I'm loyal to ThunderClan, I promise."

Fireheart pressed against him briefly and left the gray warrior to have a quick wash while he went to wake Longtail. The pale warrior shivered as he crawled out of his nest, but his eyes were determined. "I'll show you that you can trust me," he promised quietly.

Fireheart nodded, still half-ashamed that he hadn't listened to Longtail the night before. "The Clan needs you, Longtail," he meowed. "Far more than Tigerstar and Darkstripe need you, believe me."

Longtail brightened at that and followed Fireheart with the other warriors out to the nettle patch. They gulped down fresh-kill while Fireheart quickly reminded them of what Longtail had told him the day before. "We're going to investigate," he meowed. "We can't decide how to get rid of these dogs until we know exactly what we have to face. We're not going to attack them, not yet—have you got that, Cloudtail?"

Cloudtail's blue eyes burned into his, and he did not reply.

"I won't take you, Cloudtail, unless you promise to do as you're told without question."

"Oh, all right." The tip of Cloudtail's tail flicked irritably. "I want every last dog turned into crowfood, but I'll do it your way, Fireheart."

"Good." Fireheart's gaze swept over the rest of the patrol. "Any questions?"

"What if we come across Tigerstar?" asked Sandstorm.

"A cat from another Clan on our territory?" Fireheart bared his teeth. "Yes, you can attack *him*."

Cloudtail let out a growl of satisfaction.

Gulping down the last of his fresh-kill, Fireheart led the way out of the camp and up the ravine. Although the sun had nearly risen, clouds covered the sky, and shadows still lay thick among the trees. There was a strong smell of rabbit not far from the camp, but Fireheart ignored it. There was no time to hunt.

The warriors advanced warily in single file with Fireheart in the lead and Whitestorm keeping watch at the rear. After what he had learned from Longtail, Fireheart felt even more strongly that the familiar forest had become full of danger, and his fur prickled with the expectation of attack.

All was quiet until they drew close to Snakerocks. Fireheart was just considering the best way to approach the caves when Graystripe mewed, "What's that?"

He plunged into a clump of dead bracken. A moment later

Fireheart heard his voice, strained and hoarse. "Come and look at this."

Fireheart followed the sound and found Graystripe crouched over a dead rabbit. Its throat had been torn out, and its fur was stiff with dried blood.

"The pack have been killing again," Longtail mewed grimly.

"Then why didn't they eat the prey?" asked Sandstorm, coming up to sniff at the limp, gray-brown body. She sniffed again. "Fireheart, there's ShadowClan scent here!"

Fireheart opened his jaws and drew the forest breeze over the glands in the roof of his mouth. Sandstorm was right. The scent was faint but unmistakable. "Tigerstar killed this rabbit," he murmured, "and then left it here. What for, I wonder?"

He remembered how Longtail had reported seeing Tigerstar feeding the pack with rabbit, and the reek of rabbit that had followed them all the way from the ThunderClan camp. Backing away from the prey, he summoned Cloudtail with a flick of his tail. "Go back along the way we came," he instructed. "You're looking for dead rabbits. If you find any, check for other scents, and then come and tell me. White-storm, you go with him."

He watched the two warriors retreat and then turned to Graystripe. "Stay here and guard this. Sandstorm, Longtail, come with me."

Even more cautiously now, pausing to taste the air every few steps, Fireheart drew closer to Snakerocks. It wasn't long before they discovered another dead rabbit lying exposed on a rock, with the same betraying scent of Tigerstar lingering around it. By this time they were in sight of the mouth of the cave. Fireheart could just make out the shape of yet another rabbit lying at the edge of the open space in front of it. There was no sign of the pack.

"Where are the dogs?" he muttered.

"In that cave," replied Longtail. "That's where I saw Tigerstar leave the rabbit yesterday."

"When they come out, they'll see the rabbit over there, and they'll scent this one. . . ." Fireheart was thinking aloud. "And then there's the one Graystripe found . . . " Understanding hit him like a rock and he could scarcely breathe for fear. "I *know* what Whitestorm and Cloudtail will find. Tigerstar has laid a trail straight back to the camp."

Longtail crouched down on the forest floor and Sandstorm's eyes stretched wide with horror. "You mean that he wants to bring the pack right to us?"

Pictures flashed through Fireheart's mind of massive, slavering dogs racing down the sides of the ravine and breaking through the fern wall into the peaceful camp. He could see jaws snapping, limp feline bodies tossed high in the air, kits wailing as cruel teeth reached for them. . . . He shuddered. "Yes. Come on; we have to break the trail!"

Not even an order from StarClan themselves could have made Fireheart try to retrieve the rabbit that was close to the cave mouth. But he snatched up the one that lay on the rock and bounded back to where he had left Graystripe. He set down his burden long enough to meow, "Bring that rabbit. We have to warn the Clan."

Ears pricked in amazement, Graystripe obeyed. They headed back toward the camp, and before they had traveled more than a few fox-lengths Fireheart spotted Cloudtail and Whitestorm coming to meet them, slipping warily through the undergrowth.

"We've found two more rabbits," Cloudtail reported. "Both stinking of Tigerstar."

"Then go and fetch them." Rapidly Fireheart explained what he suspected. "We'll dump them in a stream somewhere and break the trail."

"That's all very well," Whitestorm meowed. "You can shift the rabbits, but what about the scent?"

Fireheart froze. Fear was making him stupid, he realized. The rabbit scent and spilled blood would still lead the pack straight to the ThunderClan camp.

"We'll move the rabbits anyway," he decided swiftly. "That might slow the dogs up. But we've got to get back and warn the Clan. They'll have to leave the camp."

Racing through the forest, ears pricked for the sound of the pack behind them, they headed for the camp. Soon they had more rabbits than they could carry. Tigerstar must have hunted all night to catch this many, Fireheart thought grimly.

"Let's leave them all here," Sandstorm suggested when they were still some way from the ravine. Her flanks heaved as she gasped for breath, and she had torn a claw, but her eyes glittered with determination, and Fireheart knew that she would run forever if he asked her to. "If the dogs find a good meal, they'll stop to eat it."

"Good idea," Fireheart meowed.

"It might have been better to leave them closer to the cave," Whitestorm pointed out, his eyes dark with worry. "That might have stopped the dogs' coming to the camp at all."

"True," Fireheart replied, "but there isn't time. The dogs could be on their way already. We don't want to meet them."

Whitestorm nodded agreement. They left the heap of rabbits in full view on the trail and sprinted on. Fireheart felt his heart pounding wildly. He should have known his old enemy would be connected with the dark force that threatened the forest. Only StarClan knew how Tigerstar had found out that the dogs were at Snakerocks, but he was using them to destroy the Clan he hated. As he dashed through the trees, Fireheart was afraid that it might be too late to stop him.

At the top of the ravine, he paused. "Spread out," he ordered his warriors. "Make sure there's no fresh-kill close to the camp."

They headed down the ravine, ranging from side to side. Cloudtail drew ahead, and not far from the entrance Fireheart saw him stop dead. He was staring down at something on the ground.

"No! No!" His voice was an earsplitting yowl, and Fireheart's fur bristled in horror.

"No!" Cloudtail yowled again. "Fireheart!"

Fireheart dashed to the warrior's side. Cloudtail was standing stiff-legged, every hair in his pelt on end as if he were facing an enemy. His eyes were fixed on the limp heap of tabby fur huddled at his paws.

"Why, Fireheart?" Cloudtail wailed. "Why her?"

Fireheart knew, but rage and grief made it hard to speak. "Because Tigerstar wants the pack to get a taste for cat blood," he rasped.

The dead cat lying in front of them was Brindleface.

CHAPTER 25

Cloudtail and Sandstorm carried Brindleface's body back to the camp, but there was no time for the mourning rituals. Apparently she had gone out hunting alone very early, and the other cats had only just noticed that she was taking a long time to return. Her burial was a hurried affair, carried out by Cloudtail and her two kits, Fernpaw and Ashpaw, while Fireheart summoned the Clan together.

They returned as Fireheart stood at the foot of the Highrock waiting for the rest of the cats to gather. Cloudtail paced back and forth, his tail lashing fiercely.

"I'll *flay* Tigerstar!" he vowed. "I'll scatter his entrails from here to Highstones. He's mine, Fireheart, and don't you forget it."

"And don't you forget that you're under my orders," Fireheart told him. "Right now we have to deal with the dog pack. We'll worry about Tigerstar later."

Cloudtail bared his teeth with a hiss of frustration, but did not argue.

Meanwhile the rest of the Clan were huddling in a shocked and silent crowd around Fireheart. Cinderpelt appeared from

Bluestar's den and limped rapidly across to him.

"Bluestar's asleep," she meowed. "Better to tell her about this when we've worked out a plan, don't you think?"

Fireheart nodded, wondering how his leader would react when she found out that all her fears about Tigerstar were true. Would the dreadful knowledge drive her into madness once and for all? Pushing his fear aside, Fireheart turned to address the Clan. "Cats of ThunderClan," he began. "This morning we discovered that there's a pack of dogs on our territory, living in the caves at Snakerocks."

Murmuring broke out among the assembled cats, along with a few yowls of defiance. Fireheart guessed that they scarcely believed him, but there was worse news to come. He couldn't help staring at Darkstripe, but the dark warrior's expression was unreadable, and Fireheart had no idea how much he already knew.

"Tigerstar has been feeding the dogs," he went on, struggling to keep his voice calm, "and he has laid a trail of dead rabbits to lead them right into our camp. You all know what lay at the end of that trail." He dipped his head toward the place outside the camp where Brindleface had been buried.

He had to signal with his tail for silence as a chorus of wailing broke out. He couldn't help noticing Goldenflower crouched with her head down as she listened to what Tigerstar had done, and he looked instinctively for the two newest apprentices. Tawnypaw was staring at him with horror in her face, but Bramblepaw's face was hidden. Fireheart wondered if he was equally shocked, or if part of him admired his father for carrying out such a bold plan.

When he could make himself heard again, Fireheart went on: "We have tried to break the trail, but the rabbits have lain there all night, and the pack will follow the scent they left behind. We must all leave—elders, kits, everyone. If the dogs come to the camp they must not find us here."

More sounds of dismay, this time a low, anxious murmuring. Dappletail, an aged, once-pretty tortoiseshell she-cat, called out, "Where shall we go?"

"To Sunningrocks," Fireheart replied. "Once you're there, climb the tallest trees you can find. If the dogs follow you, they'll think they lost the scent on the rocks, and they won't look for you."

To his relief, the Clan grew quieter now that he had given them definite orders, though the cats still crouched in grief for Brindleface. Her kits, the apprentices Fernpaw and Ashpaw, were pressed close together with looks of stunned horror on their faces. Fireheart thanked StarClan that the day, although gray and chilly, was dry, and that there were no sick cats or very young kits to make the journey.

"And what about the pack?" Dustpelt asked. "What are we going to do about them?"

Fireheart hesitated. He knew the pack was too strong for his warriors to attack directly. Tigerstar would never have led them to the camp unless he had been certain of that. *StarClan help me*, he prayed silently. As though his warrior ancestors had heard him, an idea flashed into his mind. "That's it!" he whispered. "We'll steal the trail." As the cats close by stared at him, he repeated more loudly, "We'll steal the trail!"

"What do you mean?" Sandstorm asked, her green eyes wide.

"Just what I say. Tigerstar wants to lead the dogs right to our camp. Fine. We'll let him do that. And when they arrive, we'll be waiting—to take them to the gorge."

Not far from Fourtrees, on the far side of ThunderClan's territory, the river foamed between sheer-sided cliffs. The current was fast and strong, and there were sharp rocks concealed just under the surface. If cats had drowned there, why not dogs?

"We'll need to lure the dogs over the edge," Fireheart went on, the details of the plan taking shape in his mind as he spoke. "I'll need warriors who can run fast." His dark green gaze swept the cats around him. "Graystripe. Sandstorm. Mousefur and Longtail. Dustpelt. And I'm going myself. That should be enough. The rest of you gather by the camp entrance, ready to move out."

As the cats he had not named began to obey his orders, Fireheart saw Fernpaw and Ashpaw pushing their way to the front of the crowd.

"Fireheart, we want to help," Fernpaw begged, fixing her shocked, pleading eyes on Fireheart.

"I said warriors," Fireheart reminded her gently.

"But Brindleface was our mother," protested Ashpaw. "Please, Fireheart. We want to do it for her."

"Yes, take them with you," Whitestorm put in, his voice grave. "Their anger will make them fearless."

Fireheart hesitated, then saw the intensity in the white warrior's eyes and nodded. "All right."

"And what about *me*?" Cloudtail demanded, his tail beginning to lash again.

"Listen, Cloudtail," Fireheart meowed. "I can't take all my best warriors to lure the dogs. Some of you have to look after the rest of the Clan." Cloudtail opened his mouth to argue, but Fireheart went on quickly: "I'm not giving you an easy job. If we fail, you're likely to find yourself fighting the dogs—and maybe ShadowClan as well. *Think*, Cloudtail," he urged as the warrior still looked unconvinced. "What better revenge could you take on Tigerstar than to make sure that his plans fail and that ThunderClan survives?"

Cloudtail was silent for a moment, his face twisted in grief and anger for Brindleface.

"Don't forget Lostface," Fireheart meowed quietly. "She'll need you now more than ever."

The young warrior straightened up at the mention of his injured friend and glanced across the clearing to see her limping toward the entrance, guided by Speckletail and the other elders. Her one eye was staring and her sides heaved with terror.

"Right, Fireheart." Cloudtail sounded utterly determined. "I'm on my way."

"Thank you," Fireheart called after him as he raced across the clearing to Lostface's side. "I trust you, Cloudtail."

As he watched the assembling cats, a movement beyond them caught his eye. Darkstripe was slinking through a gap in the thorn hedge, closely followed by Bramblepaw and Tawnypaw.

Fireheart shot after them and managed to catch up with them as they pushed their way through the thorns. "Darkstripe!" he snapped. "Where do you think you're going?"

The dark warrior turned. There was a flicker of alarm in his eyes, though he faced Fireheart boldly. "I don't think Sunningrocks is safe," he meowed. "I was taking these two to a better place. They—"

"What better place?" Fireheart challenged him. "If you know one, why don't you share it with the rest of the Clan? Unless you mean you're taking them to Tigerstar?" A surge of fury made him long to spring at Darkstripe and claw him, but he forced himself to stay calm. "Of course, the ShadowClan leader wouldn't want his kits to be eaten by the dog pack," he realized out loud. "You're taking them to him before the dogs get here, aren't you? I suppose you arranged all this at the last Gathering!"

Darkstripe did not reply. His expression darkened, and he would not meet Fireheart's eyes.

"Darkstripe, you disgust me," Fireheart hissed. "You knew Tigerstar meant to bring the dog pack down on us—and you never said a word to any cat! Have you no loyalty to your Clan?"

"I didn't know!" Darkstripe protested, his head swinging up. "Tigerstar told me to bring his kits to him, but he never told me why. I never knew about the pack; I swear it by StarClan!"

Fireheart wondered how much worth an oath by StarClan could possibly have in this treacherous warrior's mouth. He swung around to face the two apprentices, who were staring at him, their eyes wide and scared. "What did Darkstripe say to you?"

"N-nothing, Fireheart," stammered Tawnypaw.

"Only to go with him," her brother added. "He said he knew a good place to hide."

"And you obeyed him?" Fireheart's voice was scathing. "He's Clan leader now, is he? Or maybe some cat made him your mentor, and I didn't notice? Follow me, all of you."

Whipping around, he led the way across the clearing to where the Clan was gathering near the camp entrance. He was half-surprised to see that Darkstripe followed him, as well as Bramblepaw and Tawnypaw. Sooner or later, Fireheart knew, he would have to have a reckoning with the dark warrior, but there was no time now.

As he reached the other cats, he summoned Brackenfur with a flick of his tail. "Brackenfur," he meowed, "I'm making you responsible for these two apprentices. Don't take your eyes off them, whatever happens. And if Darkstripe so much as sniffs at them, I want to know about it."

"Yes, Fireheart," Brackenfur mewed, looking bewildered. Nudging the two apprentices, he herded them away, among the other cats.

Seeing Whitestorm close by, Fireheart padded over to him and jerked his head at Darkstripe. "Keep an eye on that one," he ordered. "I don't trust a single hair on his pelt."

Then he addressed the warriors he had chosen to run ahead of the pack. "If you haven't eaten today, I suggest you eat now," he meowed. "You'll need all your strength. We'll go soon, but first I have to talk to Bluestar."

As Fireheart turned toward Bluestar's den, he realized that Cinderpelt was beside him. "Do you want me to come with you?" she asked.

Fireheart shook his head. "No. Go and help the others get ready to leave. Do what you can to keep them calm."

"Don't worry, Fireheart," the medicine cat assured him. "I'll take a few basic remedies with me, just in case."

"Good idea," Fireheart meowed. "Get Thornpaw to help you. You can leave as soon as Bluestar is ready to join you."

When he looked into Bluestar's den, his leader was awake and grooming her fur. "Yes, Fireheart? What is it?"

Fireheart padded into the den and dipped his head. "Bluestar, we have discovered the truth about the evil in the forest," he began carefully. "We know what the 'pack' is."

Bluestar sat upright and watched Fireheart with unwavering blue eyes as he told her what he and his patrol had seen that morning. As he went on, her face grew blank with horror, and Fireheart's fears rose again that the discovery would drive her into madness.

"So Brindleface is dead," she murmured when Fireheart had finished. Bitterly she added, "Soon the rest of the Clan will follow her. StarClan have sent Tigerstar to destroy us. They will not help us now."

"Perhaps not, Bluestar, but we're not giving in," Fireheart

insisted, trying not to be panicked. "You must lead the Clan to Sunningrocks."

Bluestar's ears flicked. "And what good will that do? We can't live at Sunningrocks, and even there the pack will hunt us down."

"If my plan works, you won't be there for long. Listen." Fireheart told her how he was hoping to lure the dogs through the forest and drown them in the gorge.

His leader's gaze grew vague, fixed on something Fireheart could not see. "So you want me to go to Sunningrocks like an elder," she meowed.

Fireheart hesitated. Telling Bluestar what she should do was a lot harder than giving orders to Cloudtail. "Like a leader," he told her. "Without you there, the Clan will panic and scatter. They need you to hold them together. Besides," he added, "don't forget that this is your last life. If you lost it, what would the Clan do without you?"

Bluestar hesitated. "Very well."

"Then we should go now."

Bluestar nodded and led the way out of the den. The bulk of the Clan—all the cats Fireheart had not chosen to come with him—were already huddled together near the entrance to the camp. As Bluestar went to join them, Fireheart flicked his tail to call Whitestorm. "Stay beside her," he mewed softly. "Look after her."

Whitestorm dipped his head. "You can rely on me, Fireheart." The glance he exchanged with Fireheart showed that he understood perfectly how fragile Bluestar's mind was.

He padded at Bluestar's shoulder as she led the way out of the camp.

Seeing the white warrior, old but still vigorous, beside her, Fireheart was struck all over again by how frail his leader looked. But her presence among them would reassure the other cats, especially the elders.

When the last of the Clan had filed out into the ravine, Fireheart turned to the warriors who remained, crouched beside the burned stalks of the nettle patch. Graystripe and Sandstorm met his gaze, their eyes filled with resolution and fear in equal measure. Fireheart was reminded of the last time he had evacuated the camp, when the fire came, and how three cats had never returned.

But he knew thoughts like that would only push him into panic. He had to be strong for the sake of his Clan. Padding over to his warriors, he meowed, "Are you ready? Then let's go."

CHAPTER 26

When Fireheart reached the top of the ravine he halted and turned to Fernpaw and Ashpaw. "You two wait here," he ordered. "As soon as you see the dogs, run straight for the gorge. Sandstorm will be next in line. When you see her, climb a tree, and then when the dogs have picked up her trail and gone, head for Sunningrocks."

He looked down at the two apprentices. Their eyes gleamed with fury, grief for their mother momentarily forgotten in their desire to avenge her death. Fireheart hoped they would remember their instructions and not panic, or even worse, try to attack the dogs by themselves. "The Clan's relying on you," he added. "And we're all proud of you."

"We won't let you down," Fernpaw promised.

Fireheart left them there and led the others farther into the forest. His ears were pricked for sounds of the dogs, but for now the forest seemed to be waiting under a suffocating silence, as sinister as any howling or crashing of undergrowth. The sound of the cats' breathing and their soft pawsteps seemed unnaturally loud as they padded under the trees.

Soon Fireheart halted again. "Sandstorm, you wait here,"

he meowed. "I don't want those two apprentices to have to run too far. You're the fastest cat in ThunderClan—you'll need to get a good start on the dogs to give the rest of us a chance. Okay?"

Sandstorm nodded. "You can trust me, Fireheart."

Briefly she brushed her muzzle against his. There was no time for more words, but her love for him glowed in her green eyes, and Fireheart was filled with a wave of fear for her.

Tearing himself away, he took the rest of his warriors along a line stretching all the way to the gorge, leaving each of them at regular intervals as he went: next Longtail, then Dustpelt, and then Mousefur. At last he and Graystripe were left alone on the border with RiverClan, as near as they could get to the gorge without leaving their own territory. "Right, Graystripe," he meowed, halting. "You hide here. If all goes well, Mousefur will lead the dogs to you. When they come, head for the steepest part of the gorge. I'll be ahead of you, waiting to take over for the final stretch."

"That will be on RiverClan territory." Graystripe sounded dubious. "What's Leopardstar going to think about that?"

"With any luck, Leopardstar won't have to know anything about it," Fireheart replied, remembering how the RiverClan leader had threatened Graystripe with death if he set paw in her territory again. "We can't worry about that now. Stay hidden on our side of the border, and if you see a patrol, don't let them know you're here."

Graystripe nodded and flattened his belly to the ground to crawl underneath the branches of a thornbush. "Good luck," he meowed as he disappeared.

Fireheart wished him luck in return and went on, more warily now, into RiverClan territory. He saw no RiverClan cats but he scented some fairly fresh traces, which suggested that the dawn patrol had already passed that way. At last he found a place to hide in a hollow at the foot of a rock and settled down to wait. The whole forest was silent, except for the distant roar of water in the gorge.

Fireheart couldn't help wondering where Tigerstar was now. Safe in ShadowClan territory, he guessed, waiting for his old Clan to be torn apart. Then he could swoop in like a carrion crow and take the ThunderClan territory for his own, gloating over his perfect revenge.

Clouds still covered the sky, so Fireheart had no way to judge the passing of time, but as each heartbeat followed the last he began to worry that something had gone wrong. Why was it taking so long? Had the dogs caught one of his warriors? Fireheart pictured Sandstorm being ripped apart by those cruel jaws and worked his paws on the hard earth in front of him, extending and sheathing his claws. He had to force himself not to go back and see what had happened. *What if this was all a huge mistake?* he asked himself. Had he led his Clan into even greater danger?

Then, above the noise of the river, he heard a distant barking. Rapidly it grew closer. The dark force had gained a voice at last, giving tongue as the pack bore down on the cats who had become their prey. The sound grew louder still, until it seemed to fill all the forest, and Graystripe appeared, streaking along with his belly almost flat against the ground.

Barely three fox-lengths behind him was the pack leader. Fireheart had never seen a dog like it. It was enormous, easily twice the size of any Twoleg pet. As it ran, its muscles bunched powerfully under a short black-and-brown pelt. Its jaws gaped to show a vicious set of teeth, and its tongue lolled. It barked hoarsely as it snapped at the fleeing Graystripe.

"StarClan help me!" Fireheart whispered, and sprang out of his hiding place.

He just had time to see Graystripe hurtling toward the nearest tree; then all he could do was run. The barking seemed to redouble, and he could feel the hot breath of the pack leader against his hind paws.

For the first time Fireheart wondered what he would do when he came to the gorge. He had imagined slipping aside at the last moment to let the unsuspecting dogs dash straight over the edge. Now he realized that might not work; the dogs were much, much closer than he had imagined.

Perhaps he would have to leap over himself.

If that's what it takes to save the Clan, then that's what I will do, Fireheart vowed grimly.

The gorge was close by. Fireheart emerged from the trees to see nothing but smooth turf between him and the edge of the cliff. Casting a hasty glance over his shoulder, he saw that he was outrunning the dogs, and he slackened his pace a little to let them catch up. The pack streamed out of the trees behind their leader, their tongues lolling as they barked.

"Pack, pack! Kill, kill!" The words slashed at Fireheart like teeth.

Then from his other side a heavy weight barreled into him, bowling him over. He fought vainly to get up as a massive paw pinned him by the neck. A voice growled in his ear, "Going somewhere, Fireheart?"

It was Tigerstar.

CHAPTER 27

❧

Fireheart struggled desperately to get free, lashing out with his hind paws to claw tufts of fur from his enemy's belly. The ShadowClan leader barely moved. The reek of his scent was in Fireheart's mouth and nostrils, and his amber eyes glared into Fireheart's own.

"Greet StarClan for me," he snarled.

"Only after you!" Fireheart gasped.

To his astonishment, Tigerstar released him. Lurching to his paws, Fireheart saw the ShadowClan leader double back and spring up the nearest tree. Before he had time to wonder what was going on, he heard a deafening howl and felt the ground shake under his paws. He spun around to see the pack leader looming over him, its dripping jaws wide. There was no time to run. Fireheart shut his eyes and prepared to meet StarClan.

Pain stabbed him as sharp teeth met in his scruff. His limbs flailed helplessly as the dog lifted him from the ground and shook him from side to side. He twisted in the air, struggling to claw eyes, jowls, tongue, but his thrashing paws met nothing. The forest spun about him. He was aware of more barking, and the stink of dog was everywhere.

"StarClan, help me!" Fireheart let out a yowl of terror and despair. This was not just his death, but the end of his whole Clan. His plan had failed. "StarClan, where are you?"

Suddenly a yowl sounded close by. Fireheart was flung to the ground, the breath driven out of his body. The grip on his neck loosened and was gone. Dazed, he looked up to see a blue-gray shape ramming into the side of the lead dog.

"Bluestar!" he yowled.

The force of his leader's impact had sent the dog staggering to the very edge of the gorge. Its barking changed to a high-pitched howl of terror as its huge paws scrabbled for a grip on the turf. The loose soil crumbled away under its weight and it fell, but as it disappeared over the edge its snapping jaws closed on Bluestar's leg, and wrenched her over as well.

Two of the other dogs, hard behind their leader, could not pull up in time. Blindly they charged over the edge of the gorge and vanished, howling, while the remaining dogs skidded to a halt, their fierce barks fading to piteous whimpers. Before Fireheart could force himself to his paws, they had backed away from the edge and fled into the forest.

Fireheart staggered to the edge of the gorge and looked over. Water foamed white beneath him. For a heartbeat he glimpsed the gaping muzzle of the pack leader struggling among the waves, before it vanished again.

"Bluestar!" Fireheart screamed. What had his leader been doing over here? He had sent her with the rest of the Clan to Sunningrocks.

Too stunned to move, Fireheart gazed down into the river. Suddenly he saw a small gray head bob to the surface, paws thrashing wildly. Bluestar was still alive! But the torrent was sweeping her downstream, and Fireheart knew that she was too frail to swim for long.

There was only one thing to do. Yowling, "Bluestar, hold on! I'm coming!" he launched himself down the steep side of the gorge and into the river.

Water clutched Fireheart like a huge paw and buffeted him from side to side. The icy cold of the torrent took his breath away. His paws worked furiously as he tried to swim, but the force of the current rolled him under. He had lost sight of Bluestar before he even entered the water; he could see nothing but the foam that bubbled all around him.

As his head broke surface he gasped for air, managing to stay afloat as the racing torrent swept him downstream. Then he spotted Bluestar again, a few fox-lengths ahead of him, her fur plastered to her head and her jaws gaping. Kicking out strongly, Fireheart closed the gap between them, and as Bluestar began to sink again he fastened his teeth in her scruff.

The extra weight dragged him down. All Fireheart's instincts screamed at him to let Bluestar go and save his own life. But he made himself hold on, while he forced his limbs to go on working and bring his drowning leader back to the surface. He almost lost his grip on her as something slammed into them, and he caught a glimpse of a dog rolling over in the current, its eyes glazed with terror as it floundered helplessly and vanished again.

A sudden shadow fell across them and was gone as the current carried them under the Twoleg bridge and away from the looming cliffs. Fireheart could see the river bank now and he struck out toward it, but his limbs were aching with weariness. Bluestar was a deadweight, unable to help herself. Fireheart knew that he could not let go of her to gulp in more air, and his senses began to spin away into darkness as his head went under again.

Barely conscious, he made one more massive effort, thrusting at the water with his paws. But when he resurfaced he could not see the bank, and he had lost all sense of direction. His limbs stiffened with panic as he knew he was going to drown.

Suddenly Bluestar's weight grew less. Blinking water out of his eyes, Fireheart saw another head bobbing in the water beside him, teeth firmly gripping Bluestar's fur. He recognized the blue-gray pelt and almost forgot to swim in his shock.

It was Mistyfoot!

At the same moment he heard Stonefur's voice from his other side. "Let go. We've got her now."

Fireheart did as he was told and let Stonefur take his place. The two RiverClan cats propelled Bluestar through the water toward the bank. Without the need to support the heavy she-cat, Fireheart managed to flounder after them until he felt the river bottom beneath his paws. On flatter ground now, carried by the river out of the steep-sided gorge, he was able to splash his way to the safety of the bank on the RiverClan side.

Coughing as he gasped air into his straining lungs, Fireheart shook water from his fur and looked around to see what had become of Bluestar. Mistyfoot and Stonefur had laid the Clan leader down on her side on the pebbles. Water trickled from her parted jaws, and she did not move.

"Bluestar!" Mistyfoot exclaimed.

"Is she dead?" Fireheart asked hoarsely, staggering up to them.

"I think she—"

Stonefur was interrupted by a loud yowling. "Fireheart! Fireheart! Watch out!"

It was Graystripe's voice. Fireheart turned to see Tigerstar racing across the Twoleg bridge with the gray warrior hard behind him. As the ShadowClan leader swerved along the bank toward Fireheart and the others, Graystripe darted in front of the massive tabby and whirled around to face him.

"Keep back!" he snarled. "Don't touch them."

Rage lent strength to Fireheart. His leader lay on the riverbank, her last life ebbing away; whatever she had said or done, she was still his leader, and he had never intended her to die for the sake of the Clan. And all this was because of Tigerstar!

He bounded upstream to stand beside Graystripe, and the ShadowClan leader halted a couple of fox-lengths away. Clearly he was thinking twice about taking both of them on at the same time.

From behind him Fireheart heard Mistyfoot gasp. "Fireheart! She's alive!"

He bared his teeth at Tigerstar. "Come one step closer, and I'll throw you in the river with the dogs," he growled. "Graystripe, make him stay back."

Graystripe nodded, unsheathing his claws, and Tigerstar let out a long hiss of fury and frustration.

Fireheart raced back to Bluestar and crouched down beside her. She still lay on the pebbles, though now Fireheart could see her chest rising and falling with each jagged breath. "Bluestar?" he whispered. "Bluestar, it's Fireheart. You're all right now. You're safe."

Her eyes blinked open and focused on the two RiverClan warriors. For a heartbeat she did not seem to recognize them, and then her eyes stretched wide, softening with pride. "You saved me," she murmured.

"Shhh. Don't try to talk," Mistyfoot urged her.

Bluestar seemed not to hear. "I want to tell you something. . . . I want to ask you to forgive me for sending you away. Oakheart promised me Graypool would be a good mother to you."

"She was," Stonefur meowed tersely.

Fireheart tensed. Last time they spoke to Bluestar, the two RiverClan warriors had spat venom at her, hating her for what she had done. Would they turn on her now, defenseless as she was?

"I owe Graypool so much," Bluestar went on. Her voice was faint and uneven. "Oakheart too, for mentoring you so well. I watched you as you grew up, and I saw how much you had to give to the Clan who adopted you." A shudder passed through her body, and she stopped speaking for a moment. "If I had made a different choice, you would have given all your strength to ThunderClan. Forgive me," she rasped.

Mistyfoot and Stonefur exchanged an uncertain glance.

"She suffered a lot of pain for her choice," Fireheart couldn't help putting in. "Please forgive her."

For a heartbeat the two warriors still hesitated. Then Mistyfoot bent her head to lick her mother's fur, and Fireheart felt his legs shake with relief. "We forgive you, Bluestar," she murmured.

"We forgive you," Stonefur echoed.

Weak as she was, Bluestar began to purr with delight. Fireheart's throat felt tight as he watched the two RiverClan cats crouched over his leader—their mother—sharing tongues with her for the first time.

A furious hiss from Graystripe made him turn his head to see that Tigerstar had taken a step forward. The massive tabby's eyes were wide with astonishment. Fireheart knew that until now Tigerstar had not known who was the mother of the kits that ThunderClan had given away.

"Don't come any nearer, Tigerstar," he hissed. "This has nothing to do with you."

Turning back to Bluestar, he saw that her eyes were closing and her breath was coming fast and shallow.

"What can we do?" he asked Mistyfoot anxiously. "This is her last life, and she'll never make it back to the ThunderClan camp. Will one of you go and fetch your medicine cat?"

"It's too late for that, Fireheart." It was Stonefur who

replied, his voice low and gentle. "She is on her way to StarClan."

"No!" Fireheart protested. He crouched beside Bluestar and pressed his muzzle against hers. "Bluestar—Bluestar, wake up! We'll get help for you—hold on just a bit longer."

Bluestar's eyes flickered open again, looking not at Fireheart, but at something just past his shoulder. Her gaze was clear and filled with peace. "Oakheart," she murmured. "Have you come for me? I'm ready."

"No!" Fireheart protested again. All his recent difficulties with Bluestar faded away. He remembered only the noble leader she had been, wise and inspiring, and how she had mentored him when he came into the Clan as a kittypet. And in the end StarClan had been kind to her. She had come out of the shadows to die as nobly as she had lived, saving her Clan by sacrificing herself.

"Bluestar, don't leave us," he begged.

"I must," his leader whispered. "I have fought my last battle." She was panting in her efforts to speak. "When I saw the Clan at Sunningrocks, the strong helping the weak . . . and I knew you and the others had gone to confront the pack . . . I knew my Clan was loyal. I knew StarClan had not turned their backs on us. I knew . . ." Her voice failed and she struggled to continue. "I knew that I could not leave you to face the danger alone."

"Bluestar . . ." Fireheart's voice shook with the pain of parting, and yet his heart leaped to hear that his leader knew he was not a traitor.

Bluestar fixed her blue gaze on him. Fireheart thought he could already see the shimmer of StarClan in her eyes. "Fire will save the Clan," she murmured, and Fireheart remembered the mysterious prophecy that he had heard from his earliest days in ThunderClan. "You never understood, did you?" Bluestar went on. "Not even when I gave you your apprentice name, Firepaw. And I doubted it myself, when fire raged through our camp. Yet I see the truth now. Fireheart, you are the fire who will save ThunderClan."

Fireheart could do nothing but stare at his beloved leader. He felt as if his whole body had turned to stone. Above his head, wind tore the clouds into shreds, letting a ray of sunshine strike down and touch his pelt to flame, just as it had in the clearing when he first arrived in the Clan, so many moons ago.

"You will be a great leader." Bluestar's voice was the merest whisper. "One of the greatest the forest has ever known. You will have the warmth of fire to protect your Clan and the fierceness of fire to defend it. You will be Firestar, the light of ThunderClan."

"No," Fireheart protested. "I can't. Not without you, Bluestar."

But it was too late. Bluestar sighed softly, and the light died from her eyes. Mistyfoot let out a low wailing sound and pressed her nose to her mother's fur. Stonefur crouched close to her, his head bowed.

"Bluestar!" Fireheart meowed desperately, but there was no response. The leader of ThunderClan had given up her last life, and gone to hunt with StarClan forever.

Fireheart rose stiffly to his paws. He had to dig his claws into the earth as his head spun, and for a moment he feared that he might fall into the sky. His fur prickled, and he felt as if his thudding heart would burst through his chest.

"Fireheart," Graystripe murmured. "Oh, Fireheart."

The gray warrior had left Tigerstar and walked silently over to watch his leader die. Now Fireheart saw that his friend's amber gaze was fixed on him with something like awe, and as their eyes met, Graystripe dipped his head in deepest respect. Fireheart stiffened in horror, longing to protest; he wanted the comfort of their old, easy friendship, not this formal acknowledgment from a warrior to his Clan leader.

Beyond Graystripe, he saw Tigerstar staring at the cats huddled on the shore, amazement and fury in his eyes. Before Fireheart could say anything, the ShadowClan leader spun around and raced across the Twoleg bridge, back toward his own territory.

Fireheart let him go. He had to deal with his own terrified, hunted Clan before he tried to settle old scores. But what Tigerstar had done that day would never be forgotten, not by any cat in ThunderClan. "We'll need to fetch some of the others," he mewed hoarsely to Graystripe. "We must get Bluestar's body back to camp."

Graystripe dipped his head again. "Yes, Fireheart."

"We'll help," Stonefur offered, standing up and facing the ThunderClan cats.

"We would be honored," added Mistyfoot, her eyes clouded with sorrow. "I would like to see our mother laid to rest in her Clan."

"Thank you, both of you," meowed Fireheart. He took a deep breath, drew himself up, and shook his drying fur. He felt as if the weight of the whole Clan had descended on his shoulders, and yet, in a heartbeat, it began to seem possible that he could bear it.

He was the leader of ThunderClan now. With the death of the lead dog, the threat of the pack had gone from the forest, and his Clan was waiting for him, safe, at Sunningrocks. Sandstorm would be waiting for him too.

"Come on," he meowed to Graystripe. "Let's go home."

KEEP WATCH FOR

WARRIORS

BOOK 6:

THE DARKEST HOUR

Rain fell steadily, drumming on the hard black Thunderpath that led between unending rows of stone Twoleg nests. From time to time a monster snarled past, its eyes glaring, and a single Twoleg scurried along, huddled into its shiny pelt.

Two cats slipped silently around the corner, keeping close to the walls where the shadows were deepest. A skinny gray tom with a ragged ear and bright, watchful eyes went first, every hair on his body slicked dark with the wet.

Behind him prowled a huge tabby with massive shoulders and muscles that slid smoothly under his rain-soaked pelt. His amber eyes glowed in the harsh light, and his gaze shifted back and forth as if he expected an attack.

He paused where the dark entrance to a Twoleg nest offered a little shelter and growled, "How much farther? This place stinks."

The gray tom glanced back. "Not far now."

"It had better not be." Grimacing, the dark brown tabby padded on, ears twitching irritably to flick away the rain-drops. Harsh yellow light angled across him, and he flinched as a monster roared around the corner, throwing up a wave of filthy water that reeked of Twoleg rubbish. The cat let out a snarl as the water slopped around his paws and the spray drizzled down on his fur.

Everything about the Twolegplace disgusted him: the hard surface under his paws, the stench of monsters and the Twolegs they carried in their bellies, the unfamiliar noises, and most of all, the way that he could not survive here without a guide. The tabby was not used to depending on another cat for anything. In the forest he knew every tree, every stream, every rabbit hole. He was considered the strongest and most dangerous warrior in all the Clans. Now his sharpened skills and senses were useless. He felt as if he were deaf, blind, and lame, reduced to following his companion like a kit trailing helplessly after its mother.

But it would be worth it. The tabby's whiskers twitched in anticipation. He had already launched a plan that would turn his most hated enemies into helpless prey in their own territory. When the dogs attacked, no cat would suspect that they had been lured and guided every step of the way. And then, if things went according to plan, this expedition into Twolegplace would give him all he had ever wanted.

The Next Generation of

WARRIORS

THE NEW PROPHECY

WARRIORS
MIDNIGHT

ERIN HUNTER

Hc 0-06-074449-9

In the first installment of this exciting new series, the children of Fireheart, Sandstorm, Graystripe, and Tigerstar learn of a mysterious new prophecy . . . one that may spell doom for the forest. Join the adventure as they set out on a quest to save the Clans from destruction.

■ HarperCollins*Children'sBooks*

www.warriorcats.com

WARRIORS

#1: Into the Wild
Hc 0-06-000002-3 • Pb 0-06-052550-9

This is the beginning of the epic adventure, in which a small house cat is drawn into a perilous forest world of battles, honor, excitement, and betrayal.

#2: Fire and Ice
Hc 0-06-000003-1 • Pb 0-06-052559-2

Young hero Fireheart grapples with the chilling revelation that one of ThunderClan's own will betray them in this action-packed installment of the feline fantasy series.

#3: Forest of Secrets
Hc 0-06-000004-X • Pb 0-06-052561-4

Fireheart is determined to uncover the truth about Redtail's death—but he is unprepared to face ThunderClan's darkest secrets.

#4: Rising Storm
Hc 0-06-000005-8 • Pb 0-06-052563-0

Fireheart, who is now second in command of ThunderClan, struggles with the challenges of his new power as Tigerclaw's sinister presence still haunts the forest.

#5: A Dangerous Path
Hc 0-06-000006-6

Tigerclaw is back and more dangerous than ever as the new leader of ShadowClan, but that's not the most terrifying thing Fireheart has to face as a mysterious force sweeps through the woods, leaving a trail of devastation in its wake.

#6: The Darkest Hour
Hc 0-06-000007-4

Fireheart leads ThunderClan as they battle the most deadly threat the forest has ever seen, and the young warrior must face his destiny once and for all.

▓ HarperCollins*Children'sBooks*

www.harperchildrens.com • www.warriorcats.com

AVON BOOKS
An Imprint of HarperCollinsPublishers